Rose clasped Madsen's hand in a firm grip. "Mr. Bold, it hasn't been a pleasure meeting you, and I hope we never meet again. Good night." And with that nicety, she flounced away.

Caught flat-footed once again, Madsen fumed first and then broke out in a grin, considering. She was determined for a woman—and beautiful when she was determined.

"Not so fast, sugar," he said, catching up to her in three strides. A firm grasp on her upper arm kept her from getting away. "Our business isn't over yet."

"Let me go." She wiggled, and he loosened his hold, afraid he was hurting her. "Will you get it through your thick head, we have no business? Now you go your way, and I'll go mine."

"Can't. For a while, your way *is* my way."

"If I talk real sweet and bat my eyelashes, will you do what I ask?"

"No."

She sighed. "No one ever has. I'm just not attractive that way. It was worth a try. C'mon, then. Let's go find the marshal."

Noticing that she was shivering and that the snowfall was becoming heavier, Madsen shook his head.

"Not tonight. Not in this weather. You're chilled to the bone." And without thinking, he tucked her shoulder under his arm, nestling her closer to his warmth.

ONE WILD ROSE

Geri Borcz

ZEBRA BOOKS
Kensington Publishing Corp.
http://www.kensingtonbooks.com

ZEBRA BOOKS are published by

Kensington Publishing Corp.
850 Third Avenue
New York, NY 10022

All Kensington titles, imprints, and distributed lines are
available at special quantity discounts for bulk purchases for
sales promotion, premiums, fund-raising, educational or in-
stitutional use.

Special book excerpts or customized printings can also be
created to fit specific needs. For details, write or phone the
office of the Kensington Special Sales Manager: Kensington
Publishing Corp., 850 Third Avenue, New York, NY 10022.
Attn. Special Sales Department. Phone: 1-800-221-2647.

First Printing: February 2002
10 9 8 7 6 5 4 3 2 1

Printed in the United States of America

One

People are like shoes—everyone's got a mate somewhere.
—Old saw

Colorado Territory, 1867

Saturday night in Deadwater. Judging by the sounds, every moonshiner, hard-rock miner, and Union rowdy within fifty miles crowded the one and only saloon, the kind of hell-raising water hole where an hombre looking to lay low could throw off the trail without attracting attention.

Dogging the cold tracks of such an hombre, Madsen Bold tied up at the hitch rail just as a brawl between two hard cases slammed out the batwing doors and onto the slushy street. Not knowing the gents, Madsen stomped the snow off his boots while he waited for the odds takers to vacate the vestibule.

A white-haired old rooster jostled his way through the crowd and offered to stable Madsen's horse, so he nodded and tossed him a coin. Then Madsen eased his way into the noisy saloon and elbowed a spot near the end of the plank-board bar.

The barkeep was a burly man wearing a dingy apron and chewing on the end of a one-cent cheroot that was stuck in the side of his mouth.

"What's yer poison, mister?" he said. "Whiskey or beer?"

"Coffee," Madsen said.

He propped his Sharps rifle on the floor against the bar, eased his saddlebags off his shoulder, and peeled off his leather gloves and stuffed them into his coat pocket. Under his sourdough coat, a brace of pistols hung low on his hips.

Without batting an eyelash, the barkeep upended a cracked glass and sloshed in two fingers deep from an unlabeled bottle.

"Here," he said, shoving the tumbler toward Madsen. "Wrap yer teeth round that. This ain't no damned restaurant."

Madsen palmed the glass before it tipped and said, "Ever hear the old saw 'The customer is always right'?"

The barkeep removed the cheroot and then offered a cheap smile filled with stumpy teeth.

"Ask me if I give a rat's ass," he said.

Madsen glared back, figured the coffee wasn't worth the trouble, and scanned the rough interior for any familiar mugs.

The ramshackle building resembled a thousand others that he'd seen while on the trail of Teddy Lee Rawlings and his accomplice. Thrown together with spit and vinegar, the shack boasted crude furniture down here and rickety stairs on the far wall that most likely led to the den of sins above.

Three sporting gals, each one looking like ten years of hard times, worked the tables.

"Don't let a quail fly through this place," Madsen mused aloud to the barkeep, " 'cause those three would strike a point."

Dressed in wilted purple feathers and dingy white frillies and none too steady on their feet, the only gals in the place each draped themselves over a smelly cowboy who had an itch he'd waited all week to scratch.

"You ain't seen nuthin'," the barkeep said.

And Madsen hadn't, not until *she* appeared at the top of the stairs, wearing a short red dress and an arresting smile.

"Sweet baby Jesus," Madsen breathed.

The barkeep barked a knowing laugh.

"Told ya. Some sight, ain't she? Rosie's sure bin good for business this last week."

Why would a looker be in Deadwater?

Only one answer popped into Madsen's suspicious mind. Teddy Lee's accomplice was reported to be a blonde of average height and easy on the eyes.

Unless Madsen missed his guess, he was staring at her. If he played his cards right, Madsen could use her to find Teddy Lee.

She certainly knew her trade, for Madsen couldn't peel his gaze away from the stairs. He watched her through air thick with tin-pan piano music, smoke, and innuendo.

"A week, you say?" he asked.

The whiffy barkeep leaned closer and nodded.

"Since word got out 'bout sweetie pie yonder, ever' saddle tramp in the territory has hightailed here to smell her sweat and get hornier'n a three-peckered billy goat. She struts in and flags fly at half-mast like a friggin' parade. Harharhar."

Legs up to her armpits and with a painted face, she wasn't Madsen's type, but she would do for tonight. It was his guess she'd do whatever he wanted, real well.

He leaned a forearm against the bar's edge and cut across the barkeep's rumbling chuckles and polecat smell.

"Where in this one-street town can I get a room and a bath, pronto? Or are you the wrong one to ask?"

Madsen blamed his gruff tone on the blonde. No, on her legs. No, on her dimpled knees. Dimples he'd wanted to wrap around his bare flanks the instant he'd spied them.

He had chased every sunrise to claim dimples like those, preferably attached to an innocent young thing who turned hellcat in bed. Just his luck, his dream dimples advertised a fancy piece.

With barely a pause in spit-polishing a glass, the barkeep gestured up the stairs with his stained rag.

"The room'll cost ya six bits, mister—"

"A day's pay? That's mighty rich."

"And the bath'll run ya a hunnerd bucks." The

barkeep shot a meaningful glance to the long-and-lanky blonde who took her sweet time descending the stairs.

Madsen blew a low whistle, thumbed up his sweat-stained hat brim, and then rubbed the two-weeks' worth of dark bristles on his chin.

"Parlor-house prices?" he said. "That must be some bath."

The barkeep shrugged.

"Reckon she makes it so. These days ain't many got that much gold to chance findin' out."

That explained the haggard gals. Madsen was used to risks. What Texas Ranger wasn't? Even if he was a former ranger now, some habits were hard to change. He'd follow his hunch and take the chance.

The dimples stepped off the stairs. Through a blue haze of cheap cigar smoke, Madsen cataloged each of the blonde's obvious assets and then slugged back his whiskey before the tonsil varnish etched the glass.

"Whoa!" he said on a quick breath.

The liquid blazed a path to his stomach and seared his chest with a pain half as hot as the sight of the leggy blonde.

"Ready fer 'nother belt?" the barkeep said.

Not trusting his voice, Madsen shook his head and glanced again to the blonde.

Sugar, what might you look like wearing nothing except that smile?

It was an image to make a dead man twitch.

As she ambled past the card tables, drunks of-

fered hoots and catcalls, and men too broke to
chance her price drooled into their suds. Two or
three men in the crowd wore natty duds and
looked high in the pockets, but she seemed not
to care.

Instead, she sashayed straight toward the end of
the bar and Madsen.

If he were inclined to worry, she might have
given him pause, for he knew he was too much
like his old man, hard-bitten and set in his ways.
For the past few years, after a series of stops and
near starts, Madsen had grown resigned to the
sorry truth that whatever women wanted he didn't
have it.

So either the color of his money attracted this
woman or she somehow knew Madsen was the
man who was close on Teddy Lee's tail. Could be
a bit of both.

Madsen mulled that over as she paused to give
him a calculated stare and a practiced pout.

"Frank," she called to the barkeep. "The man's
glass is empty."

Madsen darted a hand out and covered the glass
before Frank could pour. One round was Madsen's limit. With the other hand, he swept his battered Confederate-issue campaign hat to the bar.

The blonde raised a painted eyebrow.

"Ladies admire a gent with manners," she said.

Madsen gave her back a wry grin.

"Whatever else I take off," he said, "depends
on the lady."

Her eyes widened, gypsy eyes, eyes so brown

they gleamed in the mellow lamplight like rich saddle leather and drew a man in with sensual promises of steamy nights filled with sinful delights, eyes that devoured Madsen as if he were a banquet on which she intended to feast.

His britches stretched uncomfortably snug.

She sidled up to him, and again he wondered why she'd cut him out of the herd.

No one knew him around here. He'd been on the move since his good friend Leander McNelly had enlisted his help in tracking down the small-time outlaw who had robbed a Wells Fargo shipment down in San Antonio.

The robbery had netted Teddy Lee a small amount of cash and a pouch of diamonds. It was the diamonds Leander wanted to recover before Teddy Lee had the chance to hand them over to whoever had hired him.

But Teddy Lee was a slippery one, checking his back trail every mile and ducking the big towns. He was smart enough to know someone was after him, but he didn't know who.

Maybe the blonde didn't know Madsen was the one tailing her, after all? Maybe she simply knew a real man when she saw one? There was only one way to find out.

"My, you're a big boy, handsome . . ." she said, her husky purr sliding like warm honey all the way to his aching groin.

"Care to find out how big I am, sugar? Or did you just mosey over here to talk?"

She gave a throaty chuckle, not at all put off by

his bluntness. She smelled sweet and clean, a stark contrast to the horse sweat and trail dust that Madsen had inhaled for the past month.

With the tip of her index finger, she traced a line up the buttons on his overcoat, measuring him, teasing him, daring him.

"Talk is money, handsome. I'm not a fruit stand handing out samples."

"You do look pretty ripe at that. I've got a lot to say and all night to say it. You got a place where we can——?"

The bartender's bruising grip on Madsen's shoulder halted him.

"A hunnerd bucks," he said, meaty palm out. "Up front."

At the same time, she brushed herself against Madsen's front, hard enough for her softness to convey a teasing hint of the curves hidden under the tight red dress. He looked into her eyes.

Madsen hated the powder and paint she wore. Her lips were scarlet, her eyelids blue, and the stuff gobbed on her face covered her skin like a plaster mask. He wanted to see her skin, to touch her cheeks without feeling the paint, but figured exploring her long legs was as close as he might get.

It had been a long month and, before then, a spell too dry without an oasis. He was a thirsty man who could think of several reasons—one hundred of them at the moment—why he shouldn't put off business to drink at her well.

But not one of those reasons looked or smelled

or offered to show him the kind of company to-night that the sultry gleam in her eyes promised he would find.

Forgoing the usual parley of time and price, Madsen forked over his money to the bartender.

"You're mine, cowboy, and you're not getting away," she said, clasping his hand in a surprisingly firm hold and then angling toward the stairs.

He didn't plan to try. Another part of him demanded the opportunity to enjoy her grip.

Madsen snatched his hat and gear from the greasy bar and followed her past the raucous voices and up the well-traveled stairs. Her rounded hips swayed in front of him like a red flag in front of a bull. The slinky fabric hugged her curves and made Madsen's mouth water.

She opened the door at the end of the dim hall, and he stepped past her into the room.

His nostrils flared with an exotic scent, untamed and lush. Like her. From force of habit, he swept the room with a critical eye for any nasty surprises.

It was small and neat. A fat black stove in the far corner emitted welcoming heat. A lace doily covered a well-kept bureau. An iron bed sported a crisp quilt hardly used.

Like her? Doubtful, but who cared? He had never begrudged a lady trying to make a buck.

Lady?

Somehow it fit.

Compared to the cheap whores Madsen had known, this fancy piece made him feel like taking the time to enjoy himself. This one time, pleasure before business.

A white-haired old gent poured steaming water into a dandified copper-rimmed hip tub that occupied the center of the small room. Madsen narrowed his eyes. Down to his flat miner's boots, the gent was identical to the codger who'd stabled Madsen's horse except for the hard warning that pulled his wrinkles into a scowl.

Either he was one very spry old bird or they were twins.

"Him and the other one," Madsen said, venturing a guess. "They work for you?"

"Friends of my mother's," she said. "This is Dill. You probably met his brother, Sully, downstairs. They're protective of me."

Empty bucket in hand, Dill mumbled under his breath as he shuffled out, while Madsen ignored him and watched the lazy ribbons of steam curl toward a painting on the ceiling.

He tilted his chin up, eyes wide. The lascivious scene staring back at him would start any man blabbering like a fool.

In a blue sky among fluffy white clouds, cherubs frolicked around two nudes. The man teetered on the edge of a scaffold, hands behind his back and stretched on tiptoe by a noose around his neck, but with a cat-ate-the-canary grin. In front of him knelt the female of every schoolboy's dreams, her eager face poised before the man's overripe personals.

By comparison, Madsen felt a smidgeon self-conscious.

"That old boy is well hung in the worst way," he said.

"It's called 'Heaven or Hell.' "

"Damnable choice to have to make."

She uttered a noise that sounded close to a snort.

"Forget about it, handsome. You'll get used to it after a while. The water's getting cold."

Madsen stepped between the bed and the tub. He tested the water with his finger. Warm and inviting. A low stool perched next to the tub, with a square of soap snuggled in the pile of a thick white towel.

He chucked his saddlebags to the bed, propped his Sharps in a corner by the headboard, and then shrugged out of his coat. A glance over his shoulder saw her lock the door and slip the key into the top drawer of the adjacent bureau.

She grinned.

"When I'm done with you, handsome, you won't be able to reach this key."

Madsen chuckled and tried a little fishing. "The barkeep called you Rosie. Is that your name, sugar?"

"Does it matter?"

"Just being friendly," he said.

"Then Rose will do. And what shall I call you?"

She started pulling pins from her upswept hair, so he turned back toward the tub and unbuckled his gun belt.

"My friends call me Mad," he said.

"With good reason, I'm sure."

She moved to his side and brushed his hand away. The gun belt slackened and hung lower on his hips.

"Here," she said, "let me do that."

Madsen flipped his hat, which landed on top of the bedpost, and then watched her tapered fingers deftly undress him. She had short, pared fingernails. Clean hands. Soft looking.

When she dipped lower, her bodice gaped, and he could see from here to Houston. Nice cleavage. Plump and white.

"I meant that's my name," he said.

"Call yourself Steve Austin. It doesn't matter to me."

He stilled her hand.

"How'd you know I'm from Texas?"

"With that accent?" She chuckled. "I knew it wasn't Ohio."

He'd never been undressed by a woman before and liked the novelty.

In short order, his dirty flannel shirt landed next to a chair that sat against the far wall. Two longjohn shirts followed close behind.

Bare-chested, he gazed at the top of her head, level with his waistband. But when she reached for his gun belt, he grabbed her wrist, tight.

"I like to keep these close," he said.

He removed the gun belt, folded the leather straps together against the two holsters, and then palmed the leather in his right hand, gun stocks up and ready to grab.

"How about I set them on the bureau?" she said. "That's close."

"Not close enough."

"Expecting company?"

"I always do," he said. "A man figures out he lives longer that way."

Her thoughts were hidden deep behind those brown eyes. She chewed a little of the scarlet off her bottom lip. Madsen guessed that in her profession she had a right to be wary. Her price might cut out the shiftless rowdies, but a rich man could get nasty just as fast as a poor man.

"Suit yourself, handsome."

"I usually do, sugar."

Then he laid his guns on the stool by the towel.

As she worked the buttons free of his britches, his focus narrowed considerably. Her hands seemed to have a slight tremor.

Nerves? No, Rose must have done this before. Probably bends her elbow too much.

For some reason, that thought dampened Madsen's enthusiasm.

Yet she didn't strike him as a drinker. Her eyes were too bright, the skin he could see glowed with health, and she hadn't hit him up for any free belts downstairs.

She dropped to her knees, and before he could savor her position, she shoved him down on the bed and wrenched his foot up.

"Hey! You always this rough?"

"You plan to bathe with your boots on and this, too?" she said, gesturing to his ankle sheath.

Madsen grumbled, leaned over, and yanked the knife off, setting it aside before she tugged his boots off. Then he stripped off two layers of long drawers and his pants until he was buck naked.

A minute later, without so much as a comment on his finer qualities, she ushered him into the water, and he sat with his knees bent in front of him. He'd taken baths in his sister's kitchen with more fuss and ceremony.

While Madsen lathered the soap and rubbed both hands over his face and neck, Rose folded his clothes into a pile with his saddlebags. The soap smelled spicy. Like her.

He ducked his head under the water, then came up to see her standing in front of the bureau brushing her hair, her back to him, almost as if she were stalling. Her strokes were jerky, but Madsen liked watching her all the same.

Something about the way the bristles moved through a woman's hair, sleek and slow and crackling, seemed seductive. Rose's blonde strands curled at the ends with a life of their own and gleamed like a sheet of flame against the back of the red dress.

"How about a back scrub?" he said, splashing warm water on his face to soften his beard.

His body tightened with anticipation when the soft swish of fabric came behind him. He had been on the move too long, and tonight would be a

welcome reprieve before he found out what he
needed to know and pushed on at dawn.

But the unmistakable metallic click of a gun
hammer caught him flat-footed, shattering his
steamy thoughts.

Madsen froze.

"Hands clear, cowboy," Rose said, "where I can
see them."

The sultry voice had turned all business, cool
and decisive.

Anger surged through Madsen. She had led him
to water, and he had dived in headfirst. Why does
a man's brains drop into his pants the minute a
woman offers her body?

Mentally kicking himself, Madsen raised his
arms at his sides, dared a glance over his shoulder,
and stared down the barrel of a six-gun. A steady
finger rested on the trigger.

Obviously, Rose had done this a time or two.

His guns rested just below his left hand, but the
tub didn't give him enough room to duck if she
decided to shoot.

"Don't even think about it," she said, as if reading his mind. "Now, turn around and face forward."

Madsen did as he was told. Gun held in front
of her, she walked a wide circle around to face
him, then kicked the low stool and sent his holsters clattering across the floor out of his reach.

"That's better," she said. "Since you don't have
the pouch on you, where is it?"

Madsen's eyebrows lifted, and then he smiled.

That answered his question of whether Rose was Teddy Lee's accomplice. Guess the two of them had a falling out.

"What pouch?" Madsen said.

"Don't play games. In case you're wondering, this gun is loaded."

"Kill me and you'll never find out."

She sighed. "Do I look like a murderer?"

"No, ma'am, I can't say that you do."

"Thank you. Now, you pick. A leg? A foot? What wouldn't you mind doing without?"

"Hold on now! I kinda like my parts the way they are."

"Fine. I can be reasonable. Just tell me where the pouch is."

"You tell me," Madsen said, and added, "Can I put my arms down? It's a mite chilly in here."

"All right, put them down." She gestured with the gun barrel. "And while you're at it, take that soap and give the rest of you a good lick and a promise."

"Why?"

"I have a weak stomach—why do you think?" She rolled her gaze heavenward. "I want that pouch. You're taking me to it, and I don't admire starting a trip with a man who smells like he's been tending camels."

Two

He was a two-bit outlaw with a ten-dollar attitude and a glare that would curdle milk.

Roselyn felt his gaze hit her stomach like a bad meal.

She squeezed her eyes closed, but his face floated in her head, a strong face, deeply creased and tanned to a permanent bronze. A beat later, she opened her eyes again.

The man in the tub with the unsettling looks certainly carried himself unlike any of the outlaws she'd rubbed elbows with while growing up. That didn't matter, couldn't matter. She wouldn't let it.

He matched the description of Rawlings: tall, black hair, brown eyes, a free spending ladies' man, and riding a blue roan.

Duke Pearson forgot to mention a disturbing air of determination and competency or that Rawlings was solid, with a muscled build, square-shouldered, sinfully appealing, and armed to the teeth. What other nuggets of information had that carpetbagging weasel left out?

She refused to dwell on that now. Saving Mama's neck was all that mattered.

Roselyn had watched all week for Rawlings to ride into town. It wasn't in a Romeo to go miles on end without stopping for agreeable company.

Once she'd spotted him, it was too late to worry if she possessed any of her errant pa's thespian talents. She'd gleaned plenty while growing up in saloons to make the play-acting real enough.

But catching Rawlings flat-footed had been easy compared to what lay ahead of her now. He was supposed to have the pouch on him. Damn Duke Pearson. At this moment, Roselyn could wring Mama's tender neck for getting them mixed up with the no-good carpetbagger.

Roselyn hadn't counted on having to force Rawlings at gunpoint to take her to the pouch Duke wanted returned, so she needed a plan.

And she needed one now.

Back in Texas, Duke had made his message clear: repay him the money Mama had gambled away, with interest, or else she'd pay and pay dearly. Wangling Mama out from this scheme or that was an old story for Roselyn, but this time the two of them couldn't quietly skip town.

Duke wasn't a man to take kindly to being double-crossed.

And Rawlings would find that out soon enough. Duke wanted the locked pouch Rawlings had stashed somewhere, enough that he'd made a deal with Roselyn. He'd given her three months to deliver the pouch in exchange for forgiving Mama's debt.

Knock! Knock!

"Rosie?" came an urgent whisper through the door. "Open up, honey. I gotta talk to you. It's real important."

The intrusion distracted Roselyn's attention for only a moment, but that proved long enough.

For a big man, he sure moved fast.

Before she could think to react, she was flat on her back on the floorboards. He soaked her front with the bath water that ran off his body. The hem of Mama's silk dress lay pinned around Roselyn's exposed thighs, and she gazed into the tight face of the naked man who straddled her.

Between his dead weight and her pinching corset, breathing was a luxury. Moving was a fleeting wish.

She tried to swallow but couldn't.

"What's the matter, sugar?" he said, plucking the gun from her hand. "Isn't this why you locked the door?"

She bucked her hips, trying to make him move. That was a mistake. It only brought her closer to his hardness.

Nestled much too intimately in the cradle of his hips, Roselyn felt her face burning and her temper igniting.

"It was a precaution, you big galoot," she said. "If my plan didn't work, I wanted to make sure I slowed you down some."

To her surprise, he grinned and then checked the gun's full cylinder.

"I can see you're a woman who likes to plan ahead." He jutted his chin toward the door. "Who's that, another friend of your mother's?"

Roselyn nodded and said, "Her name's Hattie Mae."

"She work downstairs?"

Roselyn nodded again.

"Answer her," he said, leaning back and easing his weight onto his legs. "Let's see what she wants."

Grateful for a deeper breath of air, Roselyn called, "Pardon me for not looking at you, Mae, but I'm not about to take my eye off my prisoner."

"You ain't holdin' the man at gunpoint, are you?"

"Not anymore," Roselyn said, and grumped under her breath.

An excited muffle of sound filtered through the door.

"Y'hear me?" Hattie Mae asked, then more forcefully, "I said, *he ain't Rawlings!*"

"*What?*"

Roselyn felt her blood draining to her toes. No, she couldn't be wrong.

As if reading Roselyn's mind, Hattie Mae continued: "It's true. The marshal's done been over to the Jensen place playing poker with Rawlings for the last hour and tryin' to figure where he'd seen his face before. When he remembered a

Wanted poster, he arrested Rawlings on the spot and slapped him in the hoosegow."

Sagging inside, Roselyn swiveled her attention between the closed door and the glittering gaze so close to hers.

Lordy, the man even had dimples. Her heart beat like a two-dollar clock.

"So y-you're not Ted—?"

He shook his drippy head, his brow crinkling as if he sorted through a puzzle.

Without thinking better of it, she smacked his wet arm.

"You could've said that before. Why the nerve— just who are you?"

"I told you, sugar."

"No, you didn't," she said, pushing on his shoulders. It was like a flea trying to budge a boulder. "You said you were mad, and I agree. And you're dripping all over me. Get off!"

Roselyn figured he relented because he wanted to, not because of her puny efforts to push him away. Before he could change his mind, she scrambled to her feet when he rose. But he beat her to the bureau drawer.

A flexed forearm easily fended her off while he fished out the door key. Then he ignored her completely for the five seconds it took to unlock the door and crack it open to gently thank Hattie Mae and tell her that he'd straighten out the misunderstanding.

He locked the door on Hattie Mae's giggles. Roselyn could've strangled her.

"What're you going to do now?" she said, arms crossed over her chest.

Rather than answer her, he took his sweet time shucking the shells from her gun. An underhand toss sent the empty gun skittering into the far corner, and a snap of his wrist flipped the shells into the cooling bath water. They hit with a plink of finality and sank to the bottom of the tub.

"Get my hundred dollars' worth," he finally said, turning the key over in his palm.

The sight of his lips shaping the words mesmerized Roselyn. Her lips tingled in response, wanting to kiss a man she knew not to kiss, and her mouth refused to work.

Earlier, she'd been too engrossed in pulling off her charade to appreciate the scenery. But looking at him now, luminously naked, every angle and plane kissed by mellow lamplight, she was suddenly aware of her own body.

She struggled to figure out what she wanted to say before managing to choke out, "Who do you think you are?"

"For the last time, my name's Mad, Madsen Bold."

He advanced on her, and she backed up, putting her arms out to ward him off. It was a useless gesture, as she discovered when he merely strode to the bed and dug into his saddlebags for his clean clothes.

Perverse woman that she was, she felt a twinge of disappointment.

That wouldn't do. This had never happened to

Roselyn, this fluttery awareness. Never. To Mama, yes. All the time.

She flitted from man to man as easily as a hummingbird in a garden of lush flowers. Roselyn adored her mama but refused to follow in her footsteps.

Some women were simply meant to swoon over a gun-toting yahoo who'd either end up dead on a spit-covered saloon floor or pull freight at the first sign of a tin badge. Not Roselyn O'Neill. No sirree bob. Appealing scoundrels were too easy to find and too hard to keep around.

Over the years, poor Mama's choices in men had proven that much. Her first husband earned himself a load of buckshot when he was caught cheating at cards, and Roselyn's own pa might have been Mama's second husband, if the man had stuck around long enough.

Roselyn envisioned a different life for herself. She'd settle for nothing less than a decent man who was content to stay in one spot the rest of his days and enjoy quiet evenings at home. No saloons. No dance-hall gals. No Wanted poster with his face stuck on it. But so far, Roselyn wasn't exactly knee-deep in possibles.

And Mr. Madsen Bold didn't count. He might be tempting to the eye, but a man eager to squander good money for a brief bit of company didn't strike her as the homebody sort. She wilted a little, and then a thought perked her up.

"Wait a minute," she said. "There's been a mistake—"

"I know, sugar, and you made it." He'd dressed and was stomping his feet into his boots when he tossed the towel at her. "Wipe that mess off your face."

Surprised, she caught the towel with both hands and blurted out, "Why?"

"You're coming to the jail with me. And you might want to change into something less skimpy. It's cold outside."

"Oh, no," she said, shaking her head. "I'm not going anywhere with you."

He ignored her outburst, strapped on his brace of pistols, and simply said, "You owe me a hundred dollars."

"No, I don't. Frank does. Talk to him."

"But I'd rather talk to you."

"Are you listening to me? I haven't got your money!"

"I've had my bath. Think your barkeep friend will give me a cheerful refund just because my pockets weren't the ones you wanted to pick?"

Roselyn had to admit he was right. Frank didn't butt his nose into what the girls did or how it turned out as long as he got his cut up front.

"I am not a thief," she said instead. "I didn't pick your pockets. It was a simple misunderstanding."

Madsen snorted.

"What's the use?" Roselyn said, swiping at the grease on her face with the towel. "Stop this nonsense or I'll scream for Dill, Sully, *and* Frank."

"That's not sweetening the pot."

Lowering the towel, Roselyn narrowed her gaze.

"All right, quit beating a dead horse," she said. "What do you really want? Name it."

She could've bitten her tongue off when his gaze glittered.

"Rawlings," he said. "I want Rawlings, and I want to know what you have to do with him."

"Nothing," she said. "I don't even know the man."

Madsen snorted again. It was becoming an irritating sound.

"If I did," Roselyn said, "think you'd be here right now?" Then it hit her. "The pouch. And you think I'm a thief? You couldn't give a fig about Rawlings. You're after the pouch."

"Don't be so surprised," he said, shrugging into his coat. "It seems you and I have a lot of things in common."

Now it was Roselyn's turn to snort.

His darkening gaze played over her, and she was powerless to stop the delicious warmth that poured down her spine.

"And they are?" she said.

He offered a faint, fleeting smile. "I count one hundred of them to be exact."

Three

They slipped out the back stairs of the saloon.

Madsen preferred it that way. The more the rowdies downstairs thought he was otherwise occupied, the fewer questions he'd rouse.

He'd called enough attention to himself already. And, as it was, Madsen had plenty of questions of his own to go around.

Rose was first on his list. She knew about the pouch of diamonds, but she didn't know Rawlings. Madsen felt certain that much was no act.

But if she wasn't Teddy Lee's accomplice, who was she? Who was she working for? What was her stake in this? Or was greed the simple answer?

Whoever she was, she had her own reasons for acting the harlot, and until he found out what they were, he didn't trust her and wasn't about to let her out of his sight. Besides, she'd bamboozled him, and that went against the grain.

No man or woman ever cheated or swindled Madsen Bold and got away with it. He prided himself on keeping what was his. Any man who let himself get cheated and did nothing about it was a man who had yellow oozing out of his collar.

So Madsen intended to stick with Miss Rose like a second skin until, one way or another, he got his money.

Looking at her now, no one could imagine the long legs and shapely curves hidden under the serviceable brown dress and blanket coat she'd donned. Madsen swore silently as the tantalizing images played across his mind without cease. And no sane person looking at her face, scrubbed pink and fresh, would suppose she'd ever stepped foot inside a saloon, let alone mistake her for a fancy piece who worked in one.

He hadn't expected her to wear Sunday-go-to-meeting clothes, but without the war paint and frills, she looked as plain as a spinster school-marm. And Madsen commented as much.

"Because I am a schoolmarm," she snapped. "Or I was."

"You?"

"And why not me? I may have grown up around saloons, but I had books."

"I was surprised, is all. I meant no disrespect."

"A miner wanted to learn to write his name, and then another asked, and then another, and before I knew it, I had a classroom. It was an honest living. Some paid in gold, most bartered work, like Dill and Sully. Grab that lantern there, will you?"

She gestured over to the wall at the bottom of

the stairs and then shivered and pulled her coat collar tighter to her neck.

"It's as dark as the inside of a dog out here," she said.

Snow fell in a powder drift through a bleak winter twilight that had a bone-chilling bite to it. Madsen snatched the lantern off its hook and aimed its brassy light on the white ground ahead of them.

"Careful you don't slip," he said, unconsciously putting a hand to her elbow to steady her. "The slush is icing over."

She shot a quick and curious glance at his helping hand before her gaze shifted and flashed him a tentative smile—sweet, silent, and lethal.

That smile did plenty to stir the fire smoldering within Madsen, and he didn't let himself think about the questions running in his mind.

He ushered her through the settlement to the small fort nearby whose troops guarded the Overland Trail. According to a couple of soldiers they passed, the marshal routinely borrowed the use of the Fort Collins guardhouse, since Deadwater had no jail.

Rumor had it that the post would soon be abandoned. Madsen figured that explained why so few soldiers were about when he and Rose entered the gates.

A wide hat brim kept the snow off Madsen's face, but he noticed that the ruffled fringe of Rose's bonnet did nothing to protect her reddening nose and cheeks from the stinging cold flakes.

Her complexion was smooth and soft looking, just as he'd imagined it would be.

The sergeant of the guard was a young man full of righteous fire who barely filled out his blue wool uniform. He refused to let them see Rawlings, let alone speak to him.

"My orders don't say nothin' about visitors," the sergeant snapped, eyeing Madsen as if he'd tangled with a skunk and lost. "Check with the marshal."

Then he spun on his heels and stalked away, dismissing them with no more expression than he'd give a keg of putrid beans.

"Where would the marshal be?" Madsen called to his back.

"Ain't my day to watch him, mister."

A moment later, Rose nodded her head in the sergeant's direction.

"Eleventh Ohio," she said. "People here have long memories when it comes to southern accents."

"I'm used to it."

But Madsen's tone suggested otherwise.

"Well, I guess that's that," Rose said. She clasped his hand in a firm grip. "Mr. Bold, it hasn't been a pleasure meeting you, and I hope we never meet again. Good night."

And with that nicety, she flounced away.

Caught flat-footed again by her, Madsen fumed first and then broke out in a grin, considering. She was determined for a woman and beautiful when she was determined.

"Not so fast, sugar," he said, catching up to her in three strides. A firm grasp on her upper arm kept her from getting away. "Our business isn't over yet."

"Let me go." She wiggled, and he loosened his hold, afraid he was hurting her. "Will you get it through your thick head, we have no business? Now you go your way, and I'll go mine."

"Can't. For a while, your way *is* my way."

"If I talk real sweet and bat my eyelashes, will you do what I ask?"

"No."

She sighed. "No one ever has. I'm just not attractive that way. It was worth a try. C'mon, then. Let's go find the marshal."

Noticing she was shivering and that the snowfall was becoming heavier, Madsen shook his head.

"Not tonight. Not in this weather. You're chilled to the bone." And without thinking, he tucked her shoulder under his arm, nestling her closer to his warmth.

"Let's get you inside," he said.

If it wasn't so cold, he would have stayed outside and kept her right where she was. Instead, he steered her toward the way they'd come, his mind back on business and sorting out his choices while she fell into step with him and tried to fill the awkward silence.

"You served in the war?" she said.

"With Terry's Rangers."

"Why, even I've heard of Colonel Terry. Is it

true his rangers were among the best Texas cavalry regiments?"

"No," Madsen said. "We were the best. Period."

"I—I'm sorry. I didn't mean to stir bad memories."

"It's not your fault only a handful of us survived the war."

"The Good Book says that to everything is a season. During those years, we all went through a season in hell."

"A season?" He stopped and faced her. "Sugar, religion and militarism aren't a good mix. Hell was coming home to chaos, to carpetbaggers and a cesspool government that punished the defeated. And it's not over yet. It won't be over for a long time. We're in one hellish season after the other."

She screened her thoughts behind down-swept lashes that glistened with melted snowflakes. He suddenly felt like a heel, and it was on the tip of his tongue to apologize.

But he'd never been much good at that.

Madsen wasn't blind. From what he'd seen, the folks left at home had suffered as much as the soldiers. He knew next to nothing about Rose, about what she might have lost or suffered or sacrificed to bring her to where she was now.

And he was in no position to judge another person's actions.

"It won't last," she said. "People are working to get their lives back. Those who can't rebuild are heading west to start over. That's what I want to do one day . . . start over."

"You'd leave your home?"

"There's no place I want to go back to. I'd like to maybe find myself a little piece of land and settle down. I want a garden."

"Flowers?"

"Those, too, but I meant vegetables. I've never had a garden, never stayed in one place long enough. I'd like to give it a try."

"Sounds peaceful," Madsen said. "Peace would be a nice change."

"What'll we do about Rawlings?" she said.

"We?"

"Well . . . since I can't shake you. . . ."

"I haven't decided yet."

They walked in crisp silence for a few moments, then Rose said, "Guess there's only one thing to do, then."

"And that is?"

"Break Rawlings out of jail."

That stopped Madsen in his tracks.

"You're not going to make it," he said. "Do you hear me?"

She looked up at him and smiled that sensual smile that sent heat rushing straight to his groin.

"Oh, I don't plan to do it alone," she said. "You're going with me."

The man couldn't seem to get the door at the top of the back stairs open fast enough.

He jerked it wide on its straining hinges and unleashed a sweltering blast of whiskey-stale air that hit Roselyn full in the face. The noise from the saloon below rode the boozy fumes and seeped up through the cracks in the boards.

Her door was at the far end of the dim corridor. She hurried along amid a burst of gusty laughter and loud voices that filtered from somewhere on the other side of the thin doors lining the walls.

He stomped into her room without waiting for an invitation.

While they had been gone, Dill and Sully had hefted the hip tub and lugged it out, obviously with some difficulty if the puddles blotching the floorboards were any indication. They had left a full whiskey bottle and two clean glasses on top of the bureau.

"Sit," Madsen said. "You have some explaining to do."

He yanked off his coat and hat, ignoring the wet snowflakes that showered the furniture and walls.

"For that matter," she said, shoving the door closed, "so do you."

Her face felt overly warm. From the stuffy room? Because he kept so close? Or because of his thunderous expression?

She couldn't decide.

One thing was clear, though. She'd let Madsen Bold get to Rawlings first over her dead body.

Something would come to her, a plan, a way to stay a step ahead. It always did.

Roselyn commanded her nerves to settle down and then took her time removing her coat and bonnet and muffler and hanging them on the hook behind the door. She wasn't so easily ordered around.

He pointed to the bed.

"I said *sit.*"

She sat.

"It seems perfectly clear—" she began.

"To you, maybe, not to me."

"We both want the pouch. Rawlings knows where it is."

"So we should take on the U.S. Army? If memory serves me, I tried that. We lost."

She narrowed her eyes.

"Are you with the Texas State Police?" she said.

"Hell, no! Don't corral me with that sorry excuse for John Law. They're little better than the outlaws they chase."

"Well, no offense, but you have the orneriness of a lawman about you."

"None taken. And you've run into enough ornery lawmen to know?"

She fidgeted with a piece of quilt.

"I've had occasion to bump into one or two in my life."

"I'll just bet you have."

He pulled a chair from the corner and straddled it. His forearms rested on the rounded chair back, and his expression was intense. Her heart pounded hard.

"To answer you," he said, "I was a ranger before the Reconstructionists disbanded them."

"*Los Diablos Tejanos,* the Texas Devils . . . so I was close—"

"Now it's your turn to answer some questions. What's your real name? Why the act? And what's your connection to Rawlings?"

She sat thinking.

"Well?"

"Which one do you want to hear first?"

"Let's start with your name. Is it Rose, or is that part of the act?"

Roselyn sighed. He didn't think much of her that was obvious. The knowledge should have made her feel better.

What did she care what he thought? She didn't need anything from a former lawman, no matter how easy he was on the eyes or how appealing he was.

From her experience, stable family men and lawmen were seldom one and the same. But for some reason she wasn't convinced.

"My name is Roselyn O'Neill. I don't work in a saloon—well, sometimes I do, but not to take up with the customers. I scrub floors, cook, change beds—"

"Your mother work in a saloon?"

"How did you know?"

"Lucky guess."

Roselyn's back bowed up, and she wagged her finger.

"Don't go getting the wrong idea about Mama.

She sings a little, dances a little, mingles, but never—never!—takes up with customers. When she was younger, she had a voice so sweet, it'd make angels weep. Folks used to come for miles just to hear her, and there wouldn't be a dry eye in the house."

"Simmer down, sugar." He held up his hands. "I made no assumptions."

"Well, see that you don't."

"That still doesn't tell me what your connection to Rawlings is."

"Money, what else?"

"It's said true riches are in heaven."

"That may be, but it's nice to have some pocket money while we're waiting to get there."

"That's why you took such a dangerous risk?"

Put that way, it did sound as if Roselyn had stew meat between her ears. And she certainly disliked the idea of his thinking that she tended to go off half-cocked.

"Nothing would have happened to me," she said. "I have Dill and Sully to see to that. One scream and they would've come running."

Madsen bowed his head into his hands.

"Rose, those two old hens are no match for the likes of Rawlings."

When he raised his head, the look he shot her was intimidating and . . . possessive?

"It was a damned foolish stunt to risk your pretty neck for pocket money."

"It wasn't exactly like that," Roselyn said, her voice rising.

"So how was it, exactly?"

"It was for Mama!"

Roselyn could've bitten her tongue off for telling this stranger so much of her business. A deep breath later, she calmed down. No point now in closing the barn door after the horse was out.

"She's a good person; really she is," Roselyn continued. "Since it's just me and Mama, she's always taken care of us and looked to make our stake. It's not her fault it doesn't work out for her. I guess it's the old country Irish in her that keeps her hoping that this time she'll hit the pot of gold at the end of the rainbow."

"What's your mother's name?"

"Fiona."

"And Fiona owes money?"

"Was that a guess, too?"

"Yes."

Roselyn nodded. He must've been a good lawman in his day. That was going to make it harder for her to sneak by him.

"She owes a low-down, no-account weasel who wouldn't think twice about hurting her until she paid."

"This weasel got a name?"

"Everybody's got a name," Roselyn said, "and some I've been reared up not to repeat."

"Spit it out, Rose."

"Duke Pearson," she said in a smaller voice.

Madsen sucked in his breath and then let out a harsh oath that Roselyn chose to ignore.

"So you know him?"

"By reputation. He's a carpetbagger. Never shakes a hand unless it has money in it. There aren't many in South Texas who don't know of him. Was Pearson behind this scheme?"

"No, this was my idea. He wants the pouch. If I return it to him, he'll forget about Mama's debt."

She crossed to the bureau and reached for the bottle.

"Would you like a drink?" she said.

"A glass of water will do."

Eyebrows raised, Roselyn switched her aim and picked up the adjacent water pitcher instead.

"Now," she said, "about breaking Rawlings out—"

"Forget it."

"But—"

"I said, forget it! We're not tangling with the army. We'll track down the marshal in the morning."

"We?" she said.

When she turned around, full water glass in hand, she found Madsen taking his shirt off.

"What do you think you're doing?" she said.

He took the glass, his fingers brushing hers. The air seemed to crackle. Did he feel it, too?

"It's been a long day," he said. "I'm going to bed."

A delicious shiver traveled down her spine.

"There's only one bed," she said.

"Plenty of room for two." He downed the water. "You don't snore, do you?"

"Of course not."

"Good. I'd hate to have to shoot you for warbling smack-dab in the middle of my shut-eye."

"But you can't sleep—"

"I can and I will. Thanks to you, I don't have anywhere to go, remember? I paid for the night with you . . . in that bed."

Roselyn had the grace to blush. He set the empty glass on the small night table and tugged off his boots.

"Then we'll just have to fit head to toe," she said.

"How's that?"

"You sleep with your head down here." She pointed first to the iron footboard and then to the headboard. "And I'll sleep with my head up there. Head to toe. That's the most decent way I can think of on short notice."

Besides, it was too cold for either one of them to sleep on the floor, and she owed the man at least a good night's rest for his money.

As she turned down the bed, he stripped off his gun belt and hung it on the post within easy reach. Then he tossed the pillow to the foot of the mattress and lay down. The ropes groaned under his weight.

"I must be getting old," he said. "This bed sure feels better than bunking on the ground."

Roselyn breathed a sigh of relief that he had left his pants on.

She hadn't realized how tired and drained she was until she took her night shift off the door hook. Turning her back, she slipped the yellowed muslin gown over her head and offered up a futile wish that he could've seen her in something nicer.

Only after she was decently covered did she wiggle out of her brown dress and petticoat and then sit on the edge of the soft mattress to pull off her wool stockings. She kept on the men's flannels she wore; it was too cold to do without them.

"Madsen?" she whispered, unwilling to turn and look at him. "Are you still awake?"

"Yes."

"I have a confession to make."

"Now? I just got comfortable."

"This is the first time I've ever slept in the same bed with a man," she said.

"If it makes you feel better, sugar, I've never slept with a woman before."

Roselyn whipped around and stared.

"I'm your first?"

For some reason, that thought softened her heart.

"Sure are," he said. She could hear his smile. "I always figured it was more polite to sleep after I left them."

She felt her ears flaming and resisted the urge to smack him.

"Just stay to your side of the bed," she said. "No foolishness. Let's get that straight right now."

"Yes, ma'am. I'll do my best to behave."

"Thank you."

After a deep, stretching yawn, she blew out the lamp that was next to the bed and melted into the tick mattress, turning onto her side, as was her habit. Not until she felt the heat of his pelvis resting against hers did she realize that her idea was a big mistake.

Maybe he wouldn't notice her position if she were quiet and didn't move?

"Rose?" she heard him whisper in the darkness. "I like this suggestion."

Suddenly, she was wide awake.

Four

Some habits were hard to break.

Madsen awoke at dawn as usual, tired, aching, and stiff from the too-soft bed. He padded through the shadows to the window to check the street.

All was quiet. And little wonder. Close to two inches of new snow landscaped the world.

Good thing he'd talked Rose out of her harebrained idea of breaking Rawlings out.

This was the kind of weather for staying close to the home fires, not for running from the law. More snow continued to fall thick and steady from a sky as gray and overcast as Madsen felt.

He'd told Rose the truth last night—he wasn't used to sleeping with a woman. Having her so near, the air from her lungs mixing with his, smelling the scent of her hair, and not reaching out with eager hands to pull her into his embrace had him tossing most of the night.

He was no stranger to thwarted desire. And his pride was such that he wasn't about to force himself where he wasn't wanted.

A movement at the fort caught his attention. He put his face to the frosted glass and peered closer.

The change was small, a minor detail most people wouldn't notice. For a man who'd stayed alive by training himself to take note of small details, it couldn't be overlooked.

Two guards walked post as they had yesterday, but now an old sod, hunched into himself against the freezing cold, hung back and paced just beyond sight of the soldiers.

More than likely morning-after drunks weren't an uncommon sight here. But it would take a bellyful of bad booze to shore up even the toughest drinker into loitering outside this morning.

Why would an old man brave this weather?

No sooner had the thought occurred to Madsen than an uneasy feeling stole over him. He whirled toward the bed where Rose still slept bundled under the covers tighter than a tick on a dog.

Or did she?

Wrenching back the rumpled quilt, Madsen stared at nothing but pillows lumped together in the empty bed. A muscle twitched along his jaw.

He swore to the walls. It took only a few moments for him to dress, gather his gear, and head for the fort.

Dill or Sully—Madsen couldn't tell which— turned as Madsen came up behind him, trudging through the drifts. The old gent didn't appear surprised to see him; he actually seemed relieved.

Madsen had a good guess why.

"How long has she been in there?" he snapped.

" 'Bout twenty minutes."

That was long enough to get into trouble.

"Saddle my horse," Madsen said, "and one for her. We'll need provisions and a diversion to get back out of the gate. Can you handle it?"

A buttery smile cracked through the wrinkled face.

"Ye betchy, sonny. Ever heared the racket dynamite'll make?"

"I said a diversion, not a disaster."

The old gent shrugged.

"Y'come t'give me grief, or am I catchin' ye on a good day?"

Madsen handed off his saddlebags and said, "Just be here with the horses."

"Dill and me'll be waitin'," he said.

On entering the opened gate, Madsen headed toward the guardhouse. The two soldiers noted his direction and let him pass.

"Hey, you there!" demanded a voice.

Turning, Madsen saw the skinny sergeant stomping toward him across the snow covered parade ground with two middle-aged privates in tow. Anyone else with any sense and more rank was huddled up inside, where it was warm.

When the sergeant got closer, he peered out from under his forage cap and said, "You're the one asking about Rawlings yesterday. With a woman."

"She here?" Madsen said.

His words hung on a frosty plume of air.

"Maybe. The marshal wants to see you." The sergeant gestured to the privates. "Take him to the guardhouse!"

Madsen tensed his legs, ready to spring, as his gaze swept over the two soldiers. They exchanged the knowing glances of men who had seen war and knew how to live to tell about it.

"Mornin', boys," Madsen said.

"We don't want no trouble, mister," one man said.

"Won't be any," Madsen returned, "unless you start it. No need to bother yourselves. I know my way."

When Madsen stepped inside the low wood-frame building, he saw a row of three cells. Not surprisingly, Rose occupied one.

She waggled her fingers at him from behind bars. Even now she managed to look angry, sheepish, and damned attractive all at the same time.

Desire, hot and powerful and raw, streaked through him.

He found he liked being caught off balance by her.

What did surprise Madsen was that the other cells were empty. That helped explain some of the sergeant's sorry attitude. The rest, Madsen felt sure, he came by natural pedigree.

Hogging the warmth of a potbellied stove was a balding man with a tin badge.

"Mornin', Marshal," Madsen said, and knocked the snow off his shoulders.

"Your name Bold?"

"It is."

The marshal jutted his chin toward Rose.

"This a friend of yours?"

"In a manner of speaking." He strode over to the cell and whispered, "You okay?"

"I'm in trouble," Rose whispered back.

"Everyone's in trouble. Why should you be an exception?"

"How're you going to spring me?"

"I have no idea."

Then he threw her a don't-argue glare and turned back to the marshal.

"Is there a problem?" Madsen said.

"You're a cool one, I'll give y'that. Shuck your hardware onto the desk."

Madsen looked around, calculating the odds. He'd lost the two privates outside somewhere, leaving the marshal and the overeager sergeant to contend with. There was no guarantee Rose wouldn't get hit by a stray bullet or a ricochet if it came to gunplay, so Madsen decided to comply . . . for now.

He set his Sharps rifle down first and then pushed his coat flaps aside and reached for his guns.

"Left-handed, butt end first, if you please," the marshal said. "Wouldn't want anyone killed by accident."

"It wouldn't be an accident," Madsen said.

"We're wasting time yammering," the sergeant cut in when both guns clunked onto the center of the desk. "Let's take him—"

"Hold your horses!" Rose said, her nose stuck out between the bars. "Wherever he goes, I go."

"Suits me," the sergeant said. "We'll take him out and hang him!"

"I was only joking, Marshal," Rose said, backing away from the bars. "I really like it in here."

The marshal held up one hand for quiet.

"Simmer down there, Sarge," he said. "You can't hang a man without a fair trial. In these parts, we give 'em a trial first . . . then we hang 'em."

"Awful free with my neck, aren't you?" Madsen said, shoving the sergeant's hand off his arm. "What's the charge?"

The marshal unlocked the cell door next to Rose's and jabbed a thumb in the air for Madsen to go inside.

"You know dad-blamed well what it is," he said. "Missy there helped that polecat Rawlings escape, and if you're with her, then you was in on it, too."

Madsen glanced hard at Rose, who screwed up her face and shook her head, then looked at him through innocent eyes. He felt her gaze warm him to his toes.

Instead of moving, he relaxed his stance and thumbed up his hat.

"If that's so," he said, "and I'm not saying it is, how come we're still here and you're not out there forming a posse to run him to ground?"

"They don't pay me to freeze my keister in a blizzard. I got you two. That'll do me for—"

Whatever else he meant to say got cut short when a roaring blast split the air. The shock rattled the walls, knocked the startled marshal off his feet, and propelled the sergeant to hightail it out the door before the ceiling caved in.

Madsen swore to himself but lost no time in reacting.

He swiped the cell keys from the marshal's hand. When the marshal tried to regain his feet, a short jab to his nose made sure he stayed down.

"Earthquake?" Rose said, eyes wide.

"Named Sully," Madsen said, working her door open and snatching her out by the hand. "Run to the gate, sugar! Don't stop for anything."

"What about you?"

"I'll be on your heels. Now go! Your outlaws are waiting."

And he gave her bottom a shove to help her on her way.

To be on the safe side, he rolled the marshal's unconscious body into the cell and locked the door. A quick toss sent the keys flying into the far corner behind the desk.

Then Madsen palmed his gun belt in one hand, grabbed the Sharps in the other, and darted out the door.

All hell had busted loose on the parade ground.

Sully had blown the supply building that sat next to the stables, raining beans and slabs of salt pork onto the snow, along with splintered boards from the building's side and half its roof.

Madsen smelled acrid smoke and heard the crackle of fire.

He dodged harried soldiers who worked to round up terrified horses that had broken out. Some horses were trampling mongrel dogs that appeared from nowhere and were snarling over pork scraps.

Madsen saw Rose clear the gate when first one bullet fanned past his ear and then another grazed his left side, searing a fiery trail of white pain across his ribs. In that second, it dawned on him that nothing was stopping her and her two criminals from hightailing it out of there and leaving him alone to face a noose.

That wasn't a prospect Madsen cared to entertain.

He turned, crouched, and returned fire in one motion. When he dove to the side to avoid another bullet aimed his way, he came up face-to-face with the startled sergeant.

The sergeant recovered quickly, let loose a cry of "You! Where's the marshal?" and barreled toward Madsen.

Half a heartbeat later, Madsen sidestepped the young man and buffaloed him with the barrel of his gun. The impact threw the sergeant's limp body forward, where he splattered face first in a puddle of beans.

"Ain't my day to watch him, Sarge," Madsen said.

"Bold!" he heard Rose shout across the confusion. "Quit lollygagging. It's time to get while the getting's good!"

Surprise hit Madsen then, and he needed no further urging. He straightened, holstered his gun, and streaked for the waiting horses.

Five

They headed south for a few miles through a steady snowfall until they came upon a tributary of the South Platte. It was a good place to divvy up to throw off any pursuers.

"This way?" Roselyn said, pointing.

She threw a questioning gaze toward Sully, and he nodded.

"Dill and me'll foller the crick down thataways," he said, " 'fore we backtrack to Deadwater. If they's any scratchy customers on our tail, we'll know it."

Then he gestured at an angle.

"Y'all cut southeast, foller the crick 'til y'come to a small cabin what's got a lean-to attached. That'll be the Bodine place. We'll meet y'there in a day or so."

As Sully talked, Roselyn noticed that Madsen kept sweeping the area with constant glances. It reassured her and made her uneasy at the same time.

"Showing our face this close to town is too risky," Madsen said.

"The cabin ain't close, and ain't nobody lived there since old man Bodine passed on to his reward last winter. It's a good place to hole up and wait out t'storm."

"Keep yer eyes peeled," Dill cut in. "She'll be sittin' high on a bank in a snaggle of quakies. It's a mite hard to spot if'n y'didn't knowed it was there."

"And if it's not there?" Madsen said.

"Then you're stuck with me until spring," Roselyn said.

She'd meant it as a joke.

He didn't even crack a smile.

Roselyn figured a man like him had little practice at leaving a town in a hurry, probably never had much reason to, and that was why he looked so glum about the whole mess. She came close to telling him he'd get used to it—she certainly had—but she stopped herself.

Such thoughts suggested permanence, and she meant to see that their unintended partnership remained very temporary.

"I know it's a bit humid out here," she said, blinking against the damp snowflakes that hit her lashes, "but is your sense of humor all wet as well?"

"My humor is just fine," he said. "Why shouldn't it be? I'm out a hundred dollars, out a good night's sleep, I'm running from the law and the army, and I'm courting lung fever. Today is still young. I figure if I'm hanged by supper, it'll give me something to look forward to."

Roselyn winced. The man was right; she'd made a mess of his life, though it was painful for her to admit it. But there wasn't a blessed thing she could do about it now.

"Know what Mama would say?"

"That we should take Frank and Jesse here and form our own outlaw gang?" Madsen suggested.

"She'd say no use crying over spilt milk," Roselyn said, ignoring his sarcasm. "And if I had known you'd quibble over every little detail . . ."

"Little—?"

"The cabin," Dill interrupted, a grin oiling his face. "She'll be there, sonny. Sully and me, we done reconnoitered, what with Miss Hattie Mae's help."

Then Sully eased his horse up along Madsen and spoke low, but Roselyn overheard him, anyway.

"Y'watch yerself, now, sonny. I allow things ain't shaped up to yer way of figgering, but it ain't all her doing. Miz Roselyn's a good girl what's got a fine head on her shoulders. Harm one hair on that head and you'll answer to me and m' brother. Y'heared me?"

"I hear you, old man."

"And?"

"Rose is safe with me. I have no intention of touching her."

"Gemme yer word on it?"

"I said so, didn't I?"

Hearing him practically spit the words at Sully,

Roselyn didn't know whether to be relieved or insulted.

The nerve of the man. Madsen hadn't heard her side of this, yet he'd already decided that the marshal spoke true and she was a guilty lawbreaker.

How like a lawman.

She watched until Dill and Sully disappeared into a curtain of snow and then felt a shiver down her spine at being on her own with Madsen. Behind those quiet, steady eyes, the man was seething. She could feel it, had felt it since he'd walked into the guardhouse and spied her behind bars.

If only he wasn't so sinfully attractive when he was angry.

The two of them rode in silence through rapidly dropping temperatures until, about twenty miles out from town, they came in sight of the Bodine place. For a while there, Roselyn worried they'd gotten lost.

But there the cabin sat, high on the snowy bank of the iced-over river and nestled in a quiet stand of aspen trees, just as Dill had promised.

There was no sign of life. No one about. No smoke curling up the chimney.

Teeth chattering, Roselyn walked her horse up cautiously, just in case. When nothing stirred, she reined in at the lean-to shed that looked to house four horses easily and dismounted in snow over her ankle boots.

"We shouldn't stop for long," she said. "Just long enough to grab a bite and thaw out a bit."

"We've got time." Madsen turned in the saddle to check their back trail as Roselyn noticed he'd done every so often. "No one's followed us."

He spoke so quietly, he almost sounded bored.

But Roselyn knew better. The way her luck was going, she wouldn't be surprised if he wasn't building up to a real hissy fit.

"The snow's covered our tracks," he said, dismounting and leading his horse into the lean-to behind Roselyn. "And the marshal won't budge far from that warm stove of his."

"What about the army?"

"By the time the fort can get men saddled, there won't be a trail to pick up. Here, I'll look after the horses."

He passed her the saddlebags from his horse and hers.

"Take these," he said, "and go in and see if you can get a fire started."

Inside the windowless cabin, it was cold, dim, and musty. Roselyn's breath frosted in the air.

It was a humble cabin, not much more than one lone man might need. She left the door ajar to let in the light and saw a table and two chairs that dominated the center of the room.

An assortment of saws, picks, and other tools decorated the pegged walls. A small wooden set of shelves held cooking pots and utensils, and two narrow bunks, topped with army blankets, were wedged L shape to the fireplace.

The firewood the late Mr. Bodine had laid in had lasted longer than he did. Roselyn judged that the bin next to the river-rock fireplace held a good two weeks' worth of wood.

She plopped both saddlebags on the table and disturbed a hundred years of dust for her trouble. After waving her hand through a coughing fit, she set about building a fire and then gathered some snow in a pot to melt for drinking and wash water.

Only a few minutes passed before the dry wood caught and blazed hot and bright. The warmth so penetrated the small room that Roselyn could close the door and shed her coat and gloves and hang them on a free peg.

Her growling stomach prompted her to pull out some jerky and hard biscuits, a can of condensed milk, a tin of tomatoes, and a few coffee beans from among the provisions that Dill had packed for her. Her fingers grazed the flask he'd included, too, and she hesitated, then decided to add it to the table fare as well.

Men usually preferred something to warm their gullet.

The cozy cabin soon filled with the aroma of coffee, and the homey combination set Roselyn's imagination to wandering to that house with the vegetable garden she'd always dreamed of. In her mind's eye rose the handsome banker, or merchant, perhaps, who'd share quiet evenings at home with her, but the image distorted out of shape when Madsen Bold's scowling face kept floating in his place.

A gust of cold air shattered her daydream and sent shivers racing up her arms. She whirled, and there stood the devil as if she'd conjured him, stamping his boots to knock off the snow.

"The storm's starting to kick up," Madsen snapped, pushing on the door to close it against the blowing snow. "It's getting colder—" He stopped short and stared at her. "What's the matter?"

"N-nothing," she said, flashing him an uncertain smile, and then she gestured to the fireplace. "Come over and warm yourself up."

He shrugged out of his hat and coat and hung them on a wall peg before moving in front of the fire, where he extended his hands toward the flames.

"Is that coffee I smell?"

"Care for a little something in it?"

She lifted the flask toward the tin cup.

"No, thanks. Just coffee will do."

Roselyn shrugged, set the flask back down, and filled his cup.

When he turned and reached for it with his left hand, she saw him flinch, and then she saw why.

A small patch of blood stained his shirt under his arm. She gasped.

"You're hit!" she said, her hand flying to her mouth. "Oh, Madsen, why didn't you say something before? Thundering hallelujah, and here you let me rattle on like a—"

"Don't bother yourself, sugar. It's just a scratch. The cold stanched the bleeding."

"From the looks, it bled quite a lot for just a scratch."

Guilt settled on her shoulders. He'd risked his life to get her out of jail, and he didn't even know her.

Ignoring his protests, she quickly rummaged in her saddlebags and came up with two clean hankies, a small jar of salve, her night shift, and a small sewing kit.

"No need for all that. It'll be scabbed over by morning."

"Nonsense," she said. "You could be dead by morning, or worse."

"What's worse than dead?"

He chuckled.

She waved his heroics away.

"Look, cowboy, I'm grateful for your help this morning—"

"You're welcome."

"But if you think I'm going to kill myself trying to dig a grave in frozen ground, think again. So unless you like the idea of your carcass being wolf bait—"

"Spare me the gory details," he said, holding up a hand. "I'm a sensitive man."

Narrowing her eyes, she said, "Take off your shirt and let me tend to your wound. And I won't take no for an answer."

Giving him no room to argue further, she helped him out of his flannel shirt and the two layers of heavy undershirts he wore. Then she bent to inspect the wound.

A groove the width of her thumb was carved out of the side of his ribs where a bullet had grazed. Lordy, it had come so close. Another inch over . . .

Roselyn bit her lip against the urge to cry.

"Someone's got good aim," she said instead.

"I've got good luck."

"Thank your stars for small favors, then," she said. "The bullet didn't go in."

"Told you I'd be fine."

"Let me be the judge of that. Sit here, near the light."

He settled into a chair angled toward the hearth as she hunkered down for a closer look. The bleeding had stopped. What blood his undershirts hadn't soaked up was dried and splotching his rib cage. The skin around the groove was an angry red.

After gathering a pan of water and the flask, she knelt at Madsen's thighs, eye level to his rapidly discoloring torso.

"Can you see all right?" he said.

"I can see you were a soldier," she said. Several faint scars marked his years of fighting and shone stark against the bruised flesh. "And accustomed to pain, from the looks of you."

Roselyn bent to the pan she'd placed at her side, swished one of the hankies in the water, and wrung out the cloth. Then she dabbed along the wound and cleaned the dried blood away.

He blanched from the pressure.

"It needs a few stitches," she said.

When she straightened, her head grazed his upraised elbow. She frowned.

"Sorry," he mumbled.

Moving his arm out of her way, he thrust his fingers through the dark strands on top of his head, giving her a good glimpse of the muscles that had crowded the sleeves of his shirt.

"You can't hold it like that for long," she said. "Here." She lifted his hand. "Lay your arm over my shoulder."

"Have you ever stitched up a man?"

Roselyn knelt and curved toward the light, positioning the thread at the eye of the needle.

"You're my first," she said, and held up the needle like a sword blade. "Are you a gambler?"

He glanced at the needle and then managed a grin.

"Do I have a choice?"

"No."

"I guess I'm a gambler."

"I like a man who's decisive." She held the needle above the water pan and poured whiskey over it. Then she said, "This is going to hurt."

And she poured whiskey over his wound.

Madsen sucked in air through his teeth but uttered no other sound.

Satisfied he wasn't going to faint dead at her feet, Roselyn brushed beneath his armpit and surveyed the ragged line of puckering skin at his rib cage.

"It's long, Madsen," she murmured past a small catch in her throat. "I'll try not to hurt you more than necessary."

"Do what you have to, sugar," he said.

"Here," she said, offering the flask. "Maybe you should take a few swallows first."

He waved it away.

"An empty belly and whiskey don't mix," he said. "Just get this over with."

When the needle pierced his skin, he never flinched. Instead, she felt his fingers splay across her back as he sucked in another halting breath.

"I'm sorry," she said.

"You're a small thing," he muttered, "to be so much trouble."

"A wise man thinks twice," she countered, "before he insults the one who's got his hide in her hands."

Roselyn bumped his arm when she raised her head to look at him. His hand rested on her shoulder.

"I learned quick not to insult you when you have a weapon in your hand." He grazed her cheek with his knuckle, and his face softened. "Are you finished carving me up yet?"

They gazed at each other for long seconds.

Lordy, how her stomach fluttered when he looked at her. She didn't want this, didn't need these trembling feelings that kept interfering with good sense. The sooner she was rid of the man, the better.

"A moment more," she said, swallowing.

With precision, she tied one knot, dabbed at the weeping puncture, and stabbed the raw flesh again.

Kneeling so intimately to him and overshadowed by his bulk, Roselyn could scarcely miss his virility. Her gaze again touched his skin, but was not entirely impersonal this time.

A fine layer of dusky hair coated the firm texture of muscles that rippled beneath her fingers. Like his face, his body was hard and bronze, as if he spent a great deal of time working outdoors.

"You know it was a bonehead move," he said, "to break out Rawlings and let him get away."

"I didn't do it." She glared up at him, daring him to call her a liar. "Sully overheard a man who helped bring Rawlings in." Then she resumed stitching and dabbing. "Rawlings had boasted about a lady friend who wouldn't let him rot in jail because he was worth his weight in gold to her. I only went to talk to Rawlings and—"

"And to get the jump on me?"

"Now that you mention it, yes."

She wrung the hankie out again as if choking it to death. What did she care what he thought?

"But he was gone when I got there," she added, "and that low-down varmint of a sergeant was pointing the finger at me."

"Guess it doesn't take much to figure how she got past the sergeant?"

Roselyn snorted agreement.

"That mean you believe me?" she said.

"Maybe."

"You can bet she wasn't homely as a lemon," she said. "There are a sinful lot of men in this world who get to feeling puffy when a woman smiles on them."

"Rose, I imagine she did a sight more than smile."

"I was being polite."

She reached a spot missing a good-sized chunk of skin and fixed her attention on the delicate work.

"Hold on to your teeth, Madsen. This isn't going to be pleasant."

Uttering a short prayer against the added pain she'd inflict, she stretched the ragged pieces together and speared them with the needle before they slipped back.

"Damn, woman! You're enjoying this, aren't you?"

"Afraid I am," she snapped. "Hold still." To distract him, she added, "If you're not a lawman anymore, that mean you plan on keeping the pouch for yourself?"

"No. I'm doing a friend a favor. I'll turn the pouch over to him."

"You do know what's in the pouch?"

"Diamonds."

"And you're not interested?"

"They're not mine," he said simply. "I shook hands that I'd return them, and that's what I'll do. I don't go back on my word, Rose."

"Ever?"

"Never."

He spoke the truth; Roselyn could feel it in her bones. If he got his hands on that pouch, Mama's chances of escaping Duke Pearson's hold were gone. Roselyn couldn't let that happen.

"There!" she said. "All done." She leaned back and surveyed her handiwork. "That wasn't so bad, was it?"

He grunted. Beads of sweat dotted his lip, and the lines around his nostrils whitened. She poured more whiskey from the flask onto the hankie and dabbed the sutures just in case. His fingers moved over her shoulder in reflex.

"You feel nice," he breathed.

"Thought you griped I was too small?"

"Changed my mind," he murmured. "I'd say you're just about right."

As he spoke, she studied each crease of his luscious mouth, unable to tear her gaze away, feeling shivers race to her stomach and lower.

This man was trouble.

"Done yet?" he said.

"B-bandage," she croaked, then cleared her throat. "I mean, I should bandage it first."

Madsen sat patiently, his eyelids drooping, while Roselyn ripped long strips from the hem of her night shift with shaky fingers. Where was good sense when she needed it? Everything she'd ever told herself about men flew out the door when Madsen looked at her as if she were the only woman alive.

A good dose of Mama is what Roselyn needed right now to set her thinking back straight.

She dabbed on some of the salve and then knelt between his thighs again to wind the cloth around his ribs. When he took a deep breath, the effort must have produced a knifing pain, because he grabbed for his injured side and closed his fingers over hers.

His sudden movement caught her off guard, and her balance tipped. Unable to move the hand he gripped, she plopped her other hand to his chest to steady herself. Beneath her fingers, the flat male nipple grew taut within the matting of curls, and a groan escaped his lips.

"I'm sorry," she said, seeing his eyes squeezed shut tight. "Honest, Madsen, I didn't mean to hurt you."

Her gaze dropped to the hand he cradled against his warm chest. She tugged, but he held firm. Her face was a scant inch away from his, his warm breath caressing her cool cheek, when his eyelids slowly opened to reveal a dark gaze burning with sensual intensity.

"That's not what hurts, sugar."

"Oh," she said, sounding breathless even to her ears.

Wedged between his muscular legs, Roselyn became aware of the hardness nudging her waist. Her mind raced in a whirlwind. Nothing had prepared her to deal with his kind of assault upon her senses.

She moistened lips gone dry. Her gaze flicked over him, drinking in the sight of a full mouth, the sweep of black hair falling over his brow, and stormy eyes. Intense, questioning, inviting eyes. They snatched her air, preempted her voice, and tugged at her resistance.

A wolf cry carried on the wind outside as the

heat built inside and coursed the length of Roselyn's body until she felt saturated in it and heavy-limbed. Her heart pounded in her ears.

She closed her eyes, drew in a ragged breath to calm herself, and knew it was a mistake. He smelled of horse, leather, and such wicked notions.

Maybe just one taste . . .

"W-want to kiss me?" she whispered.

"I want to do a lot more than kiss you, Rose."

Delicious shivers undulated down her spine, but when he stayed still, she said, "What's wrong?"

"I can't. I gave my word I wouldn't touch you that way."

"It's all right," she said with a desperation she didn't understand. "I won't tell anyone. No one will know."

"I'd know, Rose."

On a whimper of frustration, Roselyn deflated. Something akin to panic gnawed at her and spread through her chest, rising into her throat until she wanted to laugh and cry at the same time.

This had never happened to her, this confusion. Never. She flushed hot and cold and wondered if she was coming down sick.

For the first time in a long time, Roselyn was afraid, afraid to grasp what lay ahead and equally afraid to release her dreams.

Deep in her heart, she admired Madsen's restraint. She was used to being around the kind of men who got overly friendly and expected a lot for very little. Madsen was a different breed.

But right now she wished he wasn't.

"I've never met anyone like you," she said, reaching up, her hand trembling, then pulling her hand back.

She was unable to peel her gaze away from his sumptuous mouth as his lips relaxed into a faint, provocative smile.

"I gave my word, and I won't go back on it," he said. "But that doesn't mean you can't touch me if you want."

Roselyn hesitated; then, encouraged by his grin, she brought her mouth up until her lips brushed his, just barely touching, teasing the curve of his smile. Once. Twice.

He uttered a frustrated sound at the back of his throat before warm, soft, and gentle lips answered her back. She inhaled an appreciative breath, and his musky scent twined around her senses.

When she leaned back, uncertain and curious at the same time, she saw the hunger he couldn't hide reflected in his eyes. She cupped his cheek in a gentle grasp, intending to taste him again, but she frowned instead.

The stubbly skin beneath her fingers was warm, too warm. Cold reality doused her passionate fires.

"You're hot," Roselyn said on a gasp. "Burning."

"I know, and it's your fault."

"Be serious, Madsen."

Cupping both cheeks in her hands, she dipped

his chin down and kissed his forehead to gauge his temperature as her mama had done when she was little.

"You've got a good fever building here," she said. "You need to rest. Let's get you covered up in bed."

"Only if you join me," he said.

"Stop your foolishness. Now, scoot."

"Anyone tell you that you're a bossy woman, Roselyn O'Neill?"

"And you're a stubborn man, Madsen Bold."

Once he was in the bunk and covered, she tucked the blanket around him, trying not to disturb his injured side, but he winced, anyway.

"You didn't do anything, sugar," he said, looking up at her. "It's a little sore, is all."

The possessive blaze in his eyes ignited those strange sensations uncurling through Roselyn again. And she couldn't seem to stop touching him. She brushed his hair back, grazing his heated skin with her knuckles and suddenly wanting to hold him so close that she couldn't tell where he began and she left off.

Oh, no. Maybe she was more like her mama than she cared to believe.

Then Madsen blinked, and the heated look vanished so quickly, Roselyn wondered if she'd seen anything there at all. In the awkward silence that fell between them, she patted his hand and turned around to tidy up the items she'd used to tend his wound.

Despite what she'd told herself about finding a

banker or a merchant, right now she wanted nothing more than to see that look come back again into Madsen's eyes.

Six

Madsen was in hell.

His throat was parched. And wasn't water what people in hell always wanted?

He felt the hot flames licking all around him, smelled acrid brimstone, and heard the damned moaning. No matter where he turned his head, he couldn't escape the raging heat or the sound.

It hurt to open his eyes, so he gave up trying. Something soft touched his cheek, and he turned his face into it, wallowing in a sweet smell that was comforting and familiar, yet the image played just out of his reach.

He grabbed onto the softness, dragging it closer, hugging it to him, unwilling to give it up even as someone tried to pull it away from him.

"Mine," he said. "I keep what's mine."

The softness enveloped him then, caressing him and crooning to him, lulling him until he sighed with deep satisfaction and dropped into a dreamless sleep.

Later, a mournful wind singing through the bare trees outside woke him. The cabin was quiet.

Too quiet. Madsen lifted his head and saw nothing but an empty room in the dying firelight.

The little swindler had left him again. Damn her. He had to catch up to her before she rode too far.

He struggled out of the bunk and lurched to the table, grabbing the edge for support and willing his head to quit swimming. His vision was blurry, and his side pained like a double mule kick.

Madsen swore to himself. No telling how much of a lead she had on him. If it was still snowing, she'd be hard to track. He should have known better than to trust her.

Suddenly, behind him, the cabin door whipped open on a frigid blast of air. And that's when Madsen realized he was buck-naked except for his bandaged ribs. The chill howled through his fevered body like a hurricane.

"Have you lost your mind?" Rose demanded, putting her shoulder into closing the door.

"Maybe I have," Madsen said, trying to steady himself. "I'm not sure anymore. Do crazy people know they've lost their minds?"

"No, that's what makes them crazy. Come, you'll catch your death. Get back in that bed."

"I thought you'd gone." She shook her head in denial, but he caught the swift shift of her eyes. "Where were you?"

Rose rushed to his side and slipped under his arm, then steered him back toward the bunk.

"If you must know," she said, helping him ease

down, "I was visiting the privy. I'm not so low I'd run out on a sick man."

But she had entertained the idea. He was certain.

What changed her mind?

She fussed a moment, tucking him back in. Madsen started to thank her for staying even though she'd wanted to leave, but when his head touched the pillow again, he was too tired to talk.

It was daybreak when his inner clock woke him and he cracked his eyes open again. His skin felt clammy. He put tentative fingers on his bandaged ribs and winced. The cabin was warm and dim, lit only by the crackling glow of burning logs that sent shadows dancing on the chinked walls.

Madsen turned his head toward the source of the shadows and saw his shirts hung over a line that Rose had strung across the room in front of the fireplace. She was silhouetted behind the shirts.

And she was bathing.

Madsen knew then he was in a hell of his own making.

Apparently, she figured he was still sleeping. For the view she offered him, he wasn't about to disavow her of that notion just yet.

He'd told Sully he wouldn't touch her, and as many times as Madsen wished that he hadn't opened his mouth, he would stand by his word. But Madsen never said anything to the old rooster about looking.

So while she swished a cloth in the tin basin

and washed, he lay quietly drinking in her details, clearly and precisely. He allowed his gaze to drift over her, caressing her from head to bare foot and all the womanly curves in between.

She wouldn't appreciate his watching, but he tortured himself all the same. It'd been too long since he'd enjoyed the half-revealed secrets of a woman at her bath, and she was a handsome woman.

He pressed his head back against the pillow, his gaze intent on her. Every nuance of what he saw burned into his brain.

When she bent forward, reaching for a drying cloth, he caught a glimpse of her between the shirts. Firelight danced off water droplets that trickled down her arm to her fingers. A curtain of hair, as bright as prairie fire, hid her face, but the wet ends clung to her naked body and caressed the lovely curve of a lush breast. He could see a rosy nub pucker in the chilly air.

Madsen's mouth grew dry. He watched the light leap and shimmer through her blonde hair when she tossed it forward and ruffled her fingers through the strands.

His gaze trailed across her bare shoulders and traced down her slender back to a naked bottom that was full, tight, wet, and teasing his tongue to taste. The wild scent that was Rose's alone wafted to his nose and straight to his groin.

He wanted her.

At the same time, he had no business chewing over thoughts about her. His job was to recover

the diamonds, and he had to keep his mind on
seeing the chore done.

Besides, she could be one of the outlaws he was
after. She was as perplexing as she was handsome,
and there were still too many unanswered questions.

Although he'd admit she was definitely a dis-
traction.

He wanted to bend her over the table, wrap her
hair around his fist and anchor her feet apart, and
lap every inch of moisture off her sweet skin with
his tongue. He wanted to surround himself with
her warmth and feel the pulsing life of her.

But now wasn't the time. Even if he hadn't given
his word, he was too wrung out to do either one
of them any good right now. There was no harm
in letting his gaze linger on her a moment more,
though.

Madsen closed his eyes as the familiar stirrings
washed over him deep inside. When his gaze came
up again, he found himself looking into eyes that
were smoky and brilliant and startled.

Both of them had the same thought.

For a mere instant, he caught his own desire
reflected back at him before she tried to hide it.

"Are you awake?" she said in a breathless whisper.

Then she peered at him as if trying to decide
whether his eyes were clear or still glazed with fever.

A gentleman would have feigned sickness.

"Fever's broken," Madsen said, grinning. "I've
been awake, sugar. You're using a pretty soap."

She was the first to look away.

With the fire at her back, darting behind the cover of the drying shirts didn't hide much, either, but Madsen kept that to himself. He liked looking at her.

"I take it you're feeling better?" she called.

"Like I fought a mule team and they won," he said.

She poked her head around the shirts and said, "I think the worst is over, but you need to rest."

"I've been in worse shape, sugar."

The grin stayed with him as he turned his face to the wall so she'd feel she could dress in some privacy. And the images of her bath remained in that place he reserved for drowsy memories.

"You know you could've lied to me," she griped.

"Next time, I will. But I figured turnabout was fair play."

"Meaning what?"

"This is twice now, woman, you've seen me without a stitch on. I can't say that I would've bothered to get out of my clothes by myself."

She came out from around the shirts, buttoning her dress to her throat, her hair plaited into a loose braid.

"You were boiling in your own juices," she said. "I had to rub snow on you to bring the fever down, and I couldn't very well do that through your clothes."

Madsen turned and threw her a mock frown.

"You didn't take advantage of me while I was indisposed, did you?"

She snorted.

"Mr. Bold, your virtue is safe with me."

"I'm relieved to hear it. I sure would hate to think I missed anything. But now that I'm back to snuff, if you want to . . ."

He lost his leering gaze when he tried rolling onto his elbow to sit up and gritted his teeth against the pain. She was at his side in an instant.

"Here, let me help you."

It was too late for either one of them to plead modesty. She slid his arm over her shoulder and pulled him upright, exposing his bare legs and thigh in the process. Then she sat on the bunk next to him.

"You're as weak as a kitten," she said. "Just what would you do if I took you up on your offer?"

He glanced at her in alarm.

"You aren't, are you?"

"No." She laughed and then said, "I bet you're hungry."

"Starved," he said, smiling.

Rose stretched to the end of the bunk and grabbed his underdrawers and pants, handing them to him.

"Need help or can you manage these on your own?"

Her nearness was enough to stir him. If she crouched to help him put his pants on, he wasn't sure his resolve would stand the test.

"I can manage," he said, taking the clothes.

She crossed to the shirts and felt them.

"These are almost dry."

"Look in my saddlebags," he said. "I've got another clean shirt, but I'd like to wash up first."

Later, after downing a plate of biscuits and milk, Madsen felt his strength returning. He finished the remaining tomatoes, the coffee, and two glasses of water and wiped his mouth with the back of his hand.

"Tell me something," Rose said, rising from the table. "Did you really track a man all the way to Canada once for stealing a horse?"

Madsen cast her a thoughtful glance and handed her his empty plate and cup.

"How'd you hear about that?"

She shrugged and dumped the dishes into the pan to wash.

"You talked in your fever last night."

"It was my horse," Madsen said.

"Must've been an expensive one."

He grunted and reached for his gun belt.

"The nag wasn't worth twenty dollars."

"Then why did you bother?"

"Because the horse was mine," Madsen repeated. "And the hombre stole from me."

After buckling on his gun belt, he slipped on his coat and hat.

"I'm going to check on our horses. If the weather's let up, we can keep on toward Denver City."

Rose fed another log to the fire and then straightened.

"How did you know that's where I was headed?"

"That's where I'd go if I was Rawlings, and you're following Rawlings, aren't you?"

"Madsen, you might be too smart for your own good. Think it's wise to travel with those ribs?"

"You wouldn't be trying to lose me, sugar, now, would you?"

He grinned and, without waiting for an answer he already knew, pulled the door closed behind him.

Outside, little had changed from the day before. The same gray overcast and dreary skies lay on the world like a heavy shroud.

Snow decorated the bare branches of the closely packed trees and piled the ground in deep drifts. No snow fell now, but the breeze had picked up, and the cold knifed right through his layers of clothes.

A smart man wouldn't travel in this weather. Question was, how smart was Teddy Lee Rawlings?

Not much if Rose were to be believed. Her story about retrieving the diamonds to satisfy her mother's debt meant Rawlings had gone and double-crossed Duke Pearson. Not a healthy move.

So how desperate was Rawlings?

Up to now, he'd skirted the big towns. But he knew Madsen was closing in, and he couldn't spend diamonds. Whatever his plan had been, his only choice now was to try to find a buyer pronto, someone who'd pay him more than whatever Pearson had offered for stealing them.

Denver City was the closest place a buyer might

be. Rawlings would light out for there, unload the diamonds, and then hightail it to parts unknown.

No, a smart man might not brave the weather, but a desperate man would.

And so would Madsen.

He thought of that painting on the ceiling back in Deadwater . . . "Heaven or Hell." Now he understood some of that old boy's dilemma, for he wasn't sure he'd live through the temptation of spending another day alone in the cabin with Rose.

Halfway around the lean-to shed, Madsen halted, the silence finally penetrating the tantalizing thoughts of Rose that fogged his mind. He cocked his head and listened.

No sounds of starlings. No crows. Nothing moved but the nearby creek water sluicing over chunks of ice. A quick glance to his side saw the horses standing tense and prick-eared.

Madsen combed the trees for any sign of intruders as the fingers on his left hand closed around the butt of his gun.

Seven

What a ninny.

As Roselyn stowed their gear and set the cabin back the way she'd found it, she berated herself for going soft and not heading out last night, as she'd started to do. With Madsen laid up and unable to stop, or follow, her, it was the perfect chance to get a jump on him.

At any other time, she'd have hightailed it without a backward glance, snow or no snow. She wasn't a stranger to dodging trouble or to using bad weather to gain some ground. Dill and Sully knew she was heading toward Denver City. All she had to do was keep traveling southeast and they'd catch up to her in no time.

But she'd stayed instead. Something about leaving Madsen hadn't set well with her.

It was gratitude, she decided. Nothing more. She was simply grateful he'd helped her out of a tight spot. He'd done for her. Now she'd done for him.

They were square in her book.

Still, there was a niggling doubt that she preferred not to examine too closely.

For pity's sake, she'd wasted enough time with the man. Rawlings might well be halfway to Denver City and unloading the diamonds by now.

As far as Roselyn was concerned, she no longer owed Madsen Bold anything, and all bets were off. The first chance she came across to give him the slip, by golly, she'd take it.

Saddlebags in hand, Roselyn was too busy listening to her own thoughts to notice anything outside. She resolutely headed out the door, never dreaming the chance she'd hoped for would grab her, literally.

She barely cleared the doorway when someone lunged at her from the side of the cabin. A dirty arm snaked around her waist at the same time a rancid-smelling hand smashed over her mouth, bruising her lips.

"Lookee here," a voice said. "If'n it ain't a she-male!"

Her scream garbled. She bucked and wiggled, wrestling with her attacker.

"Willie," said another voice, brimming with laughter. "Yer fightin' like two wildcats with only one tree a'tween 'em. Can't y'hold her still?"

Roselyn recognized that polecat's voice. Anger surged hot through her.

"I'm a'tryin' to—"

One solid kick to Willie's shin cut him off. He yelped and danced on one foot.

Then, twisting to the side, Roselyn pumped her

elbow and drove it home in his soft middle a second before she brought her knee up and into his groin.

A sound like a blacksmith's bellows deflating exploded from his lips. He doubled over, his grip vanishing as quickly as it had appeared.

Ready to give the familiar polecat a tongue-lashing, Roselyn dropped the saddlebags, whirled, and stepped into a backhand that came from nowhere, clipping her jaw.

Her head snapped backward, and a million tiny lights burst into her vision as she pitched forward to the snow.

"That weren't a nice thing t'do, lady," said a breathless voice above her head.

Roselyn clung with defiance to consciousness and struggled to put her knees under her body. She raised her head to the laughing man, who was mounted on a dun mare.

"Hello, Jackie," she snapped. "Glad to see you're out of jail."

"Well, I'll be go to hell . . ."

Jackie Trambull was a short, stocky cutthroat nearing fifty, with sunken eyes, sporting a stringy gray beard, and carrying a sweet spot for Roselyn's mama that had never been returned. He thumbed up the brim of his pancake hat and then dismounted as fast as his bulk allowed.

"Rosie, z'at you?" he said, helping her stand and dusting the snow off her skirts. "Sure didn't s'pect t'meet up with you in these parts."

"So what are you doing here?" she said.

"I was wonderin' the same 'bout you."

"We're passing through. Last I heard you were placer mining in California."

Jackie shrugged.

"Sheriffs ain't too friendly out there, so me 'n the boys figgered on tryin' our hand 'round here. We was just lookin' for a place to warm up 'fore we ride on. How's that purty ma of yers?"

"Fine, last time I saw her." Roselyn flung off his rough hand and touched tentative fingers to her throbbing chin. "What's the big idea of letting this mangy skunk manhandle me?"

"Ain't no call t'go gettin' y'feathers ruffled, Rosie. How's we t' know it was you?"

"I'd wear a sign," she said, casting her glance around, "but you can't read. The man with me . . . what have you done with him?"

Jackie hooked a blunt thumb over his shoulder.

"Preacher's holdin' services w'him yonder in them trees."

"He'd better be alive."

"He is, 'less he riled Preacher. Y'know he's got him a temper."

"So have I," Roselyn said, glaring at the man still protectively cradling his privates.

"Y' 'member Willie here?" Jackie said, scratching his chin hairs. "Maybe not." Then he gestured to the man who'd slugged Roselyn. "And this here's a new man, Henry Tugg. He didn't mean to hit you, now, did y', Henry?"

"No, ma'am," he said, a smirk belying his words. Henry was maybe a dozen years younger than

Jackie, raw-boned, hungry looking, with dirty blond hair hanging to his shoulders. Roselyn had never seen him before, but she'd seen plenty like him with saloon girls. His kind enjoyed using their fists on anyone weaker.

"Say y'sorry to the lady," Jackie said.

"I'm right sorry, ma'am. Won't never happen again."

About that time, Preacher appeared from around the lean-to. He never aged. As far back as Roselyn could remember, he'd looked the same— tall, lanky, silver hair, a wind-scoured face tipped by a silver goatee, and an air of religious solemnity that was at odds with the sawed-off scattergun strapped to his hip.

"That's God's truth," he said, slowly striding forward. "It won't."

Then his arm swept up. He palmed his gun and fired both barrels.

Henry Tugg died before he knew he'd been hit. The impact of the shots lifted him completely off his feet. His body flew backward, a small crater blasted where his chest had been, and sprawled into a patch of reddening snow. The stench of blood rose sickeningly sweet and clung in the air like an ominous portent of trouble to come.

Roselyn swallowed a scream and recoiled from the grizzly sight, but she found it hard to dredge up any sympathy for the man.

"How do, Rosie," Preacher said, tapping the brim of his brown hat with one hand and shucking the spent shells with the other.

"That wasn't called for," she said, willing her heart to quit racing. "I didn't ask for it."

"Nope, he was the one askin' for it."

"Doesn't judgment and justice belong to a higher spirit?"

" 'Vengeance is mine, saith the Lord,' " quoted Preacher, holstering his gun. "And He surely works in mysterious ways."

Apprehension slithered down Roselyn's spine.

If she'd entertained the notion of letting Jackie stall Madsen while she hightailed it out and met up with Dill and Sully, she dismissed any thoughts of doing so now. Preacher was fast, well armed, and dangerous.

No telling what might happen if he and Madsen tangled. And they would tangle. Given their natures, Roselyn knew that as certain as her next breath. She sighed to herself.

She didn't want this, didn't need this now. But Madsen was here because of her, so he was her responsibility.

Jackie jutted his chin toward the body and said to Willie, "Get rid of that, and don't bother erectin' a marker."

As he moved, Roselyn turned her back on them and then sprinted around the lean-to and into the stand of aspen trees. A few yards past a deadfall, she spotted Madsen perched on the lip of a rock, trussed up like a Christmas goose.

"Madsen!" she said, running to him and kneeling in the snow to untie the ropes. "You heard?"

"Don't tell me," he said. "Friends of your mother's?"

Roselyn nodded, her fingers too cold to fight the hard knots.

"They're passing through," she said, staring at a trickle of blood on the side of his mouth. "Are you all right?"

"I've lived through worse."

"Please take care, Madsen. These men are on the run."

"I've tangled with dodgy men before."

"But I know them. Let me handle this my way."

"Doesn't look like you've done so well so far."

Her fingers flew to her sore chin, where his angry gaze had settled.

"Preacher killed him for it," she said, her fingers shaking.

"If he hadn't, I would've."

The words were spoken so low and deadly, Roselyn shuddered.

"I don't want to see any more killing," she said. "You or them. This was a mistake, believe me."

"I don't know what to believe from you. You acquainted with anyone who doesn't have a criminal bent?"

She ducked her gaze.

"I guess I deserved that." Without thinking, she cupped his dusky cheek in her palm, stifling the urge to kiss his cut and make the hurt go away. "Now you know why I want to dig in someplace and put roots down to China. I didn't mean for any of this to happen."

"So what happens now?"

"I don't know."

And that's what worried Roselyn.

Jackie and Preacher were unpredictable. When they took offense, they shot first and listened later.

"Please?" she said, picking at the stubborn knots again. "A woman's touch is lighter than a man's. Your word? Let me handle them?"

The doubt she saw in Madsen's eyes told her that it was against his better judgment, but he nodded, anyway, just as Jackie towered over her.

"Who's he?" Jackie said.

"My intended." Roselyn straightened up to look Jackie in the eye. Odd how the lie tripped so easily off her lips. "Now, release him from this rope getup, and I mean this minute."

"Figgered that was it," Jackie said, "what with the calf's eyes you is makin' at each other." He sniggered aloud.

Apparently, Preacher harbored doubts. As he untied Madsen, he said softly, "You two bespoken?"

"You calling the lady a liar?" Madsen said just as quietly.

They exchanged a hard, steady look, each taking the other's measure in the same glance.

Roselyn had seen enough.

"Stop it!" she said, laying her voice across them like a whip.

Both men stared at her.

"I done knowed Rosie since she was knee-high," Jackie said into the silence. "Can't figger Fiona allowin' her baby gal to traipse 'round the country with a gent she ain't bespoken to."

To Roselyn's relief, Preacher shrugged and finished untying the ropes. Once Madsen was free, he rubbed first his wrists and then the back of his neck.

"My guns?" he said.

Under his woolen coat, Jackie hitched up his britches over his gut, and his mouth hardened.

"Y'won't be needin' 'em for a spell . . . 'less I reckon wrong and yer up to no good, mister."

"You always were a trusting sort, Jackie," Roselyn said. Putting what she hoped was just the right amount of sincerity into her voice, she added, "I don't traipse around with strangers. And if you hadn't noticed, I'm a big girl now. I can fend for myself."

Either Madsen had the good sense to keep quiet or he was rigid with fury. Roselyn couldn't tell which, but the glare she glimpsed out of the corner of her eye promised volumes.

She nodded for emphasis and then expanded on her theme to give it more weight.

"Mama thinks very highly of Madsen here. She's delighted he's to be her son-in-law."

More snow began falling, and Roselyn shivered with nerves. Jackie was like a dog with a bone. Once he started gnawing on something meaty, he kept at it.

"Boys," Madsen said. "Can't you see the lady is freezing? Let's go inside the cabin and discuss this where it's warm."

Although he'd spoken evenly, Roselyn noticed his tight brow and the whiteness to his mouth. The wound at his ribs was acting up, she decided.

" 'Peared to me you was goin', not stayin'," Jackie said, shooting a hard warning to Madsen. "Y'ain't said what yer doin' in these parts and how come y'ain't hitched. I better like what I hear or else—"

"Or else nothing," Roselyn said, letting her words hang in the frozen air as she turned toward the cabin. "You're not my pappy."

"Me and Preacher's close enough!" Jackie shot back.

His wishful thinking made Roselyn want to lose her breakfast.

Once inside, she fed more logs on the banked fire to bring it back to life and picked up the empty coffeepot.

Her hand shook. Madsen alone couldn't hope to stand up to both of them. And she couldn't let him try. She needed to come up with a good story to throw Jackie and Preacher off their trail.

Lordy, the day was spiraling downward at an alarming rate. If Roselyn had thought at the jail that things wouldn't get worse, she'd been wrong.

Eight

In the best no-nonsense schoolmarm voice Madsen had ever heard, Rose embroidered how they came to be at the isolated cabin.

She weaved a whopper of a tale about traveling to Denver City to visit Madsen's dear old mother. Even he almost bought it except that they now sat some sixty miles farther north than necessary. That minor detail apparently escaped Rose's notice.

And that she lied so smoothly got him to pondering about what she'd told him had happened at the jailhouse. The truth was in there somewhere. Madsen just hadn't figured out where yet.

While she talked, he sipped hot coffee and bided his time sitting on the edge of the far bunk and watching Jackie Trambull and Preacher pass a jug of corn liquor back and forth between them. Slow-witted Willie sat cross-legged on the dirt floor, next to the heat of the stone fireplace, playing one-handed poker and losing.

Her tale embellished both ways against the middle, leaving out mention of conning Madsen out of one hundred dollars or of Rawlings and the diamonds. Smart girl. No point in giving these hardcases a whiff of pickings that were easy compared to months of backbreaking placer mining.

They were rough hombres used to rough ways but far from stupid. While Trambull rolled a smoke at the table, Preacher kept studying Madsen with a restless gaze. His eyes spoke a language all their own that was not to be mistaken.

The two men knew her story didn't play. They just didn't know why.

Thanks to the butt end of Preacher's gun, the base of Madsen's head throbbed. Maybe that was why he'd gone soft and given his word to Rose to let her handle her friends.

And he'd keep his word . . . until they forced his hand.

His side ached, too, and he felt the fever churning in his gut again. He said nothing about any of it.

Madsen was outnumbered. His Sharps was propped in the far corner near the door, and without his guns, chances were slim of fighting his way out just now.

They'd overlooked his boot knife. He'd use it when the time was right.

But not yet.

Preacher was begging for Madsen to pull something foolish. He was no fool. A knife was no match for a steady finger on a scattergun.

Instead, Madsen was a patient man. The more they drank, the easier they'd be to take.

When Rose finished, Trambull took a long swig of the jug, then leaned his chair back on two legs. He hooked blunt thumbs in the waistband of his britches and glanced over at Preacher. They shared a private understanding before the look shifted back to Madsen.

Trouble was coming.

Madsen tensed his muscles.

"Purty story, now, weren't it?" Trambull said.

Rose's confused gaze swiveled from one to the other.

"Right entertainin'," Preacher said, taking another sip from the jug.

Then Trambull slammed his chair down to the floor.

"And I ain't swallerin' a word of it."

He leaned across the table, a faint, unpleasant smile peeking through his stringy beard, and pinned Madsen with a pale gaze.

"I figger you sweet-talked this little gal with promises you ain't gonna keep and she's too shame faced to let on t'her friends how y'hoodwinked her and her mama."

"You don't know me at all," Madsen said with quiet certainty.

"Oh, I knowed you, mister," Trambull said. "Seen yer kind plenty."

"He's done no such thing!" Rose cried.

"Stay out of this, Rose," Madsen warned.

"I will not. This concerns me." She turned on Trambull. "Haven't you been listening? Am I talking to myself?"

Then she threw her hands up in disgust, waved the whole discussion aside, and turned her back on them.

"Don't y'worry none, Rosie," Trambull said, standing and taking no heed of her outburst. "We'll see he does right by you. Won't we, Preacher?"

Madsen stood when Preacher did.

"Are you saying what I think you're saying?" Madsen said.

Trambull palmed his gun.

"If'n yer a man of y'word," he said, angling the gun slowly in the firelight so the orange flames reflected off the loaded cylinder and the barrel, "then I reckon y'ain't gonna mind gettin' hitched right now. Preacher here can do the deed all legal like. So what's it gonna be? Stand up with her or die like the mangy dog I figger y'are?"

Inside, Madsen seethed. Outside, he clenched and unclenched the fists at his sides.

No one had ever accused him of going back on his word, and he didn't take kindly to hearing it tossed out now.

But of all the things that had crossed his mind in the seconds before Trambull spouted off, none of them were as painless as salvaging Rose's honor.

That she had any honor to salvage was questionable, judging by the looks and the kiss she'd given him. It was the idea of the chore falling to Madsen that caught him flat-footed.

To his surprise, old feelings rushed up at him then as fresh as the pain in his side. He'd never faced a parson at the point of a gun, never had occasion to, but there was a lesson etched into his memory.

Once, long years ago, he'd stood at the threshold of marrying and heard a woman turn him down. He still remembered how her soft voice echoed in the silence of the crowded church hall.

Madsen never blamed her. As it turned out, she'd made the right choice. But knowing that didn't make the hurt any less.

For a reason that was a mystery to him, he couldn't bring himself to do that to Rose even if their betrothal was a tall tale. These were her friends, such as they were. If they heard the truth, it had to come from her.

"Watch your mouth, mister," Madsen said. "I do what I say I'm going to do."

He pointedly stared toward where Rose had whirled around, her mouth gaping open. Then he jutted his chin.

"She doesn't want to marry me," he said. "Go ahead. Ask her."

Gauging by the shock on her face, he knew exactly what was going through her mind. And he couldn't wait to hear how she wiggled out of this one.

"You're enjoying this," she snapped, "aren't you?"

"Afraid I am," he said, crossing his arms over his chest.

Rose had told these boys that he was her husband-to-be. She couldn't very well backtrack now and admit that she was a liar, that she and Madsen were nearly strangers, and that she'd seen him buck-naked more than once and had slept with him more than once.

It didn't matter that nothing happened between them. The damage was done.

Jackie Trambull and Preacher would never believe anything different.

No, Rose had talked herself into this scrape. She would have to release Madsen from his word and let him take on her unsavory friends in his own way.

And he was looking forward to the chore.

Nine

Eyes wide, Roselyn watched Jackie level his gun on Madsen and thumb back the hammer.

Think!

Except for the crack and sizzle of the fire logs, quiet stretched into eternity, shrouded in contempt and the inevitable certainty usually reserved for deathbed vigils or funeral wakes.

By golly, not today.

For a moment, her mouth worked, but no sound came out. The seed of the idea that had rooted earlier in her mind now grew and blossomed. It took only a second for her to decide.

She picked up the steaming coffeepot, fighting to control her features and quiet her emotions, before turning to face Jackie head on. All eyes were riveted on her as she calmly poured herself a cup of coffee.

"Put that gun away," she said with quiet authority. "I won't have any more killing here." Then she stared at Willie over the rim of the cup. "Go check the horses."

"I done checked 'em."

"Then go shoot a rabbit for dinner!"

Her voice had risen with a strength and pitch that suffered no argument. She waited while he turned a questioning gaze toward Jackie. A brief nod sent Willie on his way.

"What's it gonna be, Rosie?" Jackie said.

Once the door closed, she whirled on him, slinging the entire contents of her cup at him. Scalding coffee splattered and soaked his shirt. While he bent over howling in pain and rage, Roselyn lunged forward and snatched the gun out of his hand.

As she'd hoped, Madsen had jumped on Preacher. He gave him no time to reach for his scattergun before a knife blade threatened to peel his Adam's apple.

She leveled the pistol at Jackie, just as he'd done a moment ago. When she thumbed back the hammer, the metallic click echoed through his harsh breathing.

"Don't ever bully me again, Jackie," she said. "I'll marry him, but when I do, it won't be because I have to explain anything we've done to the likes of you or because you pointed a gun in our face."

Jackie mopped his shirtsleeve over his dripping wet beard and considered the fury in front of him through widening eyes.

"Now, don't go gettin'—" he began.

"I've heard enough lecture out of you," she shot back. "Get out!" She wheeled on Preacher, too. "Both of you— Out! I want a private word with Madsen."

"Rose?" Madsen growled.

"You gave me your word," she said. "Let him go."

She watched the emotions roil in his eyes before he nodded and reluctantly lifted the blade away from Preacher's throat.

"Don't get any squirrelly ideas," Madsen warned him.

Her bluff had worked.

Jackie grabbed Preacher's arm and snapped, "C'mon."

After a moment's hesitation, Preacher finally nodded and shrugged into his coat.

"Reckon we can wait outside t'door," Jackie said, "just so's lover boy there don't go getting hisself no squirrelly ideas."

Poor Madsen looked like a lost man, and Roselyn felt a sudden, vast tenderness for him. He hadn't bargained on any of this when he rode into Deadwater, and she wouldn't blame him if he never spoke to her again.

Sure he was shocked, but he wasn't really surprised . . . was he? Did he think she'd stand quietly by and let him be killed?

Then again, maybe he had.

Giving him the slip was still uppermost in her mind, but not at the cost of his life.

Once they were alone, Roselyn released the hammer and dropped the gun to the table. She felt Madsen's strong grip seize her by the upper arm and spin her around.

"You're letting them think I dishonored you,"

he snarled. "What kind of woman lies about something like that?"

Her chin hitched up a notch.

"The kind who's trying to save your ungrateful hide."

"Save me?" he said in a strangled tone. "Nothing doing, sugar. I don't like being railroaded."

"Keep your voice down!"

She pressed her fingers to his firm lips and unwillingly remembered the edgy pleasure that had spiraled through her when she'd kissed them.

"Don't weigh those men short," she said. "If they knew we were after diamonds, how long do you think either one of us would keep breathing?"

"Thought they were your friends," Madsen said when her fingers slid away.

Roselyn grunted.

"Friendship and affection only cut so much with men like them. They'd ventilate their mothers to get their hands on those diamonds."

"Don't try to ride my wrong side. Maybe a woman of your background and gentle upbringing doesn't mind a shotgun wedding, but that's where I draw the line."

He wasn't going to make it easy, but what had she expected? She ignored his sarcasm and inhaled a calming breath, trying to appear unscorched by the condemning eyes burning into her.

"It won't come to that."

"How can you be so sure?"

"Because I have a proposition for you."

Madsen cocked a brow, and his eyes narrowed.

"I'm listening."

"Give me two days head start to find Rawlings—"

"You'll get out of my sight over my dead body."

"Which Preacher will be glad to oblige," she pointed out.

On a snort, Madsen propped his boot on the seat of the chair and slid the long hunting knife into his ankle sheath. His confidence was infuriating.

"What's in it for me?" he said.

"Simple. No shotgun wedding. It's a fair trade."

Roselyn had him over a barrel—a gun barrel, to be precise—and watched him mull that over for a moment. He was no fool. He'd realize he had no choice but to accept her offer.

Except, to her surprise, he laughed.

"What if I'm already married?" he said, straightening.

That stopped Roselyn cold.

Why the low-down varmint! The ugly possibility had never once occurred to her.

The heated way he looked and acted toward her certainly hadn't given the impression there was a missus pining away at home somewhere. Then again, for all Roselyn knew, he might have a passel of little Bolds spread from here to Texas, too. Frowning back at him, she planted her hands on her hips.

"And are you married?"

"No."

Again surprised, this time by the relief his answer brought, she blurted out the first thing that sprang to mind.

"Why not?"

"Not that it matters, but I haven't found a woman who'd have me."

She sniffed.

"I'm not surprised."

"Until now," he added.

His gaze softened, the intensity that disarmed her so smoldering in the depths of his dark eyes. The feeling caressed her skin, wrapping around her like a silken noose.

"Pardon me?" Roselyn lost her edge and blinked, then blinked again, and blurted out, "What are you saying?"

Madsen shrugged.

"I've decided if I have to marry you, then that's what I'll do."

Caught in a trap of her own making, Roselyn shook her head. He was calling her bluff, trying to turn the tables on her so she'd back down.

Even so, she wanted to cry.

In her dreams, whenever she'd envisioned talk of marriage, it was after a picnic in a sunny green meadow filled with the scent of wildflowers. The day was always warm and perfect and romantic.

There was not one romantic bone in Madsen Bold's body.

"Nice try," she said. "As tempting as you make the prospect of marrying me sound, you don't really want to do that. And I certainly don't want to marry you if I can help it. When I tie myself down, it's going to be to a nice quiet banker who knows how to treat a woman like a lady. He'll bend on his knee and propose proper."

"That's not what you told Trambull."

"I lied through my teeth."

"Why fuss against mouthing a few words if it'll save our hides? It's harmless."

His casual expression hadn't changed, but Roselyn suspected it was a mask for emotions that ran deeper and hotter and wilder.

"Harmless?" She hooked a thumb over her shoulder. "He's a real preacher, a Methodist elder—"

"Then a marriage would be real enough."

She examined each flick of Madsen's eyes and thought of his big body, of the contours and landscape of his warm skin, of the way she flushed hot and cold when he touched her.

"Only if we made it so," she said. She paced in front of the fireplace, then pivoted. "And neither of us has any intention of doing that. Do we?"

The rapid thud of boots outside crunching through snow caught Roselyn's attention seconds before she and Madsen heard the tense voices on the other side of the wooden door.

Time was running out.

She could almost pretend he'd give up tracking Rawlings and let her have the diamonds to take to Duke Pearson.

Almost.

"Two days' head start," she said.

"One."

"Deal."

Then Roselyn wondered if she'd won any concession at all when Madsen's features relaxed into a biddable expression, as if he harbored a secret.

The door burst open, and Willie rushed inside on a gust of cold, snowy air.

"Posse's a'comin'," he said, scrambling to fetch what little gear the trio had left. "Seen 'em a mile off. Done got themselves an Injun tracker, too."

Trambull and Preacher had wasted no time gaining their saddles. As Madsen made it to the doorway, Trambull wheeled his dun and pitched Madsen's guns.

"Best take care of my gal," he warned.

Madsen snagged the gun belt in midair and nodded. He was strapping on his pistols when Preacher kneed his horse forward and paused just shy of the doorway.

"Sooner or later, mister," he said as Trambull and Willie lit out southwest toward Central City. "You 'n me. Our business ain't finished."

Then he jumped his horse on their trail and was soon swallowed by the land and snow.

Madsen was under no illusions about the soft-spoken Preacher. The man was as dangerous as a rattler.

And they'd meet again sooner rather than later, Madsen decided. Of that, he was dead certain.

Following fresh tracks in new snow was easy. But even without the Indian guide, the posse would follow the chimney smoke right to the cabin.

Madsen suspected they were after Trambull and Preacher, but he and Rose didn't plan on waiting to find out if he was right. They both shared the same thought: Tracked was better than caught.

They moved through the hills southward, staying within a glimpse of the river. Being a former ranger just naturally made a man skeptical, so Madsen kept checking their back trail.

After an hour and no sign of anyone following, they stopped in a little hollow alongside the river to give the horses a breather. Deer tracks were plentiful.

"Look!" Rose whispered in wonder, and Madsen turned his head in the direction she was staring.

Two mule-deer does and a yearling walked out of a game trail leading into a draw that ran back up the mountain. The curious yearling stopped to stare at them, but the does were more skittish.

One doe was older, judging by her gray body that was almost as large as a buck's. Her face was longer and covered with more white. Probably the mother.

She studied them, decided she didn't much care for what she saw, and signaled the alarm with her tail. In a blink, all three disappeared into the draw.

"Think the buck deer is close by?" Rose said.

She was bundled against the cold so that only her eyes showed above her muffler. Inwardly, Madsen smiled at the memory of the long legs and enticing curves hidden beneath the layers of her clothes.

Rose was more troublesome than any woman he'd ever met, but something about her piqued his interest beyond mere lust. He wanted to believe she wasn't somehow in cahoots with Rawlings. And he realized with a start that he'd be sorry to find out if she was.

"I doubt it," Madsen said. "Young bucks like to keep to bachelor herds, and the older ones stay to themselves in deeper cover. They don't mix with the does except during the rut."

"That's typical male. Have your fun and then run off, leaving the womenfolk to look after the younguns."

"If that's so, then how do you explain the wolf?" When Rose cast him a questioning glance, he said, "Wolves mate for life."

Madsen could see the smile glitter in her eyes.

"God gave she-wolves big teeth," Rose said, "to keep the he-wolves in line."

With a laugh, Madsen said, "So I take it you figure men are either buck deer or he-wolves?"

Rose nodded.

"Which one are you?"

"I have to think on it," he said, mounting. "When you decide, let me know."

He started up out of the hollow when he heard the yawning snarl of a cat behind him, followed by a horse's answering scream and Rose's displaced shriek.

Instinctively, Madsen hauled on the reins and

spun his roan on its haunches. He caught sight of a young mountain lion streaking up the draw where the yearling had gone.

Rose's riderless horse was tearing down the rocky bank in panic and across the chest-deep river. It gained the relative safety of the opposite side and stood blowing, its reins loose and dragging the ground.

Rose lay sprawled on an ice ledge over the river, fumbling to get her feet under her on the slippery surface. If the ledge gave way under her weight, she'd fall face first into freezing water.

"Stay still!" Madsen called.

"Do I have a choice?" she said, making it up onto all fours.

Her muffler had slid down around her neck, the loose ends dangling to the ice like forgotten reins. She swatted them back out of the way and shoved her braid over her shoulder.

"You can always go swimming."

"No, thanks. Next suggestion?"

Her snappy reply told him she wasn't hurt, and he went weak with relief. Damn woman was going to be the death of him.

He dismounted and edged down the boulder-strewn bank, halting just before the rocks met the dirty ice. Up close, the ledge wasn't as bad as it appeared at first glance.

The surface of the ice was pitted and uneven where chunks had been washed away, but it was several inches thick. Rose was on her hands and knees, disgruntled and adorable.

Madsen broke out in a grin and crossed his arms over his chest.

"It appears to me that I could leave you there. Go find Rawlings on my own."

"You do and I'll hunt you down like a dog. Now, are you going to help or just stand there and gawk while I drown?"

"You're not even wet."

"Don't quibble over details."

Hunkering down, Madsen figured he'd had enough funning and motioned to her.

"Can you crawl to me?" he said.

Her head snapped up.

"Oh, you'd like that, wouldn't you?"

"I promise I'll try not to enjoy it."

She grumped under her breath and inched toward him over the bumps and dips like a drunk on a Saturday night saloon floor. He really did try not to chuckle.

"Stretch, Madsen," she said, "and give me your hand."

"Just a little closer."

"Give me your hand, you insufferable man! If I'm going into the water, you're going with me."

Even as she shouted, he was reaching for her. He braced one boot in between two boulders, grabbed her by the hand and forearm, and snatched her flush to his body, smothering her in his embrace and savoring her light weight.

Madsen tried hard to stay immune to her nearness. And failed.

Instead, he locked her close with one hand and

anchored her head with the other and silenced her annoyance with his mouth. Soft. Wet. Wild. He became lost in the sheer pleasure of her taste.

She parted her lips under the pressure of his demanding tongue, and he ravished her mouth like a hungry man. He traced the curve and texture of her lips, circling the sensitive edges of her mouth and absorbing the ripples of pleasure that passed through her.

Only when the sound of the horses nickering penetrated the sensual fog did he raise his head. Dreamy eyes gone smoky with desire gazed back at him.

"Am I forgiven for being insufferable?" he said, reluctant to release her.

"I haven't decided yet," she whispered.

Again, he touched her lips with his mouth. Tender, full, and slick.

"How about now?" he murmured, pulling back and wondering if she realized she was clinging to his neck as if she'd never let him go.

"Getting close, I think," she said, drawing him nearer.

Madsen drank in her whimper, brushing his mouth feather-light against hers before pressing a firmer kiss. Then he slanted his mouth over hers again, coaxing the warmth from her hidden crevices, kissing her long, slow, and thoroughly.

"You're shaking," he said, sweeping away the strands of hair that had escaped from her braid. "Don't tell me you've never done this before."

"Why would I? I'd never met you before."

Her softly spoken words jolted Madsen to his boots. No woman had ever said that to him. Although she was an exasperating woman, she had a gentleness that tugged at his heart.

He lowered his gaze and stared at her damp mouth, at the chafed spots on her cheek where his whisker stubble had scraped the tender skin. He glided the pad of his thumb over her lips, wanting much more than he had a right to.

"You don't play fair," she said.

"I know. C'mon, sugar. I'll get your horse."

He took her by the hand and led her across the rocks, silently cursing himself for a fool. Rose O'Neill was the last woman he should get mixed up with, and yet she was the one woman he burned for like hell on fire.

They followed south while they still had daylight left. Short winter days combined with overcast skies made night come early.

As they rode, Madsen took in sounds out of habit—the wind rustling through bare branches, the faint rush of water, a Steller's jay chirping, and the answering chatter of a ground squirrel. When the sounds subtlely changed, Madsen became uneasy.

He pulled up, turned in his saddle, and waited.

Minutes passed until he heard stirring. Could be they'd startled more deer?

Madsen wasn't sure.

Motioning for Rose to stay quiet and follow, he turned his horse and scrambled up a bank into the cover of the trees. Then he heard it—the tinkle of a bridle.

Rose's quick indrawn breath told him she'd heard it, too. A rider was coming, maybe two. Maybe more.

"The posse?" she whispered, eyes wide.

Madsen had no wish to tangle further with the law if he could help it. But there was no guarantee that whoever was coming was the law.

"Keep your horse quiet," he whispered back, and then patted his roan's neck and said, "Shhh. Easy, boy."

Madsen thumbed back the thong on his pistol and palmed his gun. When a man lives by his gun as long as Madsen had, he learns it as intimately as a lover's body.

He knew right off by the weight that something was wrong. A quick check of the cylinder found it empty.

Cursing softly, he palmed his other gun. Another empty cylinder. Damn Jackie Trambull.

Passing the pistols stock first to Rose, Madsen whispered, "Reload these from the box in my saddlebag."

He didn't question if she knew how. What she'd shown him so far told him she could handle a gun and shoot one straight, if it came to that.

Then, shucking the Sharps out of its scabbard, Madsen eased off his roan quiet-like and pointed the rifle barrel through the branches. He didn't wait long before two men came into view, riding slow and steady, following their tracks.

Madsen had a clear shot, yet let them come on. He wasn't begging a fight, but if they started one, he'd oblige.

They were too far off and the skies were too dreary for Madsen to get a good look to see if one of them wore a badge. What worried him more, though, was that the Indian tracker was nowhere in sight.

If he was busy flanking them, Madsen and Rose would be open targets. Worse, in a moment, the men would spot where they were hiding in the trees, and they'd be caught in a crossfire.

Ten

Roselyn wasted no time reloading the pistols and slipped one back into its holster at Madsen's side.

"Here," she whispered in his ear, unable to stop herself from savoring the warm, earthy smell of him. "It's ready."

His other gun she kept for herself, just in case. The Sharps could drop a flea at this range, but if Madsen needed help, she intended to be ready.

"There's a way out over there," he said, motioning at an angle with his chin. "You wanted a day's head start? You've got it now, sugar. Get on your horse and follow that narrow trail."

Taken aback, Roselyn stood dumb for a moment. Sure, she'd wanted to get the jump on Madsen, but not like this, not by running out on him.

"Stick to the south," he added, "and you'll come on Platteville."

"Madsen, I—"

"Go! I'll cover you."

But instead of going, she tightened her grip on

the gun, braced her back against the pine trunk, and stared right at him.

"Fine time to get heroic," she said through gritted teeth. "Two guns are better than one. I'm not leaving."

"Leave now, sugar, or forget about a head start." He whipped around to face her, his eyes narrowing. "I won't be so generous again."

"Only cowards cut and run," she said. "I've done a lot of things in my life I'm not proud of, but how dare you think I'd stoop so low? Like it or not, we're in this together, Madsen."

Roselyn refused to stare straight at this newfound sentiment for fear she'd see she was her mama's daughter, after all. She understood none of this.

Somewhere lay an answer to this question she'd never known to ask. But she accepted Madsen's unsettling presence in her life as she'd accepted every change, with backbone and with hope.

While they were thrown together, she wanted to hear it all, feel it all, remember it all, so when this time slipped away, she'd have the memory to look back on.

And that's all it could be, a memory.

Madsen was a man of his word; there was no doubt. As much as Roselyn admired him for that, it didn't change things. Mama depended on Roselyn too much for her to let him interfere with retrieving those diamonds.

For a moment, Madsen frowned at Roselyn as if he, too, sorted through a problem that had no answer. Finally, he nodded.

"Make yourself useful, then," he snapped, turning his attention back to the riders. "Scan that ridge behind us. If you see somebody sneaking up on us, shoot."

"You or them?" Roselyn said.

"Them," he said without looking at her. "Your eyes are already boring into my head."

"But they're pretty eyes."

"Yes," he said on a sigh. "They are."

Her scowl turning to a satisfied smile, Roselyn combed the crest of the ridge for intruders. When she saw nothing out of the ordinary, she peered back over her shoulder through the trees that screened them and watched the riders follow their tracks.

Only two had shown themselves so far, their features hidden beneath the brims of their hats.

Closer. A little closer.

Suddenly, Madsen called out, "You gents looking for something?"

The riders reined in and snapped up their gazes, giving Madsen and Roselyn the first clear look at their faces.

"Easy there, sonny," came the grouchy reply. "We done found it. 'Bout froze our backsides to the saddles doin' it, too."

Roselyn gasped, put a hand on Madsen's arm to still him, and then laughed with overwhelming relief.

"Sully!" she cried. "You old rascal. You scared the life out of me."

She passed Madsen's gun back to him and then climbed on her horse to greet the two old miners.

"Saw y'ran into a speck of trouble back yonder," Sully said, hooking a thumb over his shoulder.

Roselyn gave them a brief account of Tugg's death and then asked, "Anyone following you?"

Dill leaned over and spewed a stream of brown tobacco juice into a pristine snowdrift before shaking his head.

"Ain't nobody botherin' 'bout us," he said, wiping his mouth with his sleeve. "We're old news. Marshal's got his hands full lookin' for 'nother old boy who done got riled and cashed in three gents. Right messy business, too."

Roselyn glanced at Madsen and received a tight look filled with I-told-you-so about not letting him handle her friends earlier.

"Preacher?" she said.

"Sounds likely," Madsen returned, and she felt a shiver that had nothing to do with the cold.

Madsen hadn't talked about it, but Roselyn had heard Preacher's parting words. In the excitement, she'd forgotten them until now.

The next time the two men met, nothing she could say would save Madsen.

And that thought hurt more than she cared to admit.

By nightfall, the four of them reached Platteville, not far from the old trading post of Fort Vasquez.

The army had occupied the post during the war and still did. As the foursome walked their horses down the town's only street, Madsen made it plain that he wasn't keen on another tussle with bluecoats.

"Keep out of trouble," he warned Dill and Sully. Then Madsen swung a lethal gaze on Rose. "And that goes double for you."

"I'll be good as gold," she said, offering him her sweetest smile. "Promise."

Madsen grunted, unconvinced.

Platteville wasn't a town a man had to worry about hurrying through. Only about a dozen peeling structures faced each other along the street, including a saloon, a general store, a small lodging house, and a livery stable.

There were no loafers about, not in this cold, although several horses stood at the hitch rail in front of the saloon. Yellow light from the frosty windows spilled onto two mangy white dogs that nosed the plank boards fronting as a sidewalk.

Few people were out. Most were inside somewhere eating supper, Madsen guessed, and keeping warm.

He reined in outside the lodging house and Rose followed.

"Dill 'n me'll see the horses to the livery," Sully said.

"We'll get you a room," Rose offered.

Madsen flipped him a coin.

"See if you can get them a bait of oats and a rubdown."

Sully nodded and then said, "Don't wait on us. I aim to find me somethin' to warm my gizzard." And he glanced toward the saloon.

Rose handed off her saddlebags to Madsen, who took his Sharps and saddlebags and headed to the door.

Inside, the front parlor was small but tidy. A knit rug covered the floor, and a cowhide settee sat against the far wall. Three chairs were in the middle, surrounding a pot-bellied stove that gave off welcoming heat.

The mouth-watering aroma of venison wafted into the parlor from the dining room off to the right. From behind him, Madsen heard Rose's stomach rumble and growl.

In a glimpse, he noticed red-and-white checkered curtains hanging over two windows and counted half a dozen tables that sported matching tablecloths. Only four of the tables were occupied.

He took in an elderly couple sitting at one table, two soldiers at another, two middle-aged men at another, and a woman eating alone who could have been sixteen or sixty, he couldn't tell because she was decked head to foot in mourning black. One table was recently vacated and still topped with dirty supper dishes.

A balding man in a homespun shirt and with skin cured by the sun wiped his veined hands on his white apron and greeted them from behind the front counter. He was friendly but not overly so.

"You the desk clerk?" Madsen said.

"And cook and dishwasher and chief gofer," he

said, turning the register book around in anticipation of business. "Have been ever since my Maddie passed on last spring, God rest her soul. Name's Peters. Just the two of you?"

It was always better to offer something to satisfy curiosity, so Madsen said, "No. We have her two uncles with us. We'll be moving on in the morning."

"It's four to a room," Peters said, producing a pen. "Them's house rules, seeing as how we ain't got many rooms. Your uncles can bunk in with two fellers here trading horses to the army, and you and the missus there can bunk with old Doc Wetherspoon and his missus."

Rose cast Madsen a questioning glance and raised her eyebrows. It was easier and simpler to let the man's assumption about them stand.

"Does that include supper?" Madsen said.

Peters grinned.

"Venison stew tonight, all you can eat. Meals are fifteen cents extra, and I'll refund your money if my cooking's no good."

"Sound all right with you?" Madsen asked her.

"Rooms are two bits each," Peters said. "Take it or leave it."

"Fine with me, sweetheart," she said, poker-faced.

Madsen cocked his head at her syrupy endearment but tossed his money on the counter and picked up the pen to sign the register. He scanned the recent guest names first for any familiar ones.

Teddy Lee's name wasn't listed, but that was no

surprise. If he'd stayed over at the lodging house, no telling what handle he used.

After signing their names with a flourish, Madsen tossed the pen onto the register and turned to Rose.

"Let's wash up and then get a bite of supper." She smiled.

"I was hoping food was in the offing."

He led the way up the stairs Peters had indicated, where six doors lined the only corridor. For a brief moment, Madsen caught sight of the back of the widow's black dress before she disappeared into the last room next to the back door.

Opening the first door on the left, he paused to let Rose go in before him.

A kerosene lamp sat on a short table between two double beds. It was already lit and turned down low, shedding just enough brassy light for Madsen to see that the room was nothing out of the ordinary.

The two men Madsen had spotted eating supper were probably the traders Dill and Sully would bunk with, and Madsen guessed the doctor and his wife were the old couple. They were folks used to sharing, judging by the blanket pushed back from a makeshift line that was strung between the beds. Once the blanket was stretched the length of the line, it would separate the beds and offer each one some semblance of privacy.

To the side of each bed stood a washstand with pitcher and bowl. One black stove in the corner gave off heat, and a large braided rug covered the floorboards.

The far bed sported the doctor's black bag, and a few of his clothes hung from hooks on that side of the wall, so Madsen crossed to the nearest bed and laid down the saddlebags. Figuring Rose probably wanted a minute or two for privacy to wash, he propped his Sharps in the corner by the headboard and turned to leave.

"Take your time," he said, his hand on the doorknob. "I'll meet you downstairs for supper. Come when you're ready." And he pulled the door closed.

"Madsen?"

He cracked the door back open and poked his head in.

"Yes, sugar?"

"Thank you."

The heat radiating from her shy smile warmed him all the way through. Nothing she did shocked him, yet everything she did surprised him.

"You're welcome," he said, and winked.

Once downstairs, Madsen didn't go straight to the dining room. Instead, he interrupted Peters, writing in a ledger.

"I'm looking for a man," Madsen said when Peters glanced up. "About my age but smaller than me, dark hair, maybe traveling with a pretty woman. Anyone like that been through here in the last day or so?"

"Can't say as I recall no one like that."

"Are you sure?"

Peters scratched at his bald spot with an inky fingernail.

"No reason I would recall," he said, " 'less they come through the front door. All I seen is you folks, a widder lady headin' to her sister's in Denver, them that's trading with the fort, and Doc there."

Peters jabbed the air toward the old couple just finishing up in the dining room.

"He come here often?"

"Ever' month. We ain't got no doctor here-abouts, so he stays a few days to tend to them what needs it."

Just to keep casual, Madsen chatted a minute more about the weather and whatnot and then strolled into the dining room. He stopped at the doctor's table to introduce himself and tapped his hat brim to the man's wife, who'd risen from her seat.

Like her husband, Mrs. Wetherspoon was plump, with smiling eyes, and on the downhill side of seventy, Madsen guessed.

"Enjoy your pipe," she said, patting her husband's rounded shoulders. "And remember your gloves when you go out."

"I'll be fine, dear," he returned. "Run along."

Judging by the fond touches they exchanged, she seemed the sort to be content wherever he was, no matter what hardships or inconvenience she faced. It took a special woman to stay with a man like that, and Madsen felt a pang of envy for the private joy they shared.

When she excused herself to go upstairs, her

husband settled in and took a pipe and a short piece of fat stick out of his jacket pocket. He turned up the wick on the table lamp and held the stick over the flame until it caught.

"Y'mind, son?" he said, pausing while the flaming stick hovered over the bowl.

Though Madsen didn't partake of pipes, cigars, or other smokes, he wasn't intolerant of those folks who did.

"Help yourself," he said.

A moment later, a billowy wreath of pipe smoke drifted to the ceiling. As the woodsy aroma drifted across, Madsen sat down at the table next to the wall, more out of habit than because it was cleared off.

Whether in a saloon or a restaurant, he preferred a spot where he could keep tabs on the door. A man lived longer that way.

The bullet wound at his ribs had settled down to a dull throb. Madsen absently rubbed his fingers over his side.

"Hurt yourself?" the doctor said, extinguishing the stick's flame by blowing a plume of blue smoke on it.

"A bruised rib," Madsen said, unwilling to create questions he'd rather not answer. "It's nothing."

"I can take a look if you want."

"No point to. Rose tended it for me. It'll be fine."

"Suit yourself," the doctor said around another puff of his pipe. "Stew's good tonight. And the coffee's the best around."

"Glad to know that," Madsen returned. "I'll try

some, then." He glanced at the nearly clean plate still topping the table the widow had vacated. "Looks like everyone shares your opinion."

The doctor leaned forward and lowered his voice to a conspiratorial whisper.

"Miz Beasley beats all I ever seen. She eats more than any two men I know, and it's a wonder she ain't as big as a barn. Finishes here and takes a plate to her room for later. She's a skittish sort, keeps to herself. I reckon being a widow and traveling alone will do that to a woman."

Information was where a man found it, so Madsen said, "She been here long?"

"Couple of days, I reckon. Waiting on the weather to clear."

Madsen nodded, mulling that over. For a skittish woman, the widow was taking a big risk. Any woman alone was easy prey for bad company happening along, which brought him to consider why he was there.

Rawlings had to have come through Platteville on his way to Denver City. But according to the register he hadn't stopped.

Or had he?

People liked to talk, and it generally happened that people knew things without realizing how much they knew. Even if Rawlings hadn't stopped over for food or shelter, someone in a town this small would have noticed a stranger passing through.

Maybe a visit after supper to the livery stable and to the saloon would yield some answers.

Eleven

Roselyn and Madsen had the dining room to themselves.

They ate by the light of a smoking kerosene lamp whose wick sorely needed trimming, and their supper was serenaded by the muted sounds of clattering dishes and pots that filtered in from the kitchen.

But it was Roselyn's first real sit-down meal with an attractive man who wasn't an old friend, creditor, or wanted in two territories, and not much could spoil it.

She had met the doctor's wife upstairs and had spoken briefly with the doctor himself until he was called away to a patient. They were plain folks and likable.

Now she listened to Madsen talk while she sopped up the last of her second helping of venison stew with her third warm biscuit and popped it into her mouth. Madsen had nice teeth.

"Don't they feed you regular?" he said, grinning.

She glanced down at her plate, wiped clean and

ready to go back on the shelf, and returned a lop-sided grin.

"Sorry, habit. Too many years of not knowing where the next hot meal was coming from." She picked up her coffee cup and, with great regret, came back to the reason they were there. "So, do we start at the livery first or at the saloon?"

"We?"

Roselyn shrugged and set her cup back down on the checkered tablecloth.

"You decide. Either I go with you or I dog your footsteps. Which is it?"

Madsen gave a long-suffering sigh.

"You're serious."

"Very."

"What happened to being good as gold?"

"If I'm with you, what trouble can I get into?"

"But I don't need you with me. I work alone."

"Not anymore. You need me to spell it out for you? Fine, I'll say it." She leaned in close over the table and lowered her voice. "You're stuck with me. We're after the same thing, even if it's not for the same reason."

In all honesty, Roselyn couldn't fault Madsen for being steadfast in tracking the diamonds or for being dependable in his friendships. They were the very qualities that drew her to him, even as they irritated her to no end.

"I know my reason," he said, hefting the last forkful of dried apple pie, "but I'm still not sure of yours."

"You think I've lied?"

The fork stopped halfway to his mouth.

"Just about every breath, sugar, starting with the moment we met."

"I admit I stretch the truth sometimes—but only when I need to—and I'll say again that I'm sorry my plan cost you a hundred dollars—"

"Which I intend to get back, don't forget."

"As if you'd let me."

He swallowed and stared at her untouched slice of pie.

"You going to eat that?"

She pushed her dessert plate toward him.

"But I'm not lying about why I'm here," she said.

Roselyn glanced around to make sure no one was about.

"Like I told you," she added, "I don't know Rawlings, and I certainly didn't help him break out of jail. I'm sorry your friend lost property in a robbery—"

"It wasn't his property," Madsen said, digging into her pie. "It was a Wells Fargo shipment he was hired to guard."

Clamping down her temper, Roselyn smoothed nonexistent wrinkles from the tablecloth.

"Don't you understand?" she said. "I don't give a fig about his professional reputation. My mother's life is at stake here."

Madsen started to speak, but she cut him off.

"If I don't get those diamonds to Duke Pearson," she said, "he's going to take what Mama owes him out of her hide. And that's the godawful truth. I won't have her hurt or dead on my account. She's my only family, and I won't let her down."

"Where's your father?"

Roselyn leaned back, studying him, and sipped her coffee again. It had gone cold. She didn't doubt for a minute that she'd just wasted her breath.

"On a stage somewhere, I guess," she said. Then, at Madsen's prodding stare, she added, "He was an actor Mama met who swept her off her feet."

"What happened to him?"

"What always happens. He moved on when the play did. Could be dead now, for all I know."

Madsen put his fork down and shoved the empty plate to the side with the others. Roselyn watched, fascinated, as his mouth caressed the rim of his coffee cup.

Lordy, what she wouldn't give to be that cup. His taste was imprinted on her lips.

She mentally shook herself.

"It'll arouse too much curiosity," he said, replacing his cup to the saucer, "if we both poke our noses around. Checking horses and saloons are men's chores that woman don't usually do."

"Nonsense, I've gone in and out of saloons all my life."

"But most decent women don't."

His words left Roselyn chewing air, and her chair became a bed of thorns. Madsen's gaze was direct and as unrelenting as his opinion. She'd

thought she had grown immune to such conde-
scending attitudes.

She was wrong.

Fishing in her pocket for coins, she laid them
along with her napkin on the table and stood. A
firm hand on her arm waylaid her.

"I didn't mean that the way it sounded, Rose.
But you've got to know that's how people see it."

Hurt blossomed in her throat. She had shaken
off idle whispering before and had always told herself it didn't matter.

But she saw the truth now in his eyes.

She could see it plainly. His interest had been
only a reflection of hers. Poor Mama. Is this how
she was left feeling? Roselyn hoped not, for her
chest ached too much.

"I know what you meant," she said. "And of
course you're right. Thank you for supper. Finish
your coffee, then go nose around and see what
you can find out. I'll be upstairs."

His hand dropped away, and she missed the
warmth of his touch.

"Will you be all right?"

The smile she offered him fell short of genuine.

"Sure. I've taken care of myself for a long time.
I'll be fine."

In the parlor, Mrs. Wetherspoon sat in a chair
nearest the warm stove, knitting a blue-and-white
afghan that draped over her abundant lap. Roselyn nodded to her; it would've been rude not to.

"A wedding present for my sister's granddaugh-
ter," Mrs. Wetherspoon said, and smiled.

"And a very nice one, too," Roselyn returned, sensing she was expected to pause and admire the work. "That's very thoughtful of you."

Her fingers constantly moving the yarn, the doctor's wife edged her glance around Roselyn, looked in the direction of the dining room for a second, and pulled back.

"You two have a spat, dear?" she said over the low clacking of the needles. "I'm a good listener if you need one."

Roselyn shook her head in disgust and sagged against the arm of the adjacent chair.

"No, not really a spat. Just some truth I didn't want to hear."

The older woman offered an understanding nod.

"Mind you don't let it bottle up," she said. "Anger can't be avoided by pretending it doesn't exist."

Roselyn's spurt of self-pity lasted until she rounded the corner at the top of the stairs and met a draft of cold air.

Apparently, someone had a big night ahead of him, since he'd used the back door and left it cracked open in his haste. The cold air was pouring in, so Roselyn hurried along the corridor to close the door before she froze to the bone.

There were many reasons why people used a back door, and most of them were to avoid seeing or being seen. She should know. More times than she cared to count she'd crept down back stairs with Mama to slip away from someone looking for his money.

As Roselyn pulled the door shut, she studied the other closed doors in the corridor. Who had used the back way and why?

It could be a simple answer. Maybe one of the horse traders was entertaining agreeable company tonight?

Then again, maybe not.

No matter what Madsen said, if he thought she'd sit quietly by and wait for him, he was mistaken. He wasn't the only one who could nose around without attracting attention.

And Roselyn headed back down to the parlor.

Madsen pulled up his coat collar against the cold and walked the dark street to the livery, haunted by the wounded expression in Rose's eyes. He should've apologized for hurting her feelings, but being sorry didn't change things.

He still had a job to do, and he'd do it.

So where did that leave him? Did he believe Rose's story about her mother? About what had happened at the jailhouse?

One followed the other. From what Madsen had heard of Duke Pearson, he knew Rose's fears for her mother were real.

Then, if he believed the story about her mother, did it make sense for Rose to help Rawlings get away? No, it didn't. So Madsen *had* to believe that she had nothing to do with the break from the jailhouse.

Had to? Or wanted to?

Both.

And he hoped he wasn't wrong.

As exasperating as Rose was, to her credit she had gumption. She hadn't led an easy life, and he'd seen her determination and resourcefulness firsthand.

But there was nothing Madsen could do to help her mother.

He'd given his word to McNelly to return the diamonds, and that didn't mean pawning them in exchange for some broken-down saloon singer, no matter how deliciously tempting her daughter was.

When Madsen entered the livery stable, the clean outdoor smell faded. The fragrance of warm hay drifted to his nose, mingled with the familiar tang of sweaty leather, horseflesh, and the sharp odor of manure.

A lighted lantern hanging from a wall hook cut the darkness, and the place was quiet except for the occasional shuffling of a horse. There was no sign of a worker.

Winter hay was piled in tall stacks to Madsen's left, and horse trappings were hung on pegs to his right. Scattered straw littered the aisle, cushioning his boot steps.

He moved deeper, passed the row of stalls, eyeing each horse until he'd seen them all. Teddy Lee's roan wasn't among them.

Madsen found the man who ran the livery. He was in the back tack room, sprawled on a cot and ventilating his tonsils.

If he'd noticed any strangers lately, he wasn't telling. Even a hard kick to the edge of the cot didn't wake him, and the empty bottle, tucked to his side, suggested he'd sleep until morning and wake with a good head.

Leaving the livery empty-handed, Madsen crossed back over to the saloon. It was the usual: a bar running along the back wall, a dozen or so round tables scattered the width of the building, and squatty spittoons dotting the floor in strategic spots.

A handful of men in work clothes lounged at the bar, while twenty or more were spread out around the tables. Half that many soldiers from the post sat in groups of two or three.

Madsen spotted Dill and Sully at a table in the corner. Full glasses of foamy beer were perched in front of each one, not their first gauging by their rosy glow, along with the remnants of two sandwiches.

Instead of joining them, Madsen headed to the bar and waited for the bartender, a white-haired string bean with a protruding Adam's apple, to finishing pouring for a customer.

"I'm looking for a man," he said. "Smaller than me, dark hair."

"Mister, you just described half the gents who come in here."

"He might've come in the last couple of days. Riding a roan horse. Any strangers like that through here?"

The barkeep shook his head.

"Sorry, if there was, I ain't seen him. Whatcha having? Beer? Whiskey?"

"Nothing, thanks, anyway."

With frustration gnawing at him, Madsen pushed away from the bar and joined Dill and Sully.

"You two outlaws have been promoted to uncles," Madsen said, laying his dark hat on the table and taking a seat.

Sully grinned at Dill and ruffled his brother's silver head.

"This here is gettin' more interestin' ever'day."

"Watch it," Dill said, glowering. "You'll spoil my manly beauty."

And he combed his stubby fingers through his mussed hair. Madsen couldn't see that it helped his craggy looks much, and then he told them about the rooms at the lodging house.

He noticed a young soldier at a nearby table glance his way, a look that lingered before passing on. His face seemed familiar, but Madsen couldn't recall seeing the boy anywhere.

"Either of you seen him before?" he said, nudging his chin.

Dill took a swig of his beer, gazing at the soldier over the rim of his glass.

"Nope," he said, dragging his shirtsleeve across his mouth to wipe the foam away. "But them boys all look alike to me." And he and Sully chuckled over their private joke.

Madsen might not remember the soldier boy,

but that didn't mean he hadn't gotten a gander at Madsen recently.

"Blue's not my favorite color," he said, grabbing his hat and rising. "Do me a favor. Don't start anything I'll have to finish. We'll be heading out right after breakfast. Be ready."

Outside, Madsen moved quickly with silent steps to the end of the sidewalk and rounded the corner, hugging the building, his hand on the butt of his gun. He didn't wait long.

The young soldier who had been eyeing him inside walked out of the saloon and turned his head, searching both directions in the murky light.

"Something I can help you with?" Madsen said, and stepped out into the open.

The boy's head snapped around, but he stayed casual and made no move for his gun.

"No, sir," he said, peering out from under his forage cap. "But there might be something I can help you with."

A soft Texas drawl curled around each word, which frosted in the night air and roused Madsen's curiosity.

"What's your name, boy?"

"Huggins, sir. Daniel Huggins."

The name took Madsen by surprise.

"Any relation to Sam Huggins?"

"My pa."

"Well, I'll be." Madsen relaxed his stance and grinned. "How is old Sam? Haven't seen him in an age."

"He died last year."

"Oh, I didn't know."

"No reason you should."

Madsen took in the determined jaw, forthright gaze, and lean frame, but that's where his friend Sam's influence ended. The high forehead, straight nose, and blond hair marked the boy as his mother's son.

"I rode with your pa a few years back. He was a good man. Do you know who I am?"

"Not your name, but I knew by your voice that you were from my neck of the woods. Figured you to be a ranger, too."

Madsen nodded and extended his hand.

"Right on both counts. The name's Madsen Bold."

Daniel Huggins shook his hand, grinned back, and said, "Are you the one called Mad Jack? I remember Pa talking about you."

"That was in my younger years. Your pa called me that and a passel worse that aren't worth repeating. Now, what's this about you helping me?"

The boy glanced through the dirty saloon window and then motioned for Madsen to walk with him down the sidewalk.

"I was at Fort Collins when you inquired after Rawlings. I figured you to be on business when I overheard you and the sergeant talking. He shouldn't have talked to you that way."

Madsen shrugged the comment off and said, "What do you know about Rawlings?"

"He's got a woman with him—"

"I know. She's his accomplice."

They stepped off the sidewalk and into the snow of a narrow alley that ran between the buildings. Huggins faced the side of the saloon, unbuttoned his wool pants, and watered the boards.

"But that's just it," he said. "I got the impression it was the other way around. He was working for her."

"How so?"

Snow crunched under Madsen's boots as he moved to the other side of Huggins, into the shadows beyond the realm of the yellow light spilling through the windows, and relieved himself, too. Two men hosing a wall outside a saloon was a common enough sight without arousing attention.

"I saw her come to the guardhouse," Huggins said. "I couldn't hear what passed between them, but I could see she seemed real angry. She was talking, and he was listening and nodding his head. I noticed because I've seen her before. She's an actress."

Madsen buttoned back up.

"You sure about this?" he said.

Putting his uniform back to rights, Daniel said, "I saw her in a play put on by a traveling company. She goes by the name Josephine Wheeler."

As renewed doubts screamed through him, Madsen braced his shoulder against the building and inhaled a deep breath of the cold air to cool off the fire burning within. Maybe Rose *had* lied to him?

She'd told him her father was an actor. And her

own play-acting could pass, judging by what Madsen had seen so far.

Before he could ponder further, three men came out of the saloon and stepped to the hitching rail to retrieve their horses. They were talking and didn't pay any attention to the alleyway, but Daniel glanced back at them.

"I've got to go before my friends inside start wondering."

"Thanks, son," Madsen said. "I appreciate your help."

Daniel stepped up on the sidewalk and then angled back.

"Oh, and I'd steer clear of saloons around here. If I remembered you, someone else might, too. The army's peculiar about having their posts redesigned by dynamite."

With that parting advice and a brisk tap to his hat brim, he walked back into the saloon.

Madsen stood in cold silence at the entrance to the alley. A pretty woman was one thing, but make her an actress, too, and he figured the guardhouse sergeant had been a goner before she finished batting her eyelashes at him.

Knowing she was an actress also went a long way toward explaining why a two-bit outlaw like Rawlings might risk double-crossing Duke Pearson. Something Rose had said in passing played through Madsen's mind.

There are a sinful lot of men in this world who get to feeling puffy when a woman smiles on them.

And Rose would know. It had certainly worked on Madsen.

Was he wrong about her, after all?

Following a wrong trail was no fresh experience for Madsen, but the hollowness that hit his gut told him how much he'd wanted to be right about Rose.

Tracking people was almost the same as tracking animals. They all left sign, and sooner or later, they all returned to familiar ground.

Catching them took patience and knowing where to look.

Now Madsen knew.

Twelve

It was a two-dog night, and Roselyn shivered in the cold bed, wishing she owned even one dog.

When she felt the mattress dip with Madsen's weight, she didn't bother opening her eyes before shamelessly rolling against his chest, seeking some warmth. The move was her undoing.

Her nose buried in the springy chest hair that was exposed by his unbuttoned undershirt. He was like a silky heater and smelled of divine insanity.

"No head to toe?" he whispered.

"Don't be ridiculous," she whispered back. "I'm freezing. Scoot closer."

And what she said was true. The wood-burning stove sat on the other side of the blanket partition, and the blanket blocked most of the heat. What little warmth managed to creep into their side of the dark room couldn't compete with the icy chill that seeped through the cracks in the wallboards.

But warmth wasn't her only reason.

When she snuggled closer, he gathered her in his arms, his legs sleekly entwining with her legs.

His fire and seductive musk surrounded her, and she couldn't stifle her sigh of contentment.

"Warmer?" he said.

"Much."

No matter what he thought of her, she savored this fleeting moment of tenderness. She was happy, safe, and comfortable, and it was a combination she'd seldom experienced before.

"You feel good," he murmured, and she heard him take a deep breath. "Too good. And smell nice."

She tucked her face into the soft crook between his neck and shoulder that pillowed her head perfectly.

"Any luck at the livery?" she whispered.

"None."

"How about the saloon?"

"Some." And he yawned. "I want to do more than talk, sugar, so do us both a favor and go to sleep."

With the barest bit of disappointment, Roselyn hushed. Then she smiled at his honesty when she felt his desire for her push strong and hard against her middle. The sensation sent sparks to every secret place on her body.

It was a joy to lie entangled with him, to imagine this kind of tenderness always. She delighted in the sensuous friction of his hands absently rubbing her back and thighs until his body relaxed and his hands rested on the curve of her hips.

Babies never slept better.

When Roselyn awoke at dawn, the sky was clear.

Sunbeams stretched upward and sparkled off the powdery snow that laced the outside window ledge.

There was no sign of Madsen. Her gaze flew to the corner where he'd set his Sharps, but the corner was empty. His saddlebags were gone, too.

Panic set in. She bolted from the bed and dressed quickly. Then she stuffed her gear into her saddlebags, grabbed her coat, and sailed out the door and down the stairs.

She all but skidded to a halt when she glanced into the dining room. Several working men were eating their breakfast, along with the Wetherspoons at another table, and there, at a table in the corner, sat Madsen, leisurely drinking coffee.

To her dismay, relief flooded through her.

The feeling stemmed from knowing he hadn't gotten a jump on her in trailing Rawlings, or so she tried to convince herself. But deep down she knew that was a lie.

For long moments, they regarded each other, his dark eyes sharp and captivating. Then he nodded and pulled out a chair for her. Her appreciative gaze traveled the length of him and back up.

He'd dressed in a blue flannel shirt and faded denims that hugged his muscular legs like a lover's caress. His hair was still wet from his morning wash and gleaming rich and dark. The soft sweep of hair in the front that refused to behave fell across his forehead and dared her fingers to brush it back.

Lordy, she could tell herself whatever she

wanted, but the aching desire she felt for him was as real as her next breath.

She greeted the Wetherspoons first and then smiled at Madsen. His return greeting was cordial, if a bit cool.

He was moody and alert this morning. Something had changed. She just didn't know what.

"Dill and Sully up?" she said, sitting, wondering if they'd gotten into trouble last night.

"They've gone to get the horses," he said. "You have just enough time to grab a bite."

Before she could ask him who put the hair in his horse apple, Peters came out from the kitchen, looking as busy as he had last night.

"Flapjacks do you?" he said, pouring her coffee before she'd even asked.

"Fine."

She quirked a brow at Madsen, who shook his head no.

"I've already eaten," he said.

"Make it a short stack, please," Roselyn said. Then she added, "Has Mrs. Beasley been down yet?"

"Ain't seen the widder this morning, but it's early yet. 'Spect she'll be heading on to her sister's, though, seeing as how the weather's clear."

When Peters returned to the kitchen, Roselyn propped her forearms on the table and clasped her hands together. Madsen frowned across their coffee cups.

"What are you up to?" he said, so low only Roselyn heard his menacing tone. "Why the interest in the widow?"

"She's traveling alone," Roselyn said, and offered an innocent smile. "So I'm going to ask her to join us. There's safety in numbers, you know."

He grunted.

"If we add any more to our number, we'll be a parade. What's your real reason?"

Roselyn leaned over and covered his hand with hers so it would appear to the other people in the dining room that they shared an intimate moment.

"Tell me what you found out last night," she whispered, "and I'll tell you what I found out."

That caught his interest. He played along, leaning forward and caressing her fingers with his.

"You go first," he said.

She traced a fingertip over the veins on the back of his hand. His hands were rough, not the smooth hands of a banker but strong and capable of touching with infinite gentleness.

On a quick glance around, she said, "Not here."

It didn't take long for Roselyn to feed her healthy appetite once Peters served her breakfast. When she finished, Madsen put some coins on the table and grabbed his coat. They bid good-bye to the Wetherspoons, and he ushered Roselyn out onto the sidewalk fronting the lodging house.

The air was crisp and cold but not freezing, since the sun had come out. Dill and Sully were saddled and waiting at the hitch rail.

Behind them, Roselyn glimpsed Mrs. Beasley's black dress as the woman crossed the street, heading toward the closed doors of the livery.

"Speak of the devil," Roselyn said, watching the wooden door swing shut. "Let's wait a minute. When the man brings her rig out, I'll invite her to ride with us."

Madsen put his coat on, glanced in the direction she stared, and said, "Talk."

Instead, Roselyn stepped between her horse and Madsen's and then handed Madsen her saddlebags. As she watched him tie them down, she told him what she'd learned last night.

"It seems the grieving widow isn't grieving as much as she'd like folks to think. That is, if she's grieving at all, or even a widow, for that matter."

"What are you saying?"

"The woman who broke Rawlings out of jail." Roselyn jutted her chin toward the livery.

"That's her?"

"Maybe. Somebody didn't want to be seen and was using the back stairs. I found the back door cracked open last night where someone had been in too much of a hurry to close it proper."

Madsen finished with her horse and tossed his saddlebags onto his own.

"Anyone could've used that door," he said, tying the leather straps.

"True, but why would they unless they had something to hide? According to the good doctor's wife, there's been a lot of footsteps that don't seem to get farther than the widow's door. What do you make of that?"

"So the widow has better luck than I do, and Mrs. Wetherspoon is a busybody. Sugar, you'll have to do better than that."

Roselyn frowned, not understanding his attitude.

"Do you have to work at being ornery," she said, "or is it a natural talent?"

Sliding the Sharps into its scabbard, Madsen ignored her jibe and rubbed his scruffy jaw. Roselyn wondered if he was more handsome without the whiskers. No, he couldn't possibly get better looking.

"If Mrs. Beasley is who she says she is," he reasoned, "she'll be glad for our company. And—"

"And if she's not," Roselyn insisted, "she'll agree to our invite to keep from looking suspicious. Either way, we'll know what she looks like and where to find her. She'll lead us to Rawlings."

"Unless she knows who we are."

"Well, there's that—" Roselyn began, and then halted when she saw his expression narrow with thought. "Why are you looking at me so strange?"

He shook his head.

"Thinking, is all."

Roselyn started to pursue it, then changed her mind. If a man had something gnawing at him, he'd usually spit it out when he was ready.

"So tell me what you found out last night?" she said instead.

"Does the name Josephine Wheeler sound familiar?"

"No," she said, thinking a moment. "Should it?"

"She's an actress. The thought occurred to me that you might know her."

"Why would I know—? Oh, you mean because of my father?"

"Or because you're Josephine Wheeler. Are you?"

His low accusing questions sent starch up her spine and ignited her temper. After the lies she'd spouted, she didn't fault him for not trusting her completely, but his judgmental attitude was becoming a tiresome habit.

"You still think I've lied, is that it? Well, I haven't. I told you my name, and I told you I'm not the woman who helped Rawlings. I won't say it again. Believe what you will."

And Roselyn whirled toward the livery to prove it to him.

Madsen watched Rose yank the livery door open and disappear inside.

Her eyes had never shifted, and her face had never changed when he had said the name. Was anyone that good an actress?

The answer came easily.

No.

He closed the distance to the livery in long and angry strides. Ignoring Sully's call, Madsen reached for the door handle, ready to put his doubts to rest once and for all.

To his surprise, when he yanked on the door, it held fast. He yanked again harder. The wood rattled on its hinges but never budged.

Madsen stilled. The skin on the back of his neck crawled.

"What's ailing y'sonny?" Dill asked, grabbing his arm.

"Something's wrong," Madsen said.

Shrugging off Dill's hold, Madsen rattled the door again, then turned and shouted for Sully.

"Hurry! Let's get this open. Rose needs help!"

Roused by the commotion, a dozen men appeared in doorways and soon joined them. The voices were a mix of confusion.

Then, fast on the heels of a woman's scream, the stable doors burst open with a cracking splinter of wood. Horses flooded through the doorway and stampeded into the street.

It was an old Indian trick. While the knot of people behind Madsen scattered out of the way, he was pinned between the sudden opening and the clamoring men directly at his back.

He scrambled to avoid the flailing forelegs of one rearing horse and landed on slippery, iced-over ground. On a grunt of pain, he rolled and regained his feet in time to catch sight of two men atop geldings emerging from the stable among the loose horses.

The man in front was smaller, his jacket fitting loose on his body, with wisps of long dark hair flying out from under his battered hat. But there was no mistaking what Madsen saw in that instant. The man in front was a *woman*.

Rose clung to the second man's saddle like a climbing vine and screamed for him to halt. Fool woman! She'd get herself killed trying to slow him down.

"Madsen!" she shrieked on the way by. "It's him! Stop him! He's getting away!"

Without hesitating, Madsen grabbed the mane of a dun horse and mounted at a run. He brutally kicked the animal into a gallop.

Blowing great plumes of breath from its flaring nostrils, the horse no more than touched hoof to snowy ground before digging in for traction and exploding large divots of ice into the crowd behind them.

Near the edge of town, Madsen saw an old-timer on the sidewalk aiming a Henry rifle toward the two riders ahead.

Terror sliced into every nerve in Madsen's body. At this short range, the buffalo gun could take down both rider and Rose in one shot.

"Don't shoot!" Madsen roared.

The cold wind rushing by his face stole his words, but it didn't matter. His shout came too late.

The Henry spat flame, and a deafening boom followed. Through the haze of white smoke, Madsen watched horrified as crimson exploded along the rider's back a half second before he slumped forward over Rose's body.

"Rose!"

Her name was torn from Madsen's throat, and his mouth flooded with the metallic taste of fear. Even during all the years of the war, Madsen couldn't remember ever being as scared as he was at that moment.

The old-timer, with unerring accuracy, had hit his target.

Thirteen

Panicked by the noise and the scent of fresh blood, the gelding ran flat-out.

Madsen could see Rose. She was covered with blood, but she was alive. Her flailing feet told him that. From her position, she couldn't dislodge the body to gain a leg up on the saddle.

And if she lost her grip, she'd hit the ground and break her neck.

Clutching a fistful of the dun's coarse hair, Madsen wrapped his fingers in the long mane. He squeezed his thigh and leg muscles to anchor himself to the horse's sides.

Snorting wind, the dun drew abreast of the running gelding, and Madsen leaned in.

"Hold tight to the saddle horn, Rose!"

"Hurry!" she screamed back. "My arms are giving out."

And he shoved the lifeless body, plunging it to the ground in a mangled heap. In the next instant, with one straining arm, Madsen snatched Rose to his side.

"Are you hurt, sugar? Where are you hit?"

She wrapped her arms around his neck in a stranglehold, and buried her face in the hollow of his throat.

"It's not my blood," she said on a watery note. "I'm fine. I'm not hit."

He hugged her shaking body tightly to his chest, slowed the dun, and slid off the horse's back with Rose in his arms.

"Don't ever leave me like that again," he said.

His heart beat an erratic rhythm as he planted his feet in the snow.

"I won't," she said, her face flushed with emotion and her cheeks wet. "I'm sorry."

Then, in a fierce and possessive embrace, he crushed her to him, repeatedly running his hands over her arms and back, satisfying himself that she was unhurt.

"I'm fine, really," she said, smothering her whisper against his skin.

He raised her head and smoothed the tangles of blonde hair from her cheeks. His warm hands cradled her chilled face.

"You sure took your sweet time coming after me," she said.

Madsen expected to see eyes filled with anger or fear, but she flashed him a watery smile. He searched her face, and the trust that glittered in her brown eyes touched him to his heart.

"But I did come after you," he said. "You won't get away from me that easily."

"Because I still owe you a hundred dollars?"

"And because you're mine."

Then he claimed her upturned mouth. His kiss was desperate, angry, fueled by uncertainty and fear and overwhelming relief.

She responded to him, standing on tiptoe and pressing into him, needing him as much as he needed her. He absorbed her body's trembles as fierce desire and unleashed loneliness surged thick and hot through his veins.

He molded her body to his, feeling her breasts strain against his chest. His mouth slanted over hers, and he deepened the searing kiss.

He nibbled her lips, flicked and savagely thrust his tongue to explore her sweet mouth and reassure himself that she was real and alive. With every soft whimper escaping her throat, he shuddered to think how close he'd come to losing her.

"The widow was no widow," Rose said. "And you were right. They knew who we were. I surprised them and upset their getaway plans."

Madsen kissed her again and then checked up when he heard Sully shout ahead of Peters, Doc Wetherspoon, and several other men on foot. He broke away from her mouth and turned his head to the racket around them.

"She's not hurt," Madsen called when the doctor came running up, black bag in hand.

"Y'sure you're all right, ma'am?"

"Yes," she said, tucking flyaway hair behind her ears. "A little shaken, is all."

Along with Dill, a few men had reached the dead body, which was lying in the snow. One man caught up to the gelding that stood ten yards away, blowing. Others were busy catching up the horses that had broken loose from the stable.

Then Madsen brushed his lips across Rose's again before reluctantly drawing her arms from around his neck. Lightly kissing her fingertips, he gave her a reassuring smile.

When Doc Wetherspoon rolled the dead man over, Madsen's suspicion was confirmed.

"Is he definitely—?" Rose whispered.

"Yes," Madsen returned, staring at the lifeless face he'd spent over a month tracking.

"Y'know this man?" Doc said.

Madsen nodded and hunkered down to check the body.

"Name's Teddy Lee Rawlings. He's a small-time outlaw wanted for robbery in Texas. No bounty that I know of. No family, either."

And no pouch of diamonds on him.

Madsen glanced up at Rose and shook his head. She caught his silent message and seemed to crumple into herself.

"We were so close," she finally said.

His pigheadedness deserved whatever harsh words she wanted to toss his way, but they never passed her lips. Rising, Madsen dusted his hands off on his faded pants and then gestured to Rose.

"Doc, she's pretty shaken up. Will you take her back to the lodging house and ask your missus to look after her? I'll take care of things here."

"Yes, of course, you're right," Doc said, gathering his bag and taking her by the elbow. "Come along, dear. You've had quite a fright."

Rose angled her head over her shoulder.

"But Madsen—"

"Go on," he said, and kissed her. "I'll be along directly."

He watched her for a moment, letting the possessiveness wash over him, embracing it without question, then he gestured to Sully.

"Check the saddlebags on his horse."

While Peters supervised, four of the men hefted the body between them and lugged it to the livery to wait for the blacksmith to build a coffin.

Sully came back about then and reported finding nothing out of the ordinary among Teddy Lee's gear. That didn't surprise Madsen.

"The other rider was a woman," he said, and when Sully arched bushy gray eyebrows, added, "Unless I miss my guess, she goes by the name of Josephine Wheeler. Can you and Dill trail her?"

"Sure-'nuff, sonny," Sully said on a gleeful chuckle, his eyes glittering with the challenge. "Figure she's headin' t' Denver City?"

Madsen nodded and said, "Follow her and don't let her out of your sight."

"Will do. What about you and Miz Roselyn?"

He knew what the old rooster was asking. But he had no answer. Once Madsen recovered the diamonds, there'd be no reason for him to stick around.

"Don't wait on us," he said instead. "When she's calmed down and ready to ride, we'll meet up with you at the Denver House. Tomorrow at the latest."

And it shook Madsen more than he cared to

admit to think that he and Rose had so little time left together.

After Rawlings was shot, Mrs. Wetherspoon had fussed over Roselyn like a doting grandmother.

She clucked her tongue at the widow's scandalous behavior while helping Roselyn bathe and set herself back to rights. Everyone had assumed the Widow Beasley had taken up with the wanted outlaw and was running off with him, so Roselyn and Madsen had figured the truth was best left unspoken.

When she came back downstairs, Peters had her coat cleaned for her as best he could and had a cup of hot tea waiting.

"Thank you," Roselyn said, seating herself. "You've both been so kind."

"Glad we could help, dear," Mrs. Wetherspoon said, patting her hand. "Your man was very worried about you— Oh, here he comes now."

It sprang to Roselyn's tongue to say Madsen wasn't her man, that she wasn't sure what they were to each other. But she kept that behind her teeth and merely smiled her gratitude when Mrs. Wetherspoon took herself off to give them some privacy.

"How are you?" Madsen said, taking her hand as he seated himself across from her.

Only a hint of tension edged his soft voice, but his mouth was grim.

"Better now that I'm clean. I'm not as fragile as they seemed to think."

"I know." His thumb massaged her knuckles. "That's why it was good of you to let them feel useful."

"And you?" she said, trying to gauge his reaction. "How do you feel?"

More than anything, Roselyn wanted him to trust her, to believe in her, but she didn't know how to make that happen.

He sighed, released her hand, and sat back.

"You were right about the widow. More than likely she was Teddy Lee's accomplice. Is that what you wanted to hear?"

Roselyn knew it was as close as she was going to get.

"Apology accepted," she said, and sipped her tea. "Now, about getting the diamonds—"

"Nothing's changed, Rose," he said in a low, harsh voice. "I want you to know that up front. I gave my word to return those diamonds, and that's what I'm still going to do."

"I believe you. But at the same time, understand that nothing's changed for me. Mama's counting on me, and I won't let her down."

Roselyn stared at him over the cup's rim. Maybe she was her mama, after all, for she couldn't help but look at Madsen and know there was something in life even more powerful than dreams.

Fourteen

They left Platteville close to midmorning, and it was well past dark when they rode into Denver City.

After a quick bite of supper, they checked in at the Denver House. The lobby was the fanciest place Roselyn had ever seen.

Two men in suits argued across a gleaming mahogany counter with a long-nosed desk clerk. He was a mustachioed man wearing a gray shirt with sleeve garters, a black vest, and an exasperated expression behind his wire-rimmed spectacles.

The men had their backs to her, but she overheard enough to know there was a problem with their bill, or rather, with their not paying it. She was too busy gawking at the furnishings to care how the arguing turned out.

Rich wood accents gleamed on the staircase banister and reflected the crystal chandelier that hung above her head. The glass prisms caught the candlelight and sparkled like diamond chips.

Mounted elk heads adorned the walls and looked down on gold brocaded chairs and settees that were arranged in small groupings. Green potted plants stood sentinel over the seating areas, while polished brass spittoons were discreetly located in the corners.

Multicolored fringed rugs covered the wood floors. The air was fragrant with beeswax and the smell of new money.

Just as Roselyn turned her attention back to the front desk, she collided with one of the suited men who'd finished bickering with the desk clerk.

The impact wobbled her off balance. The man grabbed her shoulders, to keep his own balance, she suspected, as much as to keep her from gracelessly plopping on her backside to the freshly scrubbed floor.

"Oh, I-I'm sorry," Roselyn said to his jacket buttons. "I wasn't watching where I was going."

Her senses registered the aroma of warm wool, cigarette tobacco, and bay rum.

"I do beg your pardon, miss," he said, dropping his hands. "My fault entirely, I assure you."

When he backed up a step, so did she. Then he tipped his bowler hat and inclined his head. She noticed his hands were smooth looking, white as a baby's bottom, and his nails were trim and buffed.

His manners seemed as impeccable as his clothes. He was a well-spoken, solid blond man of middling age in a crisp white shirt, brown tie, brown coat, and dark brown pinstriped pants. The well-heeled look more than adequately hid his empty pockets.

English, Roselyn guessed, upon hearing his textured voice. He smiled, and to her surprise, his blue eyes stared back at her with interest.

"No harm done," she said, and offered an embarrassed smile in return.

"You're too kind. Please, allow me to make up for my boorish manners."

He reached into the breast pocket of his jacket, disturbing the smooth lines of his lapel, and passed her a slip of paper.

"This gent bothering you, Rose?" Madsen said, stepping to her side and dwarfing her in his shadow.

His menacing tone and glower caught her off guard.

Jealousy?

No.

Must be her wishful thinking.

"Purely an accident, sir," the man said. "I meant no disrespect."

He and Madsen exchanged a brief look. Roselyn could tell that the Englishman knew Madsen didn't like him.

But whatever further argument the man thought to advance died in his throat after a quick glance at the brace of pistols on Madsen's hips and the Sharps in his hand.

"Again, my apologies," the man said with a slight bow. "If you'll forgive me, I must run now. I do hope to see you there."

And with a curt nod to Madsen, he joined the

other man, who was waiting for him, and continued on his way.

Roselyn glanced at her hand and saw he had given her a ticket.

"What's that?" Madsen snapped.

"How's your Shakespeare?"

"Saddle sore, but thanks for asking. Now answer my question."

"This is to a matinee reading at the opera house," she said, and held up the ticket. "Edgar Bryce as Hamlet. Hamlet? The play by William Shakespeare?"

Madsen's mouth thinned. He was obviously unimpressed.

Roselyn blew a tired breath and said, "Might be a good place to find an actress, wouldn't you think?"

Then, stepping up to the counter, she pointed the ticket over her shoulder.

"Was that Edgar Bryce?" she asked the desk clerk.

"Him?" The clerk snorted. "No, ma'am. He's Hugh Cathal, the company's owner. He only thinks he's as good a gent as Mr. Bryce."

"We'd like two rooms," Madsen cut in, bringing the desk clerk back to business.

The clerk smiled, as much for the color of their money as at them. He gave them rooms side by side, up the stairs and to the right. Madsen opened Roselyn's door for her and entered first.

She waited in the corridor while he checked the interior for any nasty surprises before satisfying himself that all was well. When he lit the lamp on the table beside the bed, she saw that the room was spacious and as nicely appointed as the lobby.

One window overlooked the street and sported a green roller shade topped by white lace curtains. A cushioned chair with a footrest and a small table sat angled to the window. Green flocked paper lined the walls. A walnut double bed took up the far wall next to a matching vanity, and a tall walnut wardrobe stood to the left of the door.

After setting her saddlebags down on the bed, Madsen handed her the key. She couldn't help but note that his hands were like roots, brown and firm and strong, so unlike the man she'd bumped into in the lobby.

"Lock the door behind me and keep it locked," he said. "Don't open it unless you know who it is."

"Are we expecting trouble?" Roselyn said.

"Could be. I don't like how that man downstairs looked at you."

Her eyes widened.

"Why, I thought he was a gentleman."

Madsen tilted her jaw up with his knuckle and rubbed the pad of his thumb across her chin.

"Shows what you know," he murmured. "An overpolite man is usually hiding unpolite ideas."

His touch felt so natural. She swayed into it, not a conscious decision, more like a flower to sunlight, mesmerized by the heat in his eyes.

"If you need anything," he said, dropping his hand away, "I'll be next door. Sing out."

She wanted to scream with frustration. Instead, she pointed to his side.

"What about your wound?" she said. "You better sit down and let me take a look at it."

She reached for his coat to help him remove it, and he grabbed her hand.

"No, sugar," he said, his voice rough. "I think the best thing for me to do is walk out the door."

"But—"

"My side's better. I'll tend to it myself."

"At least let me get you the salve." Roselyn fished in her saddlebags and handed him the jar. "What about Dill and Sully? Were they going to meet us?"

Hand on the doorknob, Madsen angled back.

"If not tonight, tomorrow. I'll let you know when I hear from them."

When Madsen closed the door behind him, she locked it, not because she felt uneasy about being a woman alone in a strange hotel, but because she knew from hearing Madsen's steps and from seeing his shadow under the door that he was standing in the corridor, waiting for her to do as he had instructed.

She'd been alone in worst places and felt she could take care of herself now, but she couldn't help the pleasure that came with Madsen's consideration.

Clutching the key in her hand, she slumped against the back of the door.

Her mouth curved into a smile, and she hugged herself, enjoying the exquisite tingling that flowed and expanded into a fierce yearning. She wasn't sure what this thing was she sought.

But it always remained a bit out of reach.

"Like your rainbow, Mama?" she said to the silent room and could almost hear Fiona's smiling voice echo in her head.

The best we can do, my little wild Rose, is reach for the rainbow and not give up. Never give up.

In that way, Roselyn and Madsen were alike—both were unwilling to give up. Yet one of them would have to—once they found the diamonds.

And that's what Roselyn was afraid of facing.

Madsen lounged on top of the bed, sitting up with his back propped on pillows that were bunched against the headboard.

His gun belt hung around the walnut bedpost within easy reach. The Sharps stood in the corner between the bedside table and the bed.

Sully had made himself comfy in the chair across from Madsen, his feet hanging off the end of the cushioned footstool. In his lap, his hand hugged the neck of a half-full bottle. The brassy light from the lamp threw his shadow against the curtains.

"You know what Rose and I are after?" Madsen said, wondering for the umpteenth time just how far to trust this old outlaw and his brother.

Sully took a swig from the bottle, coughed, and then wiped his whiskers and mouth with the back of his hand.

"Yer a worryin' sort, ain'tcha?"

"Let's just say I'm cautious. I like to know who I've got at my back."

Smacking the cork down in the bottle, Sully leaned forward.

"Whatever y'thinkin', sonny, yer wrong," he said, his bushy gray brows knotted in a frown. "Miz Roselyn's been good to Dill 'n me. We done promised to help her and her ma, and that's what we aim t'do."

"So then you're only helping me because of her?"

"That's one reason."

Madsen figured that was the score, but he had needed to make sure. As soon as he got his hands on those diamonds, he could expect Dill and Sully to turn on him.

An understanding passed between them.

"What's the other reason?" Madsen said.

Sully relaxed into the cushion, a wicked twinkle in his eye.

"On account," he said, "we ain't had this much fun in a coon's age."

Madsen couldn't help himself; he laughed out loud.

About then, Rose sailed through the door.

"Sorry it took me so long," she said, closing the door behind her. "I was dozing when you knocked."

She made a sultry picture, with her sleep-softened face and her blonde hair hanging loose around her shoulders and parted in the middle. Madsen felt himself strain against his pants.

He shifted uncomfortably.

"Tell her what you told me earlier," he said.

On a grunt, Sully yanked one boot off and rubbed his foot through his sock, while Rose crossed over to sit on the edge of the bed. Madsen moved his legs to give her room to scoot close to him.

When she did, he smiled to himself.

"Find out anything?" she said to Sully.

"The lady's gone to roost at a roomin' house on the edge of town. Dill 'n me follered her, like y'said. She didn't stop nowhere or talk to nobody, so we done figgered she's got them diamonds on her—"

"Or hidden in her room?" Rose said, turning to Madsen.

His gaze traced her saucy lower lip before he nodded and said, "Dill is keeping an eye on the rooming house right now. If she tries to skip town, we'll know about it."

Sully kicked off his other boot and massaged that foot, too.

"I done told Dill I'd catch me a couple hours' shut-eye and then spell him. Y'mind if I bunk in here, sonny?"

"You might as well," Madsen said, taking Rose's hand and rising from the bed. "We'll come up with something better in the morning."

"What are you thinking?" Rose said.

Madsen put his around her and kissed her nose, his silence ripe with meaning. She blushed.

"I meant your plans about the actress," she said.

"Oh, that," he said, and grinned. "Simple. I'm thinking she might be in the play tomorrow. You can use your ticket to keep an eye on her while we check out the rooming house."

Rose nodded and said, "Then I'll see you in the morning."

On the way out, she bid Sully good night.

Madsen walked her back to her room, anyway, and again waited until he heard her key click in the lock. It was probably an unnecessary precaution, but there was no telling when a red-eyed ya-hoo might stumble into the wrong room and let drink do the thinking for him.

At least that's the reason Madsen gave himself. He raised tentative fingers to the door and traced the wood grain for a long moment, wishing he was on the other side beside her.

When Madsen returned to his own room, Sully had stripped down to dingy longhandles and was crawling under the covers.

"Want me to wake you in a few hours?" Madsen asked.

"Don't bother yerself, sonny." His gravelly voice drifted up from the pillows. "I'm a light sleeper."

The old rooster was snoring by the time Madsen had stripped off his shirt and pants and had blown out the bedside lamp. He laid down, listened to the gurgling snorts, and then buried his head under his pillow.

An hour later, a bleary-eyed Madsen rapped gently on Rose's door.

"Sugar, it's me. Open up."

Silence. Then a rattle of the key in the lock and the door was flung open wide.

"What's wrong?" she said, her eyes rounded, her hair sleep-tangled and sensually mussed. "Who's hurt?"

Her gaze traveled up and down him, taking in a shirt sagging open, pants thrown on in haste, bare feet, and a gun belt dangling from his hand.

"No one . . . yet," Madsen said, leaning his shoulder against the doorjamb. "But I'm not making any promises."

Then she cocked her head, obviously hearing the train next door as it alternately released steam and chugged rusty wheels up a steep incline.

"If I have to tolerate snoring in my left ear," Madsen said, "I'd rather it came from a mouth not surrounded by whiskers."

"You're such a romantic," Rose said, relaxing her hand against the door. "If you don't watch it, your silver tongue will turn my head."

"I'm a plain man, Rose. I haven't had a whole lot of practice at the sweet nothings that women set store by."

She waited, not giving him an inch. He was a fool to stand there in the hallway; even a little afraid she'd turn him away.

But he couldn't make himself go. He needed her, even if she'd hate him later, when he returned the diamonds.

Her eyes were dark, expressive, questioning. A wealth of secrets lay behind them.

As though she drew all of the hallway light into them, never had they shone so richly brown or gleamed with such sultry promise.

"I'm tired," he added, "and need a good night's sleep. Let me in, please?"

"Tired? Is that the only reason?"

Her lush scent reached out to him, touching him softly, luring him, as her tongue moved lightly over her bottom lip. He knew a sharp, sudden hunger that drove out any other thoughts.

"No, sugar," he said, and sighed. "I missed you."

His confession hung between them in the silence. He wanted her tongue in his mouth, wanted her taste in his mouth, wanted to take her inside himself and never let go.

Then, an eternity later, Rose offered him a tantalizing smile.

"For not knowing sweet nothings," she murmured, "you do all right."

She clasped his hand gently and tugged him inside the shadowy room. Her hand in his felt so right. His doubts and uncertainty ebbed away.

Madsen closed the door on the outside world and locked them inside a world of their own making. When he turned, Rose hid her gaze behind down-swept lashes. Her night shift lay puddled at her feet, and she wore nothing but fragile moonlight.

He'd imagined her just so the first time he saw her. And how many times since?

Too many to count.

Even as the thought formed, he was reaching for her.

Roselyn met him in the middle of the room and answered him with a sigh, a drawn-out kiss, a hand that inched around his neck and encouraged him closer.

The apple doesn't fall far from the tree, so the saying went. And Roselyn finally knew it was true.

Without a whimper, without so much as a fight, she'd accepted that she was her mama's daughter when Madsen's simple declaration cut to her heart. He wasn't the kind of man who needed much from anything or anyone, and it was obviously difficult for him to ask.

Even knowing he'd leave her, she wanted what time with him she could steal. And she wanted him, right now.

Only he created the insistent throbbing she felt deep inside, and only he could soothe it.

What a fool she was.

Standing on tiptoe to kiss him, she slid her tongue across his lower lip, tasting the sweetness of him. He lifted a hand to cup her chin, tracing a rough finger down her cheek and along the line of her jaw. His arousal rose against her thighs.

A moan escaped her throat, and she closed her eyes as his lips caressed her neck, her throat, and the valley between her breasts. Her hands were impatient to revel in the texture of his skin, in his muscular strength and breadth.

"You have too many clothes on," she said.

Then fingers ripped at buttons, and hands swept clothes aside until they were both caressing and exploring.

When her hands slid down his waist and over his hips, he murmured, "Patience, sweetheart. We've got all night." Then he raised questioning eyes to her. "Haven't we?"

He could have whispered of forever or the hundred other lies that had swayed women down through the ages, but not Madsen. He was a man of his word. Roselyn understood then that he was seeking no promises and giving none.

He wanted her to be certain as well.

"Stay with me tonight," she whispered against his mouth. "I want you to stay."

Tomorrow and all the tomorrows after that were for worries and fears. Tonight was for feeling alive. Tonight was for making memories.

In answer, he kissed her throat, her jaw, her lips, and lifted her in his arms and carried her to the big walnut bed.

Fifteen

Madsen was starved for Rose's touch. He was all hard, searching desire, and she was warm and yielding and soft as doeskin.

She offered a pale, perfect figure of beauty in the moonlight. And for this fragment of eternity, he dared to believe she was really his.

He laid her gently on the rumpled sheets, burying her in the softness of the bed, and covered her with his body against the chill in the room. Enticed by the perfume of skin as supple as the wind, he scorched a path down her chest with his lips to her narrow waist and back up again.

Her eyes were sultry, so filled with wonder, and she gave him the slow smile that he'd pictured a million times in his dreams.

His heart pounded, and the blood roared in his ears. He had never felt such urgency for anyone.

She leaned her head, her teeth tugging on his lip. Satiny strands of hair flowed over his hands, teasing and arousing. He slid between her thighs, his erection pulsing against the damp heat there.

She sought his mouth again, and teasing turned

hot and needy when Rose pressed her impatient body to his. Madsen heard her breathing quicken.

He memorized the feel of her eager, questing hands, and he groaned.

"Please, sweetheart," he gasped against her mouth, pushing her palm until it cradled all of him. "Touch me, Rose."

Her slender hands on him were pure heaven. She was tentative at first, then delicious in the glide of her fingers skimming around and over, back and forth.

When he could bear her gentle teasing no more, he slipped his hand between them and touched that most intimate part of her and savored the silky moisture raining on his fingers.

He entered her, and waves of sensation washed through her and into him. Her white heat clutched him, drawing in his strength, burning him to his soul.

With a pause and a half-held breath, Madsen closed his eyes and waited until he could no longer feel himself apart from her.

"Madsen?" she whispered, stirring sensuously under him.

"You feel so good," he said.

"Is it over?"

He was shaking with need but mustered a wry chuckle.

"It will be if you don't hold still."

Finally in control once more, he wrapped her dimpled knees around his bare flanks, something he'd wanted to do from the instant he'd first spied them. Her thighs were strong, lissome, greedily clamping him tight.

His hungry body began to move, and she lifted to him, seeking more of him, her blonde hair splayed out across the pillow and glistening in the pale light like rich silver. She drew him deeper, demanding, matching his hunger with a wildness that thrilled him.

Her arms tightened around his shoulders. His mouth sought hers.

He swallowed her cry and then soared, aching, intense, a shuddering eruption, as sweet as the curve of her hip, as her earthy whispers in his ear, as his body dissolving into hers until he could no longer tell where she began and he left off.

Slowly the shimmer faded, leaving Roselyn listening to Madsen's quiet breathing, apart from each other but no longer separate. Never again separate.

He lay curled on his side, Roselyn tucked in his arms. His lips were nestled against her cheek. Her head was pillowed on his shoulder. She loved listening to his breathing.

If she could just lie here for the rest of her life. No one-horse towns in her past. No Duke Pearson in her future.

But that was a futile wish.

Nothing had really changed. With daylight would come her responsibility to her mama and the ever-present problem of laying hands on those diamonds before Madsen could.

For now, though, she had this moment. She closed her eyes, surrounded by his strength and warmth, feeling safe and wanted and rich beyond measure.

And thinking words of love that she was afraid to say. As long as she didn't say them, she wouldn't have to face the disappointment and regret when he rode away.

"Rose? You awake, sugar?"

"No. You're a dream, and I can do what I want in my dreams."

She snuggled into his bare shoulder and kissed the tender spot below his ear.

"We need to talk, Rose."

His words rumbled in his chest. She felt—as much as heard—them like another heartbeat.

"I like how you taste," she said. "Let's talk about that."

He pulled away from her, and she could feel his eyes on her.

"I'm serious," he said.

"So am I."

She licked the hollow of his throat and then trailed her tongue up his bristly chin until her lips hovered a breath away from his. For a moment, she stared into the dark mist of his eyes, sharing the same thin sheet of air.

Slowly, she kissed him, giving her heart in that kiss, saying more than she could ever put into words.

"You were saying?" she murmured.

"Woman, you talk too much."

Then he suddenly rolled, pressing the full weight of his chest and thighs against her, anchoring her so that she was spread-eagled beneath him.

His touch was everywhere, as was his mouth, plunging her into a dizzying whirlpool of feeling, her senses drowning in the hot current flowing between them. He caressed her as if he could never have enough of her, and her body responded with an urgency that more than equaled his own.

Her fingers ran down the valley of his spine, stroking his hips, palms holding him tight, urging him closer. Their bodies fit so well together.

No longer teasing or tentative, together they swept upward into the storm before exploding into a million tiny bursts of sunlight.

When Roselyn floated back to the bed, Madsen was there to catch her. He gave a warm kiss to her forehead, to her nose.

"I was thinking," he said, against her mouth. "Maybe I can help your mother."

Roselyn sat up, pushing him flat to the bed and straddling him, barely able to contain her excitement.

"Oh, Madsen," she said, sprinkling kisses over his face. "I was hoping you'd say that. Together we can get the diamonds and return them to Duke, and then we can—"

"Whoa! Hold up, there." Gentle pressure on

her shoulders backed her off until searching eyes stared up at her. "I didn't mean that."

"But you said—"

"I said *help* your mother. I meant I can wire my friend—he was a ranger, too. He can protect your mother."

Her spirits deflating, Roselyn shook her head in denial, sending her hair flying about her shoulders.

"You don't understand. Mama and me . . . we're in too deep to tread water. The only thing that'll protect her is to pay off Duke Pearson."

Madsen took Roselyn's hand from his chest and tenderly kissed her fingertips.

"My friend Leander can put her someplace safe," he said. "Someplace out of Pearson's reach."

A cold shiver hit Roselyn's core. Madsen was asking her to risk the only family she had.

His idea might work now, but what about later? What then, when Roselyn and her mama were just a warm speck in Madsen's memory, if he remembered her at all?

No, Roselyn couldn't take the chance. If she didn't pull Mama out of the fire this time, she'd have to face Duke Pearson again sometime down the road.

And next time, he wouldn't bother with friendly terms.

Shaking her head again, Roselyn withdrew her hand and scooted off the bed.

"For how long, Madsen? A week? Two weeks?

A year? Your friend can't protect her forever, and Duke isn't a man to forget. I thought maybe you . . . me . . ."

Roselyn swallowed hard and turned to collect her night shift off the floor so Madsen couldn't see the tears welling up in her eyes. She loved him for offering to help, but she didn't believe he could help short of going back on his word and letting her have the diamonds to pay Pearson.

And going back on his word was one thing Madsen Bold would never do.

"That you . . . me, what?" he said.

Madsen swung his legs over the edge of the bed and stood, advancing on her.

"What, Rose?" He gestured to the bed, all tenderness gone. "Did you think this would change my mind about returning the diamonds?"

There was no point in denying that the thought had crossed her mind. It had.

"In a way," she said, clutching the ragged shift to her chest, suddenly feeling vulnerable and conscious of her nakedness and wary of his overpowering strength. "Maybe I was hoping that. We make a good team."

He stopped in front of her and raked his fingers through his hair. His gaze was direct and bleak in the moonlight that spilled through the lace curtains.

She wanted to turn away from the accusation in his eyes, but she forced herself to face him.

"So that's all this was?" he said. "A bribe?"

"I didn't say that—!"

"You didn't have to, sugar."

His voice was flat, resigned. Disappointed? No, he'd gotten what he wanted.

And, for that matter, so had Roselyn.

But it wasn't enough. Now that she'd had a taste, she wanted a lifetime more of lying in his arms, of hearing his voice, of having him near.

"Don't look at me like that," she said. "I'm not a stranger."

"You *are* a stranger," he said, turning to yank on his shirt and pants. "I don't know who you are."

He didn't bother buttoning his shirt.

"I'll go wake Sully to spell his brother," he said. "Lock the door behind me."

"Madsen? Don't go."

He paused at the door without looking back.

"We've had our roll in the hay," he said, and she flinched at his coldness. "Good night, Rose."

His icy words lingered in the air long after he'd gone.

Roselyn stood staring at the closed door, her heart aching, wanting to call Madsen back, wanting to call back their lovemaking. Her body still burned with his touch, and she could still taste him.

But maybe it was better this way. It would make the leave-taking easier when she headed back home with the diamonds.

Roselyn had been alone before, but she'd never known what it was to feel lonely. Now she did.

And it hurt.

Sixteen

There was no fool like an old fool, so the saying went.

Even if Madsen wasn't that old, he felt like it this morning. He'd risen at dawn after a sleepless night and washed and dressed out of habit, not because his mind was focused on what he was doing.

The brown pair of pants and white shirt he pulled out of his saddlebags were the last clean clothes he owned. That much registered as he tamped his feet down into his boots without trying for quiet.

He'd left Dill sound asleep in the bed, snarfing and snoring as bad as, if not worse than, his brother had done. No wonder the two old roosters were bachelors.

But Madsen stared out the window at the sun creeping up on another frosty day and hardly noticed the warbling anymore.

He was too engrossed in listening to his own raging thoughts. A simple chore of tracking down a thief had turned into something more complex than Madsen had ever imagined, all because he'd walked into a run-down saloon and tripped over his heart.

There was no denying it. Rose O'Neill was a complication, one he had never expected to encounter in his life. He'd ridden alone for a lot of years and without question figured he would always ride the trail alone.

Now he was having second thoughts.

Could he blame Rose for wanting to change his mind? In all honesty, no.

After all, what happened between them last night was his fault for needing more than he was willing to give.

Had he expected her *not* to try to change his mind? Expected, no. But deep down he had hoped she would come to him because she wanted to.

God, how he had hoped.

The hollowness in the center of his chest threatened to suffocate him.

It had been a mistake to go to Rose's room, to take advantage of the situation, but he'd gone, anyway. In so short a time, he'd gotten used to having her around, and he couldn't stop himself from seeking her out.

But it wouldn't happen again.

So knowing that, why couldn't he forget her steamy eyes, her sultry fragrance, her lingering touch? Madsen ran a weary hand over his scruffy face.

The answer crept up quietly.

Because he'd foolishly thought more had passed between them than just simple need. Because he loved her.

There was so much about Rose that appealed to him.

He liked her gentleness, her strength, her resourcefulness, her compassion, the way she embraced life without complaint. Rose was unbendingly loyal when it came to someone she loved, a trait that Madsen admired.

He liked the way she fit in his arms, the way she cried out his name in her passion . . . the way she made him feel like the luckiest man alive.

Yet, most of all, she was too stubborn for her own good.

She was desperate to save her mother, and he wasn't proud of using that to his advantage, but he'd told her the truth when he'd said maybe he could help. Now there was no maybe about it.

He wanted to help. And despite what Rose had said, he would help.

Skipping breakfast, Madsen got directions from the desk clerk and headed to the telegraph office. His friend Leander McNelly was aware of Duke Pearson and that his influence stretched south of San Antonio down to Laredo.

So there was no need to waste words explaining what he already knew.

Madsen's wire was brief and to the point.

Rawlings dead. Have located accomplice, an actress. Josephine Wheeler. Duke Pearson involved.

Any connection? Find saloon singer Fiona O'Neill and keep her safe from Pearson. She's to stay put until she hears from me or her daughter, Rose.

Madsen had no plan yet, but he would figure something out. For now, getting Rose's mother out of Pearson's reach was a good start.

On his way back to the hotel, Madsen stopped for a bath and a shave and found a laundress who would do his wash. Then he went to check on Sully.

Madsen expected to get his hands on the diamonds today, and he refused to let himself imagine the pleading look on Rose's face once that happened.

The slightly stooped man in the opera-house foyer took Roselyn's ticket and flashed her an admiring grin as she removed her coat.

She'd taken care in dressing this morning, as much to bolster her sagging spirits as to look as differently as possible since the last time Josephine Wheeler had seen her. Roselyn wore her best dress, a burgundy-and-brown skirt and jacket that she saved for special occasions.

It was the kind of outfit that lent her an air of demure respectability and made the gun hidden in her reticule come as a surprise.

She'd hung the dress in the wardrobe last night to let the wrinkles drop out, and the few that remained fell in the folds of the skirt and weren't unsightly. Her hair was brushed to a high sheen and pulled back on the sides and held by combs, with the length secured by a deep brown snood that she knew was a good contrast against her honey-colored hair.

Now she gave the man a blinding smile and asked if Edgar Bryce would be reading today, knowing full well if he were breathing he'd take the lead.

True to Roselyn's guess, the man tripped over himself in his haste to be helpful.

"Mr. Bryce never misses a performance," he said. "Thoughty gent, too. Always tips his hat comin' and goin'. No airs on him."

Then Roselyn asked sweetly, "And Miss Wheeler? Will she read Gertrude or Ophelia?"

The man wore a blank look for a second, then scrunched his nose as if catching a whiff of fresh manure.

"Josie a friend of yours?" he said.

When Roselyn shook her head, he relaxed.

"Well, then, I don't mind tellin' you I ain't sure she's doin' either one. If she shows up, she will. Can't never tell with that one."

Actors were notoriously unreliable, but Roselyn wondered why Mr. Cathal continued to tolerate such absences, and she commented as much.

The gossipy man leaned his head in to her and confided, " 'Cause Mr. Cathal's sweet on Josie, but y'didn't hear that from me."

Roselyn patted his arm as if it were their little secret, although she suspected rumors of the romance probably had run through the company like a wildfire. She thanked the man and soon settled into her seat.

If Wheeler showed herself onstage, there still remained the problem of picking her out from the other actors. Roselyn hadn't gotten that good a look at her back in the Platteville stables beyond dark hair, medium height, and younger than her mama.

The theater was small, with tiny balcony boxes left and right that sat empty. Half the seats down center were empty as well. Roselyn suspected most people in mining country preferred seeing theatrical pieces that featured lively music with dancers or singers.

Madsen would, Roselyn thought.

Thinking of him tightened the ball of misery in the pit of her stomach. Roselyn had never been interested in a man before, not seriously.

She'd made up her mind long ago about what she wanted, and Madsen Bold had none of the characteristics she required. In the wee hours of the morning, she'd decided it was better to forget about him. He wasn't sedate or settled or even romantic.

Instead, he was tough and practical, all hard muscle and hard will. Sure, he was decent, courteous in his own way, and with an affectionate side that tugged at her heart and refused to let go, but he was also stubborn, pure and simple.

His integrity wouldn't give an inch, and that could get Mama killed. So it was up to Roselyn to quit mooning over a man she couldn't have and outsmart him.

By the time poor Ophelia died off, so had most of the audience. One heckler offered to put a few of the cast members out of their misery as well, but he was soon persuaded to be quiet by a burly stagehand.

Roselyn was left among a handful of people who stuck it out to watch the entire sorry reading.

She was no judge—she'd seen only a couple of productions in her life put on by traveling companies—but from what she saw, *Hamlet* wasn't the only tragedy here. It needed more than Edgar Bryce's voice and talent to save it. No wonder Mr. Cathal had a problem paying his hotel bill.

If Josephine Wheeler had been on the stage, Roselyn couldn't swear to it. The cast had donned costumes and made up faces to lend drama to the reading, and it was easy to hide in plain sight. Roselyn couldn't place the woman.

She rose to leave, shrugging into her coat and hoping Madsen or Sully and Dill had better luck. Then an idea occurred to her.

Wouldn't it be rude not to go backstage and thank Mr. Cathal for giving her the ticket? And if Roselyn could nose around while there, all the better.

It was risky to show herself backstage. Wheeler might recognize her first and know for a fact they were closing in on her. Then again she might not.

It was a risk Roselyn had to take.

Seventeen

From a narrow alleyway with a clear view of the two-story rooming house, Madsen had watched a dapper man in a bowler hat and overcoat go inside.

He emerged a few minutes later with a dark-haired woman on his arm. Although the sun was shining, she was bundled against him to block the cold breeze.

"That's her," Sully whispered.

"Doesn't look like she wasted much time mourning Rawlings," Madsen said, his eyes narrowing. "Now, does it?"

"Don't know who the dandy is. Ain't seen him 'afore."

"I have. Saw him last night in the lobby. Calls himself Cathal."

Witnesses to the robbery had reported that Teddy Lee's accomplice was a blonde, but with the information Madsen now had, he decided she'd worn a wig as a disguise. He watched an older woman wearing an aproned dress and holding a broom follow right on their heels.

"The landlady?" Madsen said.

Sully nodded. She was arguing with the couple, judging by her angry gestures, but they were too far away for Madsen to hear clearly.

Then again, he didn't need to hear them. Landladies seldom argued on a cold front porch with paying tenants.

Madsen got his answer when Cathal and Josephine Wheeler turned deaf ears to the sputtering landlady and headed toward the center of town. She hurled a few more words into the air after them before abruptly retreating back inside, where it was warm.

But seeing them did leave Madsen wondering. Suppose Cathal was partnered with Miss Wheeler in the scheme to double-cross Duke Pearson?

If he was, the shooting back in Platteville must have come as an unexpected bonus to them. It was a slick arrangement, from what Madsen could tell.

As far as Pearson knew, Teddy Lee was the double-crosser. And Teddy Lee, the poor sap, died not knowing he was simply a convenient scapegoat.

Whatever their plan had been, Cathal and Wheeler both had money problems, which told Madsen the diamonds were intact. They hadn't found a buyer yet.

It was merely a matter now of finding where the diamonds were stashed.

Madsen motioned to Dill, with instructions to keep tabs on the actress, while he and Sully checked out her room.

"If'n they head in to the opry house," Dill said, "want me to hightail it back here and stand lookout case she changes her mind?"

"No, stick with her," Madsen said. "We'll only need a few minutes. If she turns back in that time, can you figure a way to stall her?"

As Dill tossed him a wicked grin and turned to go out of the alley, Madsen swung his attention to Sully.

"You know which room is hers?"

"Back side of the house, facin' this way," Sully said, pointing. "I seen the light come on last night, and I seen her pull the curtains to."

"Head to the back door, then," Madsen said, "and act like a hungry man looking for a meal—"

"Won't be much actin' to it."

Madsen gave Sully a shove to help him on his way and said, "Go on, you mangy old coot. Keep the landlady busy and I'll slip in the front door."

Given a smile of singular sweetness and a soft voice, the stagehand readily admitted Roselyn backstage. He even offered to usher her to Mr. Cathal rather than make her wait while he fetched him.

Raised voices filtered into the chilly, dim corridor she traveled and halted abruptly when the stagehand rapped on a hollow door and received a bellowed "What the bloody 'ell do you want!" in reply.

Roselyn shooed his hand off the doorknob,

smiled a dismissal, and opened the door herself, her reticule close to her palm. To her surprise, rather than interrupting Josephine Wheeler arguing with Mr. Cathal, she stared into the livid face of Edgar Bryce.

It didn't take a genius to figure that he and Cathal probably argued over money.

Without the stage makeup, Bryce was a middle-aged man with tiny lines of maturity around his mouth and eyes. His sandy blond hair was streaked with silver, and he was sporting a paunch in the middle.

He was seated at a mirrored dressing table when she entered, wearing an azure quilted bed robe, but good manners propelled him to his feet as she stepped into the dressing room. Cathal was already standing, his back to a dressing screen.

He was clad as neatly as the night before, in a gray suit, but today he simply stared, a blank look on his face and no light of recognition in his cold blue eyes.

"Gentlemen," Roselyn said, deciding it was best to adopt a southern-belle demureness. She'd seen enough of them to pull it off. "Please forgive my intrusion."

Cathal didn't even bother to apologize for the language he must have known she had overheard or to act flustered about it.

Ignoring him for the moment, she glided toward Bryce, who stared at her through compassionate brown eyes that sparkled with a warm and genuine smile. She extended her gloved hand and smiled back.

"How do you do, Mr. Bryce? I'm Roselyn O'Neill, and I wanted you to know how much I enjoyed your performance today."

The high color in Bryce's face receded as he cupped her hand in both of his.

"What a gracious lady you are. That's kind of you to say, missus—"

"It's miss."

"Miss . . . O'Neill, is it?" he added, cocking his head and still sandwiching her hand in his. "You have an accent I haven't heard for many years."

"Texas, sir," she said.

"Texas," he repeated as if testing the word. "I thought so. In my younger years, it was my privilege to visit several towns down there. I still carry many fond memories of the people I met."

He nodded, studying her for a moment. Under his scrutiny, Roselyn felt puzzled more than uncomfortable. Could he see through her act?

Gently extracting her hand, she swung on Cathal then and smiled a noticeable degree cooler.

"And I wanted to thank you for giving me the ticket," she said. "It was very generous of you."

"Not at all." He gave an impatient wave. "It was my pleasure. Think nothing of it. Now, if that is all, will you excuse us?"

He glanced at her and dismissed her in the same brief look. So Madsen had been right; Cathal was no gentleman.

Behind the natty clothes and high manners hid a small ferret of a man. Roselyn tamped down on a spurt of temper, finally grasping what Hugh Cathal had taken her for last night in the hotel lobby.

Now he showed no sign of interest or even that he'd ever seen her before.

To his kind, the woman he bumped into was common enough to leer at and common enough not to merit recalling. In the next second, Roselyn realized his attitude might work to her advantage.

If Cathal didn't recognize her when he'd seen her up close, then chances were good that Wheeler wouldn't recognize her, either.

And the test came sooner than Roselyn expected.

Madsen lurked at the side of the rooming house until he heard the landlady talking to Sully. Then he skirted the house, bounded up the porch stairs, and up to Wheeler's room.

She'd locked the door, but a quick flick with his boot knife to the flimsy latch and he was inside. What he saw spoke volumes about the occupant.

The bed was unmade, the sheets soiled. Dirty clothes landscaped the room. Shirts, dresses, petticoats, and underdrawers were strewn on the bed, puddled on the rug, and tossed over the chair. Several opened bottles and pots cluttered the vanity.

More clothes spilled out of a trunk in the corner that gaped open. Shoes were haphazardly scattered on the floor. The cloying smell of old perfume and stale sex assaulted his nose.

At first glance, it appeared the room had been ransacked, but Madsen had the sneaking suspicion that wherever Wheeler went, her room always looked this way. Women like her seldom put much stock in mundane housekeeping chores. He much preferred Rose's fondness for order and neatness.

The mess did tell him one thing: Wheeler felt safe here. She wasn't planning on hightailing it out of town just yet.

Putting his ear to the door, he listened for signs of anyone coming up the stairs. When he heard nothing, he made quick work of his search.

He unearthed the black dress and veil from under the clothes rubble as well as the men's shirt and britches Wheeler had worn in Platteville. A hatbox beneath the bed held several wigs, a blonde one among them. He checked the mattress, the pillows, under the rug, the floorboards, and even the trunk for a false bottom.

Nothing.

He'd searched every nook and scrap of cloth in the room and found no diamonds. With no time to indulge his frustration, he left the room as quietly as he'd come in.

Madsen was easing down the stairs when he heard floorboards creak around the corner.

Someone was coming.

Without missing a beat, he pivoted on the riser so it appeared he was climbing up the stairs rather than coming down.

"Hey, you there!" came a high-pitched female voice behind him. "Where d'you think you're goin'?"

Madsen turned toward the voice as if he had all the time in the world. He met a pinch-faced woman wielding a broom, the same woman he'd seen earlier arguing with Wheeler on the porch.

"I'm looking for Josephine Wheeler," he said. "She in?"

"No, she ain't. What d'you want with her?"

"She owes me money for a horse."

The landlady relaxed her grip on the broom and snorted.

"Stand in line, mister. Any money Miss Hoity-Toity gets comes to me. She owes me back rent."

Madsen thumbed up his hat brim and cleared the stairs, shaking his head in sympathy for their shared plight.

"If that don't beat all," he said. "Can't trust nobody nowadays. If she can't pay, I'm taking my horse back. Don't let on I was here, will you? I don't want her knowing what I aim to do."

The landlady took in his Confederate-issue hat, patted his shoulder, and walked him to the door.

"The war's over," she said. "I ain't like some people and hold a grudge. Don't got to worry none about me, mister. I ain't seen you."

"Much obliged, ma'am."

Once outside on the porch, Madsen tapped his hat brim and received a long-suffering smile in return. Then he strolled across the slushy street, confident he'd get to Wheeler before she knew he was on to her.

Sully joined him in the alleyway a few minutes later, crumbs in his beard and munching on a chunk of bread.

"How'd we do?" he said.

"Looks like the lady carries them with her," Madsen said. "She may be partnered with that dandy. You up to siding me if it comes to it?"

Hiking his britches, Sully puffed out his chest and said, "I reckon I am, seein' as how I was totin' hardware when you wasn't nothin' but a twinkle in yer pappy's eye."

"Good enough," Madsen said. "Let's go get them."

Eighteen

A woman's voice caught Roselyn's attention. She turned around to the doorway of the dressing room and stared straight at a slender actress in a red wig and a frayed, medieval-style scarlet dress who was about Roselyn's same height, although a few years older than she.

Beneath the painted face, the woman had high cheekbones, a spiteful grin, and haughty eyes. Roselyn had seen those eyes before and remembered them.

So here at last was Josephine Wheeler.

"This another of your tarts?" Wheeler snapped at Hugh Cathal. "At least your taste is improving."

"Excuse me," Roselyn said, and took one step forward. "You mean it *would be* improving if I were his tart. Since I'm neither his nor a tart, it looks to me as if his taste is as bad as it's always been."

Then Roselyn punctuated her opinion with a syrupy smile.

"Josie, please," Cathal said, reaching out a placating hand.

Wheeler shrugged away his fingers and reached

up to yank off the red wig. Dark hair was coiled and pinned flat to her head.

"Must you be dreary, Josephine?" Bryce said, the very soul of civility. "It's bad enough you decided to grace us with your presence once again."

"Don't get used to it, old man," she said, her dark eyes mocking him as she tugged at the tight bodice of her costume. "I've had a bellyful of you and this two-bit outfit, and I don't intend to stick around much longer. I've got bigger things ahead of me."

"How fortunate for us," Bryce said.

"Did you tell him?" Wheeler said to Cathal, smacking the headpiece into his chest.

"Not yet. We were just discussing it when—"

"Lost your nerve again," she said. "Didn't you? You're so spineless."

Then she turned a cat-ate-the-canary grin on Bryce.

"What Hugh doesn't have guts to tell you, old man, is that he's retiring the company."

"Wouldn't it be more accurate," Bryce said, "to say he's run his father's company into the ground and there's no way for it to recover from his poor management?"

Cathal blanched, and his silence was telling.

"Watch who you're talking to," Wheeler said. "Hugh is taking me to New York, where we sail for England. I'm going to be the biggest thing to hit the English stage, and when I am, you and all the other bumpkins can eat dirt."

Bryce fixed his gaze on Roselyn then.

"Please excuse her lack of manners, Miss

O'Neill," he said. "She can't help it. She was raised in a pigsty."

Turning vicious eyes on Cathal, Wheeler said, "Are you going to let him get away with that?"

"You're quite correct," Bryce said, cutting off Cathal before he could reply. "I do apologize—"

Wheeler's face cleared immediately.

"For insulting pigs," Bryce finished.

Before the echo of his voice died, Wheeler launched herself at Bryce, fingernails first. Roselyn scampered off to the side and out of the way, but she noticed that Bryce held his ground.

Dislodged hairpins flew into the air, causing the dark coil of Wheeler's braid to wiggle about her shoulder like a snake. Cathal stepped in, caught Wheeler by the waist, and hauled her backward before her flailing arms could connect.

He'd reacted so fast, Roselyn figured Wheeler had given him a lot of practice with her temper. No one noticed Madsen appear until he spoke.

"Looks like one big happy family to me," he said.

He filled the doorway and commanded their startled attention by shoving back the flaps of his coat and resting his palms on the brace of pistols at his hips.

"You!" Wheeler said, going limp in Cathal's grasp.

"I've been called worse, Miss Wheeler," Madsen said.

Despite what Roselyn had told herself, her pulse sped up. She didn't imagine Madsen could get more handsome, but he'd obviously bathed and shaved since she'd seen him last, and her heart tripped in her chest.

"Afternoon, Rose," he said, his voice like rough velvet across her raw senses.

"Madsen," she returned with a nod. "You clean up good."

"So do you, sugar."

It wasn't profuse flattery, but thrilling nonetheless. Roselyn felt her cheeks grow warm from the heat that leaped into his eyes.

"Any luck?" she said.

"Nope. I figure it's right here."

Roselyn nodded agreement. If Wheeler hadn't stashed the pouch in her room, it was likely she had it with her here at the theater. The prospect of being so close to success should have excited Roselyn, but she felt sadness more than victory.

Bryce swiveled his gaze from one to the other and then stepped forward and introduced himself.

"I seem to be the only one not acquainted with you, sir. How do you do?" Madsen shook the hand Bryce extended. "From your dress and demeanor, Mr. Bold, I take it you're the law and are here on business. Am I right?"

"In a manner of speaking. You don't seem too surprised."

"Actors must deal with all sorts," he said, glancing at his now-former employer. "There are few surprises left in my profession."

Madsen kept his gaze on Wheeler and said, "Would you excuse us, Mr. Bryce? I'd like a word with Miss Wheeler, and it doesn't concern you."

Instead of leaving, Bryce propped his hips on the dressing table and crossed his arms over his chest.

"On the contrary," he said. "If the play's closing, I'm out of a job, and that very much concerns me. I'll stay put if you don't mind."

"Suit yourself. Just keep out of the way."

Once Josephine Wheeler's initial shock wore off, she collected herself, and Roselyn watched her put her costume dress and the haughty mask back firmly in place. By comparison, Cathal had paled noticeably behind her, and his shirt collar seemed to have shrunk on him.

With a contemptuous toss of her hair, Wheeler said, "Nothing you say could interest me."

She made to storm out, but Madsen blocked her path.

"Let me pass," she said, low and deadly.

"Dill? Sully?" he called over his shoulder. "Watch this door. If anyone comes near it, shoot."

"Anyone?" came the reply.

"*Anyone.*"

Then Madsen closed the door behind him and palmed his gun.

"Where are they, Miss Wheeler?"

"I don't know what you're talking about."

"Don't play games. I'm in no mood."

Cathal made a choking sound. Wheeler stared down at the gun and laughed.

Roselyn discounted Cathal as a man who couldn't lick his upper lip. They were obviously in cahoots. But of the two of them, Wheeler was the more dangerous.

"Go ahead, shoot," Wheeler said. "That's what you're going to have to do to get any answers out of me. You can't, can you, big man? You don't have the guts to shoot a woman."

While Roselyn searched Madsen's tight face, she questioned the smugness on Wheeler's. The woman was confident. Too confident.

Why? What made her so recklessly positive the diamonds wouldn't be found?

Where could they hide something of value? Rooms, belongings, and furniture were easily searched. So it would have to be a place where the woman was assured no one would consider looking. . . .

Suddenly, Roselyn knew where.

"Madsen might not shoot a woman," Roselyn said, quietly slipping her gun from her reticule and pointing it at Wheeler. "But I would, and I will."

She cocked back the hammer.

"Now take off your dress," she added, stepping closer.

"What?"

"It's over, Josephine. Don't be shy on our account. You're an actress. You've shared a dressing room before."

"I will not—"

"We can do this the easy way or the hard way. Either take the costume off or choose. An arm? A foot? A leg? What do you think you can do without? I have six bullets, and I can use all six until you do as you're told. It's your choice."

"You wouldn't dare . . ."

Her bravado slipping, Wheeler inched back from Roselyn's advance until Cathal's chest blocked her retreat.

"Bugger it, Josie!" he said, clutching her shoulders. "She is serious. Tell her what she wants to know!"

"Shut up, you fool!" Wheeler said. "She's bluffing."

In the next instant, Roselyn squeezed off a round. The bullet notched a hole in the slipper on Wheeler's foot, a fat hair from blowing her big toe off.

"The woman's crazy!" Wheeler shouted, dancing in place. "Do something about her!"

"She seems to be doing fine by herself," Madsen said, shifting his stance to lean his shoulder against the door. "But I think I'd do as the lady asks if I were you."

His voice was calm, almost amused. He was giving Roselyn his trust, and she could have hugged him for it. As it was, she had to suppress her satisfaction behind a stoic face.

No one else moved.

A knock and a shout sounded from the other side of the door, "Ever'thin' all right in there?"

"Fine, Sully," Roselyn called back.

She pointed the smoking gun again.

"How sure are you that I'm bluffing?" she said to Wheeler.

"Pardon me for interrupting, Miss O'Neill," Bryce said, still perched behind her on the dressing table, "but I am curious."

A quick glance over her shoulder and she saw the confusion on his face.

"It's simple, Mr. Bryce," she said, returning her attention to the two lovebirds. "Miss Wheeler has a cache of stolen diamonds sewn in her under-clothing. We're here to retrieve the diamonds and to see them returned."

"Are you Pinkertons?" he said.

Josephine Wheeler lost her haughtiness then and sagged against Cathal.

"Close," Madsen said, and grinned. "We're Texas Devils."

Cathal's face glistened with sweat. His glance shifted from Madsen to Roselyn and settled back on Madsen; then he raised a beseeching hand to him.

Because Madsen was bigger? Or because he was a man? Roselyn couldn't decide.

"Can't we be reasonable?" he said. "We'll share the diamonds with you. Who will know? Bloody hell, who will care?"

When Madsen opened his mouth to speak, Roselyn beat him to it.

She pointed the gun at Hugh Cathal, cocked the hammer once more, and said, "We will, Mr. Cathal. We'll know."

With the diamonds tucked safely inside his shirt, Madsen watched as the tubby marshal locked Wheeler in one cell.

Even with her dignity in shreds, she'd recovered enough to spit fire.

"I'll get you for this, Bold," she said, whirling around, her fingers clenching the iron bars.

"You know where to find me," Madsen said.

"Watch your back. I have a long memory."

"Funny thing about that advice." Madsen thumbed up his hat brim. "Duke Pearson's probably thinking the same thing about you, and I hear he's not as forgiving as I am. You only cost me time. You cost him a lot more than that."

Letting her chew on her bile for a bit, Madsen heard Wheeler suck in a breath before she dropped her grasp on the bars. Pearson wasn't aware of Wheeler and Cathal's part in the double cross that Madsen knew of, but bad news had a way of traveling fast.

Madsen didn't doubt for a minute that Pearson would find out. And when he did, he'd be serving hell for breakfast.

The marshal shoved Cathal into the other cell and turned the key in the lock. A hollow metallic sound echoed with finality not only on Wheeler's schemes but on Madsen's chance with Rose.

He'd never forget the angry look in her eyes when Cathal wrestled the pouch from Wheeler and handed it over to Madsen; she'd hidden it in a concealed pocket of her petticoat. Rose's hurt had cut deep into Madsen, but he could do nothing to ease her frustration.

Maybe in time she'd see he was right?

He could still hope. Rose didn't trust Madsen to help her mother, and he couldn't demand her trust. Somehow he had to convince her.

He'd left her to explain things with Bryce while Dill and Sully had helped him escort the two love-birds to jail.

In thanks for their help, Madsen had given the old codgers money to treat themselves to a steak supper. Last he saw, they were headed to the near-est saloon.

"Probably a reward due here," the marshal said, pulling on the bars to make sure the door was se-cure. The ring of keys dangled from his other hand. "I'll wire, and if there is, where you want it sent?"

Madsen mulled that over while they walked back into the marshal's office at the front of the build-ing and then said, "See that it goes to Miss Fiona O'Neill, care of Wells Fargo, San Antonio, Texas."

The marshal seated himself in a creaky chair behind a scarred desk and scratched notes on a piece of paper. Madsen sat in an equally squeaky chair opposite him.

For the next half-hour, Madsen made his report to the marshal, outlining the robbery, the death of Teddy Lee Rawlings, and the roles played by Wheeler and Cathal, with a possible connection to Duke Pearson. The crime was out of the mar-shal's jurisdiction, but whoever was sent from down south to retrieve the pair of lovebirds would need the information to pass on.

His duty completed, Madsen's next stop was to send another wire to Leander McNelly, this one briefer than the first.

Job done. Heading home.

Details could wait. No need to crow success or to go into lengthy explanations. Leander knew Madsen well and would rest assured he'd kept his word.

Throughout his life, Madsen had always prided himself on not compromising his integrity. Integrity was the only thing of value a man had left when everything else was stripped away. He'd learned that lesson well from the war.

But those years were distant from him now, and his future yawned before him like one long, bleak winter in the Rockies. Integrity couldn't wrap her arms around him, turn warm and languid and easy in his embrace, or fill him with desire and need and love.

Madsen stepped outside into the frigid twilight and ran a weary hand over his face. Time was running out.

He'd be leaving soon to return the diamonds, and he had yet to come up with a plan to resolve Fiona O'Neill's debt to Pearson. Rose had been painfully right: Leander could protect Fiona, but not forever.

Nineteen

Roselyn sat across the table from Edgar Bryce, enjoying a glass of red wine with her supper and feeling its smooth warmth flow through her muscles and relax her tenseness.

The restaurant was small but busy. No tin plates here. The dishes were real china.

With dark falling outside, she could see herself in the frosty window glass as the lights inside reflected her and the people at the tables behind her. Beyond her reflection, across the street, shops closed up for the night as riders trotted past on their way toward the saloon a few doors down that was just gearing up for the evening.

She missed her mama and wondered how she was faring. Pushing bites of sliced elk roast through the onion gravy on her plate, Roselyn deliberated on her rapidly dwindling choices.

It was her own bad luck that Hugh Cathal had interfered. If not for him, Roselyn would have the diamonds and one less worry.

Instead, Madsen had his paws wrapped around the pouch of diamonds, and while a small part of

Roselyn hoped he would do the right thing and hand the pouch over to her, she knew that was a futile wish.

"I guess I should be shocked by what you've told me," Bryce said, dabbing his mouth with his napkin. "But if the company hadn't folded this way, it would have folded another. Hugh never had his late father's business sense. Throwing in with the likes of Josephine was just one bad decision in a score of bad decisions for Hugh."

"Mr. Bryce—?"

"Edgar," he said, refilling her wineglass. "Since we've shared an adventurous afternoon, I think we can forgo formalities, don't you?"

Then he refilled his own glass and set the bottle down. Roselyn returned his wry grin, finding it easy to be in his company. He was self-possessed and gracious, and she didn't feel the need to be witty or clever or even pretend to be something she wasn't.

He looked dapper in his brown three-piece suit, the silver at his temples lending him a dignified air. The years had worn away Edgar's youthful handsomeness, but they'd left a rock-hard center of strength and sturdiness that appealed to the opposite sex.

Roselyn wondered why some woman hadn't snatched him up long ago and said as much.

"There was someone once," he said.

In the fragile silence that followed, Roselyn realized he had revealed as much as he intended to.

She reached across the table and closed her fingers around his.

"I'm sorry," she said.

"For what?"

"She hurt you, didn't she, this memory?"

"Pity we can't snare the past and bring it back," he said, glancing down at her fingers. "It's hard to know what's in the heart of someone else. We can only know what's in our own."

"So what will you do now, Edgar?" she said.

He sipped his wine and shrugged.

"Retire, perhaps. I haven't decided. I learned years ago to put a little aside for the lean times. God knows, there have been many in my career. What about you?"

"I'll go home," she said.

"To Texas?"

"Right now, yes. Back to Texas."

"What about Mr. Bold?"

"What about him?"

"Nothing, except I got the impression that you and he were . . . ?"

She set her fork down on her plate and lifted her glass.

"We're friends, nothing more," she said, and drank her wine. "Well, maybe not friends— No, that sounds like we're enemies, and we're not." She gave up and finished off the glass. "I don't know what we are."

"I see."

Edgar poured more wine.

"Do you really?"

"No, but I won't pry."

"He's upset with me," she said. "Thinks I tried to bribe him."

"And did you?"

"Maybe . . . but not for the reason he thinks."

"And what reason does he think?"

Polishing off her glass, she held her hand out for another refill, which Edgar obliged. As he poured, the light glowed through the wine, splashing a shimmering rainbow of reds and pinks across the white cotton tablecloth.

Roselyn thought of her mama.

"For the diamonds, of course," Roselyn said.

"So he thought you wanted to steal them?"

She propped her elbow on the table and cupped her chin in her palm.

"Nope, I'm not a thief. Madsen knows I don't give a fig about those diamonds. It's what I mean to do with them that rubs him the wrong way."

Then, seeing the confusion written on Edgar's face, she blurted out the whole sorry story of Fiona and Pearson's threat.

"He'll hurt her," Roselyn said. "And it'll be Madsen's fault, because he's too stubborn to bend an inch."

Edgar reached over, took her hand in his, and gave it a squeeze.

"Is there anything I can do to help?"

Shaking her head, Roselyn downed the rest of her wine.

"I appreciate your offer," she said, lifting the

bottle and finding it empty. "But there's nothing—unless you want to come to Texas with me."

Once said, she brightened with the idea.

"You can meet Mama. You'd like her. She's handsome, you're handsome. I bet the two of you would get on like a house afire."

Edgar laughed and said, "Thank you for the compliment. If Fiona is anything like her daughter, I think I would enjoy meeting the lady."

Roselyn's smile turned wistful.

"Mama sings like an angel," she said. "I can't carry a tune. I guess I take after my pappy. Did I tell you he was an actor? Probably not as good as you, though."

"Would it help if I spoke with Madsen?" Edgar said.

The appearance of the waiter cut Roselyn short, so while Edgar was busy with him, she gazed out the window. Here and there brassy light spilled out of windows and onto the street, mixing with the moonlight that veiled the world in a silvery softness.

She watched people go by on the sidewalk, thinking about Madsen and mulling over what she was going to do. As if she'd conjured him up, she caught sight of Madsen on the boardwalk across the street, heading toward the hotel.

Roselyn stood so quickly, her chair almost tipped.

"Forgive me, Edgar. There's Madsen, and I have to talk to him."

"But you haven't finished—"

"Don't get up," she said, her head a little swimmy. "Thank you for supper. It was delicious."

Wending her way through the crowded restaurant, she hurried to fetch her coat, shrugging into it as she sailed out the front door, not even bothering to button up against the cold blast of outside air.

"Madsen!" she called from the sidewalk, and waved.

On hearing his name, he stopped and angled around. She hiked her skirts to cross the muddy street and tried to dodge the ice patches. With her gaze down, she didn't see the horse and rider who almost knocked into her, not until she heard the man cursing.

"Hey, watch your mouth, buster!" she yelled as he maneuvered his way around her.

Her foot hit a slick spot then, and she lost her balance. Down she went with a yelp and a teeth-jarring bump on her backside. Roselyn sat in the middle of the dirt street, trying to get her bearings, and couldn't remember falling.

Madsen was beside her in an instant.

"Rose! Are you hurt?" he said, helping her to stand.

She wobbled against him.

"There you are," she said, gingerly touching her bottom, and then her eyes flared. "Tell that jackass he should watch where he's going."

Madsen held her at arm's length, searching her face, and his brows knotted in a frown.

"Have you been drinking?"

"Just a little wine with supper—"

"A little? Compared to what? Sugar, you're sloshed."

While Madsen smoothed down her coat and buttoned it, Roselyn patted her hair back in place and looked him straight in the eye. Lordy, he had beautiful eyes, rimmed with thick, dark lashes any woman would envy.

"I'll have you know I have never been *sloshed* in my life."

"I'm no expert, but it appears to me you just fell off the wagon. C'mon, let's get you back to the hotel."

He circled her shoulders with his arm and guided her onto the shadowy sidewalk. She snuggled into the space under his arm and laid her head against him. He felt so right.

And that's what was wrong.

She wrenched out of his embrace and whirled to face him.

"Now what's the matter?" he said.

"You." She jabbed her finger into his shoulder. "You're what's the matter, and you know it."

Madsen didn't pretend to misunderstand. He grabbed her finger, and the rest of her followed until she was plastered against his chest. With a thumb and forefinger, he nudged her chin up.

"Trust me," he said. "I can help you and your mother. I will help."

It was too dark on the boardwalk to read his eyes, but she heard the earnestness in his voice.

He believed what he said, and she wanted to believe, too.

But it was such a risk. Roselyn wished she could see the gaze beneath the hat brim more clearly.

"If you want to help," she said, "give me the diamonds and let me take them to Pearson."

With both hands, he hugged her to him, resting his chin on the crown of her head.

"You know I can't do that, Rose," he said, his voice low and rough.

"I know why you lie, but you don't have to."

"I'm not lying."

She pulled back, shaking her head, and he let her slip from his grasp.

"Listen to yourself, Madsen. It's not that you *can't* do it. It's that you *won't* do it. Can't you ever unbend?"

Convinced of the answer, Roselyn took two weary steps toward the hotel, slowed, and then pivoted.

"When do you leave?" she said.

"Not until tomorrow."

"That soon?"

"No point to linger."

The subtle kiss of the cold night air on her face and neck helped to clear her head. She inhaled a deep breath, fragrant with wood smoke and the aroma of roast beef, and felt the weight of responsibility settle on her shoulders.

"Rose?" he said.

She struggled with herself at first, then surrendered. After tomorrow, she'd never see him again, and she refused to live the rest of her life with regrets.

"I want to wake up with you in the morning," she said. "I want to feel your warm breath on my neck, the stubble on your cheek. . . ."

An indrawn breath hissed between his teeth.

"I'm on a short string, Rose. Do you know what you're saying? Are you sure?"

In his question, she heard his silent need for her assurance that he was wanted, that he was the reason, the only reason.

Nodding, she said, "Whatever happens, it's us tonight. I don't expect anything from you."

A wire was delivered to the hotel that Madsen picked up on his way by the front desk. Leander McNelly was as brief and to the point as his friend Madsen had been.

Will do. The Mosley place.

His message was clear. Leander would find Fiona O'Neill and hide her at a friend's ranch outside Laredo and then keep an eye on Pearson.

"Good news?" Rose said.

And Madsen shared with her what he'd done. She thanked him for his consideration, but the doubt in her eyes told him she didn't believe it would help.

Madsen stuffed the paper into his pocket on the way up the stairs. At her door, she stopped and handed him the key.

He slipped it from her grasp and opened the door, surprised at how his fingers trembled. Inside, the room was dark but for the moonlight filtering through the lace curtains and flowing across the bed like a silver river.

He closed the door in the semidarkness, but she walked over to the window, pushed the curtains aside, and pulled the green roll shade down.

"Light the lamp, please?" she said.

"You want the light on?"

"I want to see you," she said. "All of you."

When the light flared to life, Madsen glanced over and saw that Rose had lain her coat across the chair and had turned the bed back. His passion for her burned as hot and steady as the lamplight that threw shadows on the wall.

He lowered the lamp wick until a gossamer sheen of pale yellow light settled over the bed, like moonlight on a hot summer night.

"That all right?" he said.

"Fine."

When he reached to take off his hat and coat, she nudged his hand aside and said, "Let me."

Her voice glided along every male nerve ending he owned with sultry promise. Then she pulled off his hat, brushed back a curl from his forehead, and kissed him. Her lips were generous, intoxicating.

"You taste sweet," he said, licking his lips. "I can taste the wine you drank."

Cocking her head, she said, "You're not a drinker, are you?"

"No. Never saw much reason to. Never cared for the taste . . . until now."

His coat came off. Another kiss. He unbuckled his guns, and she looped the gun belt over the bedpost. The diamond pouch made a slight bulge on one side of his shirt. He slipped the button and pulled the pouch out, handing it to her.

She looked at the pouch and then at him. He watched her expression but saw nothing except a reflection of his own hunger and desire. Then she buried the pouch inside his discarded coat.

His shirt followed next, and then she pulled his long-john shirt over his head and sprinkled kisses on his bare chest. Her fingers fluttered over his skin, dipping in the mat of dark hair, rubbing, stroking.

When she went down on her knees to unbutton his pants, he rested his hands on her shoulders. Goose pimples rose on his skin from the chill leaching into the room and from the heat building at his core.

"Ticklish?" she said.

"No."

"Let's see . . ."

The teasing sound of delight was rich within her voice. She smiled up at him and kissed his bared belly.

He sucked in a breath. Whatever blood he had in his brain slammed downward.

He couldn't think; he could only watch . . . and feel.

Her pink tongue darted out and followed the

slim path of dark hair that disappeared into his pants. The slick raspy sensation created more tingling than Madsen could stand.

"Like to play games, do you?" he said.

She laughed. It was the first genuine rumble of happiness he'd heard from her, and the sound reached out and enfolded him, wrapping itself around his heart.

He grabbed her shoulders and hauled her up against him, letting her feel the full impact of what she did to him before he captured her mouth with a desperate need that shocked him with its intensity.

"Open for me," he said. "Let me taste you again."

Cupping his face between her hands, she responded to his plea, exploring and caressing, tasting and savoring in return. Madsen twisted and lowered himself to the bed, drawing Rose down on top of him.

"Not yet," she said, nibbling down the warm expanse of his throat.

She slid away from his embrace, an elusive form retreating into the dimness beyond the realm of the lamp. Flat on his back on the bed, he watched her tug off his boots and socks and peel off his pants until he was wearing nothing but a smile and mellow lamplight.

He'd never really cared about a woman's opinion before, had never taken enough time to bother, but what this woman thought mattered to him more than he wanted to admit.

"Do I pass muster?" he said.

The eyes gazing at him glittered with heat and something more. She had her hands on his calves, and her lips followed.

"You're beautiful," she said, her breath a warm, moist murmur against his skin, her lips forging a path up his thighs with tiny nips and kisses. "Hard and soft at the same time."

Slender hands closed around him, measuring him, approving of him, fondling and playing in gentle rhythms. He closed his eyes, unable to hold on to half-formed thoughts, his senses saturated and alive, letting her taste and explore, savoring her unhurried caresses, and dared to imagine a lifetime of such loving attention.

"I like how you taste," she said, her touch penetrating, lingering, and reverberating along each nerve. "Salty sweet, like teardrops."

"I want you," he said, reaching for her.

But she slipped out of his grasp, fading back into the dimness at the side of the bed.

"Not yet," she said again.

Madsen's hands clenched and unclenched fistfuls of the sheets as he watched her in the shadows slowly peel off her jacket, then her skirt, then her petticoat, and toss them onto the nearby chair. He'd never been so aware of his own breathing before.

One by one, the layers fell away like petals of an exotic flower until she stood open and ripe to his gaze, long-limbed and golden in all nature's glory.

He lay on the bed in full bloom.

She freed her hair from the confines of the snood and the combs, shaking it out and sending a shower of uncontrollable blonde waves over her shoulders and down her back. He watched her pad toward him, catlike, stalking, slow and sleek, rounded hips that fit his hands perfectly, her eyes glittering with mischief.

Waiting, anticipating, he was unable to move, unwilling to move, wanting whatever came next. And wanting it now.

The bed dipped with her slight weight. Then she straddled him and pinned his wrists over his head. He stared up into eyes brimming with possibilities, eyes that would haunt his dreams forever.

His throat was tight with emotion, his heart slamming against his ribs. The satiny strands of hair chased her lips across his chest, his shoulders, and the hollow of his cheeks.

Then she swallowed his moan in a soul-stealing kiss.

"Do you know what you're doing to me?" he said, gripping the bars of the headboard with iron fingers.

"Making a memory."

Her thumb grazed his lips, and he opened his mouth to nip the pad with his teeth. With every breath, he inhaled the fragrance of the spicy soap she liked to use and the warm perfume of her body.

"You're doing a lot more than that," he gasped out. "A hell of a lot more."

"Don't you move," she said.

His body was slick, glistening with need, but he obeyed. Then she rubbed herself against him, the supple friction of her breasts brushing against his chest, his cheeks, his mouth, her hair spilling over her face and capturing him within a silky cocoon.

She paused over him, her muscles tense, teasing and torturing the part of him that cried out for her touch the most.

"Tell me, what do you want?" she whispered in his ear.

"You, Rose," he managed to say. "Now!"

And this time she obeyed. She slid onto the hard tip of him like hot oil, and his breathing quickened with the exquisite rocking. Slowly, her soft wetness embraced all of him, devoured him, the current flowing from her to him, and her mouth muffled his cry.

"I love you, Madsen," she said against his mouth. "Always."

Then Rose moved in slow motion, but he couldn't answer her, couldn't speak. The pulsing had already started.

Madsen felt the slices of sunlight streaking through him and struggled for breath, drawing out the moment as a musician holds a single note until the tone becomes so sweet, it shatters into tiny fragments of sound that echo into eternity.

They stayed together for long moments, neither willing to break the bond. Madsen could barely retain a coherent thought. His body was soaked.

His senses were overflowing. And his mind was drained.

Rose rolled to the side, and he went with her, pillowing his head on her breast, listening to her heartbeat mingle with his. She was a woman built for comfort and soft in all the right places.

Everything about her seemed achingly familiar, and he felt as if he belonged there and nowhere else. He entwined her fingers with his, touching her with his heart, and then pulled the covers over them to ward off the chill as their bodies cooled.

Just as he felt sleep well up around him, he thought he heard Rose murmur about the hundred dollars she owed him. He smiled but couldn't manage to open his heavy eyelids.

There had been women in his life before, but none who stayed and none who had cared for him or loved him as his Rose did.

"You're priceless to me," he whispered, pulling her close to him and cradling her softness. "Priceless."

Twenty

Roselyn climbed down off her horse to let it drink in the cold running stream of the Huerfano River and munch some of the blue grama grass that dotted the bank. She tossed her braid over her shoulder and shaded her eyes against the late-afternoon sun.

Off to her right lay the Sangre de Cristo Mountains. The Wet Mountains lay to her left. Texas waited far beyond the valley in front of her.

And a week's ride behind her. . . .

She didn't want to think about what she'd left behind in Denver City, but she couldn't get the image out of her mind. Even now she saw Madsen sleeping peacefully, his hair tousled on the pillow, his face relaxed and softened and adorable. A face she loved.

The memory weighed heavily on her, almost as heavily as the pouch of diamonds hidden in the bodice of her brown traveling dress.

His unwillingness to compromise his word had left her no choice to save her mama. In Roselyn's life, she'd stretched the truth when she had to, had shammed when she had to, but in all she'd ever done, she'd never been a thief.

Now she was. Stealing from Madsen had been the hardest thing for her to do.

A black-tailed jackrabbit scampering by caught her attention, probably scared out of the brush by a mule deer. But when she turned to her horse and saw it standing tense and prick-eared, she had second thoughts.

Someone was nearby.

She was reaching in her pocket for her gun, but she was too slow. A shadow fell across her face.

"I hope you're not thinking to shoot me," came a man's voice from her side.

Surprised by a voice she thought she recognized, Roselyn snapped her gaze around, staring into the sun, at the same time, her hand came up, gun barrel pointed toward the voice. She could see nothing beyond bright white light until she backed up and shaded her eyes.

Then the man came into focus.

"Edgar! Are you following me?"

She relaxed her grip and lowered the gun. Edgar Bryce offered a sheepish grin and walked forward, looking less like an actor and more like a rancher. He'd traded his three-piece suit for faded denims and a blue cotton shirt.

He pushed his wide-brimmed hat to the back of his head and led his horse past her to the stream.

"If the offer still stands to join you on the way to Texas, then, yes, I'm following you."

He spoke easily and casually, but her nerves prickled all the same. The diamonds nestled between her breasts felt like a boulder.

The idea of his coming along seemed fine in Denver City, with the wine flowing and people surrounding her in a crowded restaurant. And with Madsen nearby.

But what did she really know about this man? About his motives?

Next to nothing.

"And if it doesn't?" she said.

He glared over his shoulder, arched a brow, a no-nonsense expression awash his face.

"If it doesn't, then I'm inviting myself along, anyway. A woman traveling alone faces too many dangers."

Some closer than others, she decided.

"I can take care of myself," she said, returning the gun to her pocket but keeping her hand on it. "I've been doing it for a long time."

"I have no doubt of that, but it gives me peace of mind to see for myself firsthand. Madsen might have been here himself, but he's been detained by two gentlemen I think you're acquainted with."

"Dill and Sully," she said.

Had Madsen sent him, then?

"Those are the ones, like two peas in a pod."

"I asked them to hold him for a couple of weeks to give me a head start. Is—is Madsen all right?"

"Was, last I saw him, although I must admit he wasn't in good humor. I assume being held at gunpoint will do that to a man."

Roselyn flinched. If she knew Madsen, he was hopping mad. But it was the only plan she could come up with to stall him while she delivered the diamonds to Pearson.

"He's upset with me now," she said. "He'll get over it and forget all about me."

While the horse quenched its thirst, Edgar turned around, a brace of rabbits dangling from his hand, and shot Roselyn a wry grin.

"He's worried that you're out here by yourself," Edgar said, holding up the rabbits. "But I've brought supper, so now you're stuck with me."

Did he know she had the diamonds? Was that what he was after?

"How did you get those?" she said, pointing to the rabbits.

"Roselyn, you wound me," he said. "I haven't always been a useless actor."

"I never said you were useless."

"You didn't have to," he said, hunkering down and laying the rabbits on a nearby rock to skin. "It's written all over your face."

He whipped out a hunting knife then and glanced up at her, his eyes guarded.

"There's a great deal about me you don't know," he said. "Before we get to Texas, I may surprise you."

And that's what worried her.

So far, he'd given her no reason for fear. If he was after the diamonds, he could have jumped her by now and taken them or shot her and left her body by the trail to rot, with no one the wiser. He could very well be what he seemed, a caring and concerned man.

But then again, maybe not.

She'd keep her guard up and her eye on him.

It was dark, and the night had grown cold by the time the frosty air was fragrant with the aroma of rabbit roasting on a makeshift spit. Roselyn had spread her bedroll on the ground not far from the campfire and sat with her back propped against her saddle. Her gun was close. Edgar had spread his bedroll not far from hers.

She had traveled light; he'd brought a few comforts, including coffee and a pot. Her stomach rumbled at the combined smells of boiling coffee and cooked rabbit.

"A piece for you, dear lady," he said, holding the spit in one hand and ripping off a juicy portion of meat with the other. "Careful, it's hot."

Roselyn thanked him as she juggled the steaming piece of meat in her hands to cool it off.

"And some for me," he said. "Coffee?"

She nodded, amazed at how adept he was at making himself to home in camp. The cry of a coyote lingered on the breeze. Somewhere out there in the dark was Madsen. Was he looking at the same stars?

Once Pearson had the diamonds, there would be no reason for Madsen to bother with her. And now she had taken away any reason for him to even remember her with kindness.

"Do you think it's a terrible thing I'm doing,"

she asked, "making Madsen go back on his word?"

Edgar wiped his greasy fingers on his pants.

"I won't try to second-guess—"

"I do," she said, dropping her gaze. "I wish there could have been some other way."

Madsen's gaze rested on the cards in his hand, but he was seeing sultry brown eyes, an arresting smile, and satiny legs that had him waking in the middle of the night drenched in sweat. Rose had been gone for three long days.

"Y'gonna play," Sully said, "or fold?"

"What? Oh, fold," Madsen said, tossing the cards facedown onto the side table.

"I figger that comes to one million six hunnerd thousand you owe us," Dill said, scratching on a piece of paper. "Sound 'bout right t'you?"

"Sure, whatever you say."

A lamp flared in the hotel room and chased away the deepening twilight. Madsen paid no attention. Instead, he paced to the window and gazed down at the nearly empty street, hoping to see Rose riding up, even though he knew she never would.

She was out there somewhere.

It gave Madsen small comfort to know Bryce was with her. He wasn't worried that the man intended to harm Rose, just the opposite. There was something about him that Madsen immediately liked, a firmness to his chin, the way he looked a man in the eye.

He was an actor, but he'd struck Madsen as an upright and honorable man. So why did Madsen have a nagging in his gut that told him there was more to Bryce's interest than friendship?

Because a man hadn't had the chance to steal didn't mean he was honest. What if Bryce wanted the diamonds?

Not knowing for sure had Madsen worried.

He worried as well that Rose might be riding into a trap. The idea of her facing Pearson on her own went against the grain.

She thought retrieving the diamonds would satisfy Pearson, but there was no guarantee with a man like him. Duke Pearson was a carpetbagger who could easily demand more, leaving Rose and Fiona on the hook, with no way off.

"What the hell is she doing?" he yelled to no one in particular.

So many questions. Not enough answers.

"From where I sit," Dill said, "it 'pears y'ain't got much truck with women."

Without looking back, Madsen tossed over his shoulder, "Keep your advice to yourself, you old maid."

"Got it bad, ain'tcha, sonny?" Sully said quietly. Yes.

The simple truth was that Madsen needed Rose like his next breath and had missed her so much the past three days, the feeling was a constant hollow ache in his chest where his heart used to be. If this was a peek at his life without Rose, he didn't much care to put up with more of it.

Yesterday, Madsen had caught a flash of blonde hair and had almost leaped through the window until the woman turned around and he saw she wasn't Rose. His Rose. She'd always be his. And deep down he needed to believe he was part of her, too.

For pulling this stunt, he would rattle her teeth when he caught up to her. Rose was going to be the death of him yet.

He knew why she'd done it.

Day and night, the echo of her voice lingered in his head. *Can't you ever unbend?*

He'd once thought he didn't know how, but she was teaching him every day. She'd taught him so much already, except the most important lesson.

She never taught him how to say good-bye.

"Did y'hear me?" Sully said from the table behind him. "I said . . . Hey, are y'listenin' to anythin'?"

Madsen angled his head over his shoulder at the two sly codgers who'd kept him prisoner. He'd awakened three days ago—the first time in his life he'd overslept—not to the passion-glazed eyes he'd expected but to a cold gun barrel pointed in his face.

Dill and Sully had turned on him just as he'd expected, but they'd caught him flat-footed, anyway. They had confiscated his guns, his Sharps, and his boot knife and had done a damned fine job of ignoring his threats.

Until now.

His patience with them was wearing thinner

than the gray hairs on their heads. Rose had her head start; now it was Madsen's turn to deal the cards.

"I've listened all I'm going to listen," he said, facing the room and crossing muscled arms over his chest. "I'm giving you a choice. Either you two can ride with me or I'll plant you where you stand."

The decision was made. If Madsen had to unbend to show Rose he loved her, then that was exactly what he intended to do.

Twenty-one

Nights were still chilly, but days turned comfortable as Roselyn and Edgar crossed into Texas, paralleling the Pecos River for a spell. Many settlers had traveled the land before them, leaving trails and roads that led into Camp Stockton.

The fort was abandoned now; it had been since the war ended. During the decade before, the army had protected travelers who made use of the abundant water supply at Comanche Springs.

Like so many before them, Roselyn and Edgar stopped to refill their canteens before moving on. She kept her gun at the ready and pulled up often to check her back trail, as Madsen had taught her to do.

So far she had spotted nothing worth mention.

But outside the old fort, she couldn't shake the feeling of being followed.

The trail ahead of them was empty except for sunshine and silence, scrub brush and scrub oak trees framed against a cloudless sky. No sound carried to her ears other than the breeze whispering through tree branches, and she wondered about that.

"What is it?" Edgar said, reining in beside her. "Maybe nothing."

Feeling uneasy, though, Roselyn wheeled her horse.

She headed him back toward an outcropping of rock that was dotted with scrub oak rather than topping the ridge ahead of them and being caught out in the open. Edgar was right on her heels.

The shot came out of nowhere.

It chipped the rock that was level with Roselyn's shoulder and spit fragments into her face. She ducked her chin into her chest, but not before she felt a sharp sting cut across her cheek.

In the cover of the scrub oak, she scrambled out of the saddle, ducking under tree limbs, and plastered herself behind the rock. Edgar jumped brush and was at her elbow in an instant, his gun drawn.

"You move pretty well for an old actor," Roselyn said.

"Told you I'd surprise you," he said, then stared at her. "You're hit!"

Roselyn swiped the wetness on her jaw, and her fingers came away wet with blood.

"This?" she said. "It's nothing. Rock chip grazed me, is all. You've probably done worse shaving."

While they waited for the next shot to use the muzzle flash to gauge the shooter's position, Edgar whipped off his blue bandanna and passed it to her. She wadded it up and put pressure on her cheek to stanch the cut.

"See anything?" Roselyn said.

"Nothing," Edgar said, peeking over the rim. "I think it's only one man."

In the next breath, bullets peppered the rock, pinning them down. One bullet cut the top of Edgar's hat, sending it flying behind him.

"Make that two men," he said, ducking.

Then he popped his bare head up and returned fire in the lull between shots but hit nothing of substance.

"I figure they think they've got us dead to rights," Roselyn said, passing him her gun and reloading his.

"Haven't they?"

She grinned.

"We're still breathing, aren't we?"

"Who do you think they are? Thieves, maybe?"

Unwilling to speculate, Roselyn shrugged.

The answer came when a man shouted from the trees, "Rosie? Y'hear me?"

She knew that voice and sucked in a breath. If Jackie Trambull was here, that meant Preacher wasn't far away.

"Who's he?" Edgar said.

"Trouble," Roselyn said, sobering. "Big trouble."

Suddenly, the weight of the diamonds felt like a shackle around her neck. Roselyn had no doubt that the pouch was what they were after.

Jackie must have overheard her and Madsen talking when he stood outside the cabin door. It was just like Jackie to bide time while someone else did the work, and then he swooped in for easy pickings. He had plenty of practice jumping claims.

"Yeah, Jackie," she shouted back. "I take it the Indian tracker didn't do the posse much good?"

Jackie barked a cruel laugh then and said, "A bellyful of buckshot's a sure cure for nosy Injuns."

A shiver raced down Roselyn's spine.

"Any particular reason you're spoiling my afternoon ride?" she said with more bravado than she felt.

"Y'know what we want," Jackie shouted back. "A man can learn a heap of things if'n he keep his ears washed. Ain't nowhere to go. C'mon out nice like and hand over them diamonds and we'll just mosey on our way."

Even if Roselyn was inclined to give up the diamonds, which she wasn't—she'd gone through too much to get this far and refused to give up now—she didn't believe Jackie for an instant.

"We're in a pickle, Edgar," she said, turning to him. "And I don't mind telling you . . . those are dodgy men out there. No matter what they say, they plan on leaving us for dead."

She was giving Edgar an out and waited to see if he'd take it. In the weeks the two of them had traveled together, he'd shown himself to be an easy and helpful trail companion.

Whatever his ulterior motive had been for joining her, he had yet to share it with her. And Roselyn had begun to think he had no motive at all beyond gentlemanly kindness.

But ending up dead stretched kindness to the limit.

This wasn't his fight. Roselyn felt confident she could hold them off while Edgar slipped back the way they'd come, circling wide around and to the safety of another trail.

Edgar seemed to consider her words, then squinted up into the sky.

"It's a few hours to dark," he said, and then returned his gaze to Roselyn's face and looked her square in the eyes. "I think we can make the afternoon interesting for them and be done in time for supper."

Madsen hauled up on the reins when he heard the report of a gun in the distance.

He and the two old roosters had kept to the saddle to shorten the lead Rose had on them, but she and Bryce had been pushing hard to the south, and Madsen hadn't overtaken them yet.

"One shot," Sully said, shifting his seat and scratching his chin. "Figure a feller's huntin' up supper?"

"Could be," Madsen said, waiting.

As he sat his horse, his gut warned him that something was wrong. Rose had taken the diamonds and bolted, wanting to get shut of him, and Madsen had been willing to let her think she'd gotten her way.

Now, though, he wasn't sure he'd made the right decision. If anything happened to her . . . He refused to even look that thought in the face.

When he heard the hollow echo of other shots follow in rapid succession, he knew Sully was wrong. The war years came back to Madsen easily then, and he divided his meager force.

He shucked his Sharps from its boot and then ordered Sully to flank the right and Dill to the left, while he would come up the middle.

"When you hear my rifle, shoot," he said. "No telling what ragtag band of thieves Rose has stumbled across."

Texas was filled with thousands of former soldiers, destitute men, men used to killing and living off the land. Some of them were good men trying to reclaim their lives; most were the dregs of the Old South, bitter and unemployed, unable to handle defeat.

The majority of the hardened men with a criminal bent had flooded the South Texas region, for there was no law in South Texas. The region was too difficult for the victorious North to govern. They didn't have the manpower to spread over such an isolated and desolate territory.

But the crowning insult for many former soldiers had been to come home in rags and face well-dressed and wealthy carpetbaggers, like Duke Pearson, who had spent the war years getting rich off the blood staining the land.

Was it any wonder desperate men turned to crime and preyed off any innocent unlucky enough to cross their path?

Nothing in Madsen condoned the actions of such men, but he understood them.

And in her way, Rose understood them, too. She could handle herself and a gun, but she needed more than an out-of-work actor to see her safe to South Texas. Madsen figured she was learning that lesson right now.

He rode up behind them not long after the shooting started and hauled on the reins, staying back far enough not to be spotted by the thieves. Sliding off his horse, he dropped to the ground, the Sharps held in one hand.

The horse stood as if fettered, munching on what short grass it could find. Madsen climbed through the scrub brush and caught the drift of the shouting.

When he pegged the voice as Trambull's, Madsen cursed to himself. Up ahead of him, he saw two horses standing back from the rocky outcropping, reins dragging in the dust.

They caught wind of him and stood ears up, heads lifted. Beyond the horses, Madsen could just make out the forms of Rose and Bryce through the scrub oaks, crouched and returning fire over the rock rim.

Bryce was acquitting himself better than Madsen had imagined. The two of them were holding their own.

Maybe he'd underestimated Bryce's ability? It was obvious he could handle a gun.

"Easy, boys," Madsen crooned to the horses.

Then he bent low to clear hanging branches and squatted down to survey the area. Between him and the cover of the rock lay ten yards of empty dirt.

It was no good place to be. He cursed again. He'd be an open target for Trambull and Preacher, but there was no other choice except to sprint for it.

Palming his gun, he emptied the cylinder over the rock rim as he ran, dodging bullets that fanned his ear or thudded at his feet and spat dirt into the air. Rose and Bryce whirled as one, guns pointed at Madsen's gut.

"Hold up there!" Madsen shouted, barreling ahead.

And they both checked up at the last second.

He heard Rose's quick intake of breath as he landed hard on his shoulder against the jagged rock, sending a fine cloud of chalky dust into their faces.

"Glad you could make it," Bryce said, turning back to give Trambull more grief.

"What are you doing here?" Rose snapped.

"Disappointed, sugar?"

His words came out harsher than he intended. He'd spent too much time dreaming of her, longing for her, scared for her. She'd seeped into his blood, and he ached now to pull her close and hold her and never let go.

But there wasn't time, and this wasn't the place.

Instead, Madsen peeked over the rim to see if he could spot either Trambull or Preacher. A ridge lay ahead, dotted with rock and brush. They were well concealed.

"I'm surprised," she said. "Where are Dill and Sully?"

He glanced over his shoulder at her. She was trail-weary and smudged with dirt, but she never looked more beautiful than when she smiled at him . . . except maybe when she was glaring at him, as she was doing now.

"They should be cutting Trambull off on both sides," he said.

"I almost blew a hole in your gizzard!" she said, and turned to face him fully.

"Lucky for me you didn't."

That's when Madsen saw the blood smeared on the side of her face. He cradled the Sharps and frowned back.

"Who did that?" he said, cupping her chin.

Her eyes were clear liquid, glittering with anger, fear, and defiance, all at the same time. She thought he'd wrestle the diamonds from her now. He could read it in her gaze, in her stiffness, in the muscles that were tense and ready to fight back.

"Cut myself shaving," she said.

Madsen grunted, wanting nothing more than to haul her close, rattle her teeth, and then kiss her mindless.

"What would you say if I asked for the diamonds back?" he said.

"Go to hell."

"Too late." He dropped his hand. "I've been there."

Then chiding himself for a fool, he jutted his chin, hoping Fiona O'Neill was worth it.

"Your horses are back there in the brush," he said. "We'll keep Trambull busy while you two make a run for it."

"But what about you?"

"Do what I tell you, sugar." Then Madsen turned to Bryce. "Run for the horses. I'll cover you. Get her to the Mosley place. It's outside Laredo. We'll join you there when we can."

Bryce nodded, clapped him on the shoulder, and grabbed Rose's arm to get her moving.

"Go!" Madsen said.

Instead, Rose surprised him by pulling his head to her and kissing him hard.

"Take care of yourself," she whispered, and then she was gone.

As the echo of her words lingered, Madsen raised the Sharps and sighted down the long barrel.

When the next muzzle flash came from the ridge, he pulled the trigger. The Sharps kicked, and an instant later Dill and Sully opened from behind rocks to the sides of the ridge and trimmed the scrub trees with bullets.

They exchanged a few more volleys before quiet settled. The sun slipped lower in the sky.

"Had enough yet?" Madsen yelled.

"Hell, we can dance all night," Trambull yelled back.

Then he punctuated his answer with a bullet. Madsen aimed the Sharps at the muzzle flash and squeezed off another shot. A string of cursing erupted from the ridge.

"Get him!"

"You get him, dammit," came the reply. "He got me."

Dill and Sully opened again, but this time the ridge was silent.

After a few moments, Madsen shouted, "Hold your fire!"

In the dead quiet, the only sound was that of horses' hooves fading in the distance. Madsen quickly cleared the rock and shouted for Dill and Sully.

"Anything?" he said, but he knew what they would find.

"I got blood," Sully shouted back.

"Whose?"

"Mine!"

Madsen followed the sound of Sully's voice and found him sprawled in the dirt, his back slumped against a rock. His legs were spread-eagled as if they had given way under him. The left side of his shirt was soaked in blood, and his left arm dangled, useless.

"Don't try to move," Madsen said, propping the Sharps against the rock and kneeling down to check his wound. "That looks pretty bad."

"One of 'em's hit," Sully said, wincing. "Sorry, sonny. Look's like they done got clean away."

"Nothing to be sorry for," Madsen said. "Rose is safe for a while. That lying son of a bitch Trambull will want to lick his wounds for a few days."

Madsen peeled Sully's shirt away and revealed gray chest hair matted with blood. He used his bandanna to stanch the flow.

Dill came up then and knelt next to his brother. He'd obviously done this before.

"Ain't no help for it," he said. "That bullet's gotta come out."

Sully nodded.

"I done been shot three times and knifed twice and lived through 'em all. I reckon I'll make it this time, too."

They field-dressed the wound and then made camp farther up the trail, behind a small grove of post oak, near a creek. After Dill dug out the bullet and slapped a red-hot knife on the wound to close it up, there was nothing to do but wait and hope infection didn't set in.

Madsen walked beyond the smell of charred flesh and out past the realm of the campfire. He stared off in the direction of the lengthening shadows.

Sully would slow them down, but Madsen couldn't run off and leave the old rooster. He had to trust that Bryce would look after Rose for now.

But Madsen didn't fool himself. Trambull and Preacher would try again. They had too much respect for profit not to.

Next time, they'd strike when they were certain Rose was easy pickings instead of in the company of a small army. And when they did, Madsen would be her ace in the hole.

Twenty-two

South Texas enjoyed two seasons—hot and cold.

Roselyn was reminded of that as she and Edgar approached northwest of Laredo and the sun climbed toward midday. It wasn't spring yet, but the days were heating up.

She had pushed to meet Pearson's ninety-day deadline and would just barely squeak through in time. They had lost close to a week when Edgar's horse had stepped into an armadillo hole and snapped its leg.

Edgar had wrenched his knee in the fall, nothing broken, but his injury was painful. The two of them had ridden double on Roselyn's horse, slowing their pace to spare both the animal and Edgar, until they came across a rancher willing to sell them another horse.

Now Roselyn lifted the braid off her sticky neck, then mopped her face with a damp hankie. Overhead, a black hawk soared high in the cloudless sky.

Sweat collected under the diamond pouch and trickled down her chest, but she could do nothing about it except endure the grimy feeling.

The diamonds were a constant reminder of Madsen. Roselyn had resolutely tried to push all thoughts of him from her mind, but he was an unseen presence that was always with her, a silent witness to every nuance of her life. Not knowing what happened to him back near Stockton was the worst.

She alternated between worrying that Jackie and Preacher had gotten him and dreading that Madsen would show up to claim the diamonds before she could deliver them to Pearson.

Nothing had changed between them. If Madsen were in one piece, Roselyn had no doubt he'd keep his word to his friend.

She knew that about him, had seen his bald-faced stubbornness from the beginning and understood it. But understanding didn't make her aching heart feel one bit better.

If he cared for her, he'd forget what he'd told his friend and stand with her. That is, *if* he cared. . . .

The sorry truth was he didn't. She'd wasted a thousand kisses, and now she wasted time wishing for something she'd never have.

"I'm wilting, Edgar," she said. "How about you?"

When Edgar removed his hat and swiped his sleeve across his forehead, the bright sunlight lit his dampened hair like pale fire. His face was flushed, but he smiled.

"Welcome to Texas," he said.

It hadn't escaped Roselyn's notice that the closer they rode to Laredo, the more edgy Edgar seemed to get.

"You all right?" she said.

"Fine," he returned, rubbing his knee, but she wasn't convinced. "Just not as young as I used to be."

She let it rest. Something besides his knee was eating at him, and she figured he'd tell her when he was ready.

Not once had he mentioned the diamonds, and Roselyn couldn't help but wonder why.

They passed Fort McIntosh, which was built near an old Indian crossing on the steep banks of the Rio Grande. Roselyn saw some of the townspeople in small canoes fording the river back and forth into Mexico.

Laredo was a sleepy, traditional Spanish plaza town, with wide, dusty streets fronted by stone buildings made from the sandstone and lime taken from the rich riverbanks. Central to the town was a rectangular plaza that was used to corral cattle for branding at roundup time and used at other times for public gatherings.

"What's the name of the place again?" Edgar said as they rounded the plaza.

"The Mosley place."

"Shall we try the sheriff's office for directions?"

"No. There's no telling who Pearson has in his pocket. He'll find out soon enough that I'm back. News travels fast. Right now, I have a better idea."

Roselyn nudged her horse toward the mouth-watering aroma of fried river perch coming from a nearby saloon. Two old men shooting the breeze sat in rockers out front and gave them directions.

"Old-timers are as good as a town crier," Roselyn said as they headed out of town. "Not much happens that they don't know about."

The Mosley place sat about ten miles east of town, past jacales made of thatch from cane harvested in the river valley. The huts were sprinkled among thorny brush where spring flowers were just beginning to bloom over the rolling land—blue violet skullcaps, the orange and yellows of Indian paintbrush, and vibrant bluebonnets.

Roselyn was busy dodging armadillo holes that mined the trail when Edgar gestured toward a low-roofed ranch house that was nestled in a clearing of cottonwoods. She shaded her eyes and studied the house and outlying buildings.

The house was small, with a covered porch that wrapped three sides. Off to the right sat a barn with a corral that had four horses loose in it.

Roselyn glimpsed wash hanging on a line to dry at the back corner of the house. If anyone was home, it was hard to tell.

"That must be it," he said. "Are you sure this is where your mother is?"

"As sure as I can be. Madsen got the wire over a month ago. What'll we do if she's not there?"

"Let's find out first before we worry, shall we?"

Edgar drew a deep breath then, and Roselyn thought he meant to say something else. But he seemed to think better of it. He just glanced at her and offered an uncertain smile.

"Don't worry about meeting my mama," Roselyn said. "You look fine."

The yard was empty except for sunshine and sparrows and a few chickens scratching around. A dusty red rooster appeared from a pen round the corner and puffed his chest out at the intruders.

Roselyn never imagined her mama in such homey surroundings.

She nudged her horse toward the hitching post just as a white-haired Mexican stepped out from behind a clump of cottonwoods. He aimed a scattergun right at their gullets.

Twenty yards from the door, both Roselyn and Edgar checked up, sitting easy, keeping their hands in plain sight.

The old man fired off something in rapid Spanish. She couldn't tell if he'd issued an order or asked a question.

"Think he wants an answer?" Roselyn said.

"Appears that way."

"You speak Spanish?"

"No."

"Me, neither."

"Any suggestions?"

Out of the corner of her eye, Roselyn glanced at Edgar and said, "Duck?"

"I would if I thought it'd help."

Then Edgar slowly raised his hand.

"*Señora* O'Neill," he said, and pointed to Roselyn. "*Niña.*"

The old man bleated again, but Roselyn wasn't paying him any attention this time.

A strawberry blonde woman in a blue checkered cotton dress had opened the front door and

stepped onto the porch. Her collar was unbuttoned. Her sleeves were rolled to her elbow. She
wiped her hands on her apron and then swiped
hair off her face that was straggling loose from its
pins.

Even from a distance Roselyn recognized her.

"Mama!" she shouted, and waved.

Fiona frantically waved back and left the porch
at a run. Roselyn jumped off her horse and ran
to meet her.

They hugged long and hard in the middle of
the yard, laughing and crying, each checking that
the other one was well and whole.

"Oh, my Rose, I'm glad you're back," Fiona said
with a watery laugh, squeezing another hug and
kissing her cheek. "I've been so frightened for
you."

"I'm fine, Mama, don't cry. Let me look at you."

Holding Fiona's hands, Roselyn stepped back at
arm's length. It had been only a couple of months,
yet Fiona seemed to have aged more.

New gray hairs nestled at her temples, and new
lines had sprouted around her mouth. Dark shadows ringed her soft eyes.

Roselyn turned toward Edgar, who had walked
their horses up to let the two woman have a private
reunion. The old man with the scattergun was nowhere to be seen.

Edgar had taken his hat off, and it now dangled
from one hand.

"Mama, come meet a friend of mine—"

But Roselyn never got the words out.

"Hello, Edgar," Fiona said in barely a whisper.

She dropped Roselyn's hand and glued her gaze to the man in front of her.

"Fiona," he returned with a nod. "It's been a long time. You're looking well."

No one moved. Eyes wide, Roselyn was too confused to do anything but stare.

Then, on a strangled cry, Fiona took two steps into Edgar's arms. He bent his head, and Fiona rose up to meet him.

They kissed for a long time, slowly and thoroughly.

Roselyn shifted her feet, feeling like the third wheel on a two-wheel carriage, and just waited, thinking they'd come up for air.

"Would you two like to get a hotel room?" she finally said to their bent heads.

Breathing heavily, Fiona pulled back, her eyes glazed with wonder, her face streaked with tears. She stared first at Edgar and then at Roselyn.

"I-I don't know what to—" she began, then broke off, sobbed, and ran back into the house.

The sorry truth hit Roselyn as she stared at the closed door. In a jumble of pent-up emotions, she turned a stony glare on Edgar.

"You've got some explaining to do," she said.

Without a backward glance, Roselyn grabbed her horse's reins and led it into the barn. Edgar limped behind her.

Sully was a tough old bird and managed to keep to his saddle until the trio straggled into Uvalde.

Madsen had wanted to fix up a travois along the way, but Sully would have none of it.

He was a proud man and refused to give any concession to his age. Madsen couldn't fault him for his orneriness.

The shoulder wound had festered, and Sully was in bad shape when Madsen deposited him and Dill at the doctor's. But he didn't let on when he took his leave of the brothers.

"I'll be back inside a week," Madsen said to Sully. "Stay out of the saloons until then."

Sick as he was, Sully screwed up his face and managed in a hoarse whisper, "Ain't y'ever heard that too little temptation can lead to virtue?"

Madsen pointed his finger.

"Just one drink, then, you old coot. One."

From what Madsen had witnessed during the war, he wasn't all that sure he'd see Sully again. He hoped he was wrong. Dill was going to be lost without him.

Before Madsen rode out of Uvalde, he saw to one more chore: He sent two messages.

The first went to Duke Pearson. For diamonds, Pearson would leave the comforts of San Antonio. Madsen was betting on it.

The second message went to Leander McNelly. Madsen's plan was simple. Once Pearson had the diamonds and Fiona's debt was cleared, Madsen would give up Pearson to his friend Leander and the Pinkerton agents employed by Wells Fargo.

The less Rose knew about the latter, though, the better. If questioned, she couldn't admit to what she didn't know. There was no guarantee Pearson wouldn't wiggle his way out, and Madsen didn't intend to give him an excuse to bother Rose or her mother again.

Now, as Madsen approached Aaron Mosley's place, he wasn't looking forward to breaking the news about Sully to Rose. He had been anxious to get to her but contented himself with knowing she was safe.

They hadn't crossed any sign of Trambull or Preacher, which was no surprise. Madsen didn't fool himself that they had given up, though. Their kind was the reason why he had joined his friend Leander in fighting to get the rangers restored.

Leander McNelly had been a war hero at seventeen—the most decorated enlisted man in the Confederate army—and had finished the war a respected cavalry captain. If anyone could bring justice to the chaos and anarchy in South Texas, it would be McNelly.

For right now, Leander had done well in choosing where to hide Fiona. Madsen figured they had some time yet before those rough hombres discovered where Rose was.

The house was out of the way and not visited often. Of a wife and three grown sons, the house was all Aaron had left after the war.

A caretaker looked after things now. Aaron never stepped foot there anymore, preferring to spend his time in Uvalde with his late wife's people, but he couldn't bring himself to let the house go.

The caretaker recognized Madsen and cradled

his scattergun to wave him in. In a few moments, Madsen would see Rose again, and he wondered how she'd greet him.

More eager than he thought possible, Madsen reined in, dismounted, and walked his horse toward the barn.

It was cool inside the spacious barn, and it took a moment for Roselyn's eyes to adjust to the dim light. Once she had her horse inside a stall that was carpeted with fresh hay, she ripped her saddlebags off and slammed them over the stall rails.

"Who are you?" she said, whipping around. "And don't lie to me. I don't want to hear any more lies out of you."

"I never lied to you, Roselyn," Edgar said. "I told you from the beginning that I might surprise you."

Yes, he had told her, she had to give him that.

"This is some surprise," she said, losing a bit of her anger.

"I wasn't sure myself until just now."

"You let me believe you were after the diamonds, and all this time—"

"Is that what you thought?"

On a grunt, Edgar hefted his saddle onto the rail and leaned on it.

"I came with you," he said, "because I wasn't going to let my daughter travel alone. I never cared about the diamonds. I'm sorry."

"It's too late for sorry, Edgar. Years too late."

Her saddle and saddle blanket hit the rail next.

"I suspected, Roselyn, when I met you at the theater, but I wasn't certain. I couldn't find the words to tell you."

"You didn't try hard enough."

"Would you believe I love Fiona?"

"Love? Yes, once," Roselyn said, throwing her hands wide. "And I'm proof of that moment of pleasure. Edgar, you turned your back on both of us with your cry of release."

"It wasn't like that. I wanted to marry your mother."

Roselyn wavered from the sincerity she gleaned in his face. She'd never had a father, and it was a hard thing to accept that she was staring at him now.

She took a deep breath, her voice dropping to a deceptive calm.

"That's a pretty lie when Mama isn't here to say different."

"Ask her yourself, then," Edgar said. "Talk with her. Listen to what she has to say."

Expelling a frustrated breath, Roselyn studied the blond man with an assessing gaze.

"If there's anything of you in me," she said, "it's surely this talent for making a muddle of my life."

Edgar refused to rise to the bait or even nibble at it.

Instead, he laid a gentle hand on Roselyn's shoulder. The gesture was her undoing. His lips curved at the corners, and pride sparkled in his brown eyes.

Her well of anger drained and filled with softness. She found it tough to stay angry with Edgar when they had been through so much together in the past few weeks.

"While it isn't my most admirable trait," Edgar said, "it's good you possess something of me."

Then he sobered, ran his other hand over his bristly jaw, and scratched his chin.

"The three of us . . ." he said, and cleared his throat before starting again. "We have so many things to discuss, Roselyn. I want you to know I'd like to stay, that is, if you'll both have me."

He hesitated, his uncertainty about his reception evident in his questioning gaze. Roselyn amazed herself by nodding her head in agreement.

"Go in the house and talk with Mama now," she said. "I think you two need to straighten things out first."

Edgar blinked away the moisture that welled in his eyes, and Roselyn watched him swallow with difficulty.

"Go on," she said, patting his hand. "I'll finish up out here."

He mutely nodded his head and gripped the shoulder beneath his hand with a soft, affirming squeeze.

They'd lost so many years. She'd once told Madsen she wanted to start over, and she'd meant it.

Now seemed as good a time as any.

Twenty-three

Madsen was dust-caked and saddle-weary and waiting outside the barn when Bryce limped into the doorway.

A warm breeze lifted the sweat-soaked hair off Madsen's neck and swirled dust around the nearby corral. The conversation he'd just overheard was none of his business.

If Bryce asked, Madsen would answer.

But he didn't ask.

Instead, Bryce hesitated a moment, took a deep breath, and then lifted eyes to Madsen that were banked with joy and purpose.

"Glad to see you made it," Bryce said.

"Looks like you almost didn't," Madsen said, gesturing to the leg Bryce favored.

"Horse threw me. The leg's a sore nuisance, but not worth mention." Bryce hooked a thumb over his shoulder. "She's inside."

"I know. She all right?"

"Obstinate like her mother, but I'd have her no other way. See for yourself."

Madsen grinned, said, "Much obliged," and

then watched as Bryce headed toward the house to confront his future.

Inside the barn, Roselyn was currying her horse, her strokes slow, thoughtful, with a sensuous sweep that recalled how those same hands had teased and inflicted sweet torment on Madsen's bare skin. He felt himself strain against his britches.

She glanced over her shoulder when he walked his horse in, and her hand halted in mid-sweep.

"Madsen! Is it really you?"

"What gave me away? Was it the hat? Or the horse?"

"The scruffy beard," she said, turning around. "It makes you rugged looking. Hard. Dangerous."

Then she threw the brush at him, but he caught it easily and tossed it at his feet.

"You sure took your sweet time getting here," she snapped, rounding the stall. "How was I supposed to know your bullet-riddled carcass wasn't rotting in a ditch somewhere?"

Before she could get up a full head of steam, Madsen grabbed her around the waist and hauled her up against his heart, letting every soft curve mold to his hardness. He felt the tension in her body, watched the emotions swirling in her eyes.

Madsen tried to fathom what she saw in him and failed.

"That mean you missed me?" he said, and raised her chin up to his mouth.

"Yes, you big galoot," she whispered. "But why I bother, I don't know."

"Sure you do," he murmured.

When his lips touched hers, the quick peck he'd intended to silence her was forgotten. Instead, once he tasted her, the smoldering ignited into flame, and he kissed her hard and long and deep.

And she kissed him back with an eagerness and burning that matched his own.

"That's one reason," Rose said against his mouth. "I need a bath." She sniffed. "And so do you."

"Is that an invitation?"

Madsen thrust his hips against hers and grinned when her eyes widened.

Rose smacked his shoulder and said, "Behave yourself. Mama's in the house, and I won't have her catching us—"

"Bryce will keep her busy," Madsen said, and knew it was the wrong choice of words when Rose pushed out of his arms.

"She's not like that. Did you . . . Did you hear Edgar?"

"Afraid so." Madsen nodded, and turned to take care of his horse. "I didn't want to intrude, so I waited outside."

"He's going to take some getting used to."

"You don't have to talk about it now, sugar. That's between you, your mother, and him."

From the corner of his eye, he saw Rose snatch up the brush from the ground and pick absently at the bristles.

"I never thanked you for what you did for Mama," Rose said. "But I want you to know I'm grateful for your help."

"You're welcome," Madsen said, hefting his saddle and wanting more from Rose than gratitude. "We need to talk about those diamonds—"

"What's there to say? I know you intend to keep your word to your friend."

"Yes, Rose, I do, but—"

"Are you very angry with me for what I've done?"

"I passed angry a few weeks ago." There was no point in dancing around bad news. "Sully took a bullet outside Stockton. He's at the doc's in Uvalde."

Rose gasped, and her hand flew to her mouth. "Will he be all right?"

"I honestly don't know, sugar. But Dill's with him. He's not alone."

"I didn't mean for this to happen," Rose said, shaking her head. "The diamonds are safe, but let's not talk about them now. My head is spinning. Can it wait until after supper?"

"But we will have to talk about them."

Rose blew a heavy breath, nodded, and said, "You haven't seen Mama yet. Come meet her."

Taking off his hat, Madsen swiped his sleeve across his gritty forehead. He was more than a mite whiffy.

"I don't much care for meeting your mother when I look like a saddle bum. Let me get cleaned up first. There's a creek nearby. I won't be long."

The caretaker ambled in about then, so Rose grabbed her saddlebags on the way out of the barn. Madsen watched her go. He wasn't a man comfortable with talking about soft things.

Maybe once he'd helped Rose deliver the diamonds to Pearson, that would convince her of what was in Madsen's heart without his having to get tongue-tied over it.

Fiona was standing at the open door to the side porch, the savory aroma of chili and beans cooking drifted out from the kitchen. Roselyn followed her mama's gaze and saw Edgar heading down the winter-brown field.

"Isn't he wonderful?" Fiona said, holding the door wide for Roselyn to pass.

The simple comment told Roselyn that everything Edgar had said was true.

"Where's he going?" Roselyn said, shading her eyes.

"To the creek."

Lowering her arm, Roselyn nodded and passed her saddlebags into Fiona's outstretched hand.

"How's his knee?"

"I gave him some laudanum to take the edge off. It'll be fine with some rest."

"Why didn't you marry him?"

Fiona couldn't meet Roselyn's gaze.

"I was afraid," she said, slipping back inside.

Roselyn heard both the regret and the shame in her mama's voice. Confused, she followed her into the mudroom off the kitchen. A Mexican woman hummed softly to herself in front of the stove, and Roselyn recognized the tune as one of Mama's favorites.

The mudroom was a storage room of sorts, long and narrow, with one small curtained window that overlooked a cluttered worktable. Brooms and a washboard were shoved into one corner below wall shelves that were littered with pans and other household odds and ends.

In the middle of the floor sat a battered tub that was filled with fresh water. The tub reminded Roselyn of the first time she'd seen Madsen.

Her chest tightened. So much had changed since that night.

Fiona shoved the clutter aside and deposited the saddlebags on top of the worktable. When she turned around, she seemed to crumple into herself.

"I've made such a mess of things this time, Rose," she said. "I won't blame you if you hate me."

"I don't hate you, Mama." Roselyn brushed the tears from Fiona's cheeks and nudged up her chin. "I don't always understand you, but I never hate you. We're in this together, you and me, and we'll see it through together. Just like always."

Roselyn tested the water with her fingers and then untied her braid and started unbuttoning her dirty dress.

"Why didn't you marry Edgar?" she repeated.

A regretful sigh escaped Fiona. She helped Roselyn into the water, then sat on the floor, laying her hands on the side of the tub and resting her cheek on them.

"He was already married to the theater," she said. "Oh, he would have stayed with us, tried his hand at this or that, but he would have hated it. I was afraid he would grow to hate us, too, if I asked him to become something he wasn't."

The words struck a chord in Roselyn. She closed her eyes and absorbed the impact of them, feeling the guilt weigh heavy about causing Madsen to go back on his word.

If only there was another way for Roselyn to get her mama out from under Pearson's thumb . . . but there wasn't.

"Edgar's a good man, Mama. Did he tell you he wants to stay?"

Fiona nodded, took the soap from Roselyn to scrub her back, and said, "What do you think? We can't recall the past. What if we've changed too much?"

"You won't know until you try." Roselyn angled her head over her wet shoulder. "And I have a feeling he may surprise you."

Supper was beans, tortillas, and spicy chili cooked by the caretaker's wife. Madsen ate his fill, polishing off the last bite of his tortilla and studying Rose's mother across the table. Fiona O'Neill was definitely *not* what he expected.

She might sing in saloons, but she was neither broken down nor old. Instead, a comely woman, she was a more mature version of Rose—the same size, same trim shape, even had the same prairie-fire hair except for the touch of gray. Sitting next to each other, Rose all scrubbed pink and glowing, her hair braided, and wearing a yellow dress, the two of them looked more like sisters than mother and daughter.

Fiona had a lilt to her laugh, a quiet charm, and a fragile sadness to her surface calm. She was far from the dried up con artist riding a rough trail that he'd pictured her to be. Watching Rose indulge Fiona, fetching for her or jumping up for more tortillas or chili, Madsen could see now why Rose was so devoted to her and possessed an iron determination to protect her.

Bryce sat across from Madsen, barely touching his meal, unable to take his eyes off Fiona. Madsen knew the kind of hunger churning in the older man's gut, because he felt the same thing every time he looked at Rose.

Even now he felt the pull of her sensuality, the warmth of her gaze touch him with mysterious depths. Rose was a mixture of curiosity and inde-pendent spirit, with an attractive serving of nerve.

Everything about her promised to bring into his life something that wasn't there. The intense pos-sessiveness that washed over him was a constant companion.

He pushed his empty plate away and sat back. The clay jug of pulque the caretaker's wife had placed on the table remained untouched.

When Rose stood to clear the table, Madsen

said, "It's time we talked about what we're going to do."

"You've got a plan?" Bryce said, adjusting his bad leg and sitting straighter in his chair.

"This doesn't concern you, Bryce," Madsen said, shoving a cup and the jug of pulque toward him. "Maybe you'd like to step out on the porch for a spell?"

Bryce let the jug sit.

"Whatever concerns them concerns me," he said. "I'll stay. I can help."

Glancing at the two women, Madsen received nods, and then he shrugged.

"Maybe you can at that," he said. "I figure to fork over the diamonds to Pearson and get the hell out."

"Just like that?" Bryce said.

Madsen handed off his dirty plate to Rose and said, "I sent Pearson a message. He'll be in Uvalde in a few days, and I'll be there to meet him. I'm going to make sure he understands that's the end of it. Fiona's debt is settled."

Fiona reached across the table, clasped Madsen's hand, and gave it a squeeze.

"Thank you," she said, her voice soft but strong. "I know I'm a foolish old woman at times. You have risked yourself for me, and I'm beholden to you."

She looked at him through liquid brown eyes, and he glanced away quickly, unable to speak for a moment. He felt his ears heating up.

After clearing his throat, Madsen said, "Don't

thank me, ma'am. Thank your daughter. She's got a stubborn persuasiveness about her."

Rose plopped the dirty dishes down with a clatter.

"I'm going with you," she said. "This is our trouble, and I'll see it through to the end. Besides, I'm worried about Sully. I want to check on him."

Madsen opened his mouth to object, but Rose cut him off.

"Either I go," she added, "or I dog your trail. You choose."

She wasn't giving him much choice. Too many times Madsen had tasted her resolve firsthand and knew she'd do it.

"See what I mean," he said to Fiona. Then, rising from the chair, he added, "We leave after breakfast, Rose. Be ready."

"I won't make you wait."

"See that you don't."

She nodded and collected the dishes to wash.

"What do you want me to do?" Bryce said, rising from the table and limping to the door.

"I want you to stay here," Madsen said, grabbing his hat off the wall peg.

Judging by Bryce's thin mouth, he'd taken insult, but Madsen was being practical. The man wasn't the picture of health, and if they needed to get gone in a hurry, he'd slow them down.

Madsen thanked Fiona for his supper and then headed to the barn to bed down for the night. When he stepped off the porch and was out of earshot of the kitchen, he pivoted to Bryce and softened the blow.

"I need you to keep an eye out for Miz Fiona," he said, "and keep your gun handy. I don't think Pearson will try anything, but if he does . . ."

"Don't worry," Bryce said, standing a little taller now. "I'll be ready for him."

Fiona washed the dishes while Roselyn dried. Edgar was out on the porch, enjoying an evening smoke.

"Has Pearson given you any grief?" Roselyn said.

"He sent one of his gun-toting brutes around every couple of weeks," Fiona said, passing her a wet plate. "A friendly reminder, he called it. But I knew better."

Roselyn whipped her gaze up.

"What if he thinks you skipped town?" she said.

Fiona patted her hand.

"That's the chance I took. It's done now, no sense in worrying about it. I figured your friend Mr. Bold had a plan."

"Mama, don't count on Madsen—"

"Things will work out fine for us, sweetheart," Fiona said, drying her hands on her apron. "You'll see."

The clean plate in Roselyn's hands blurred. She couldn't worry her mama. Fiona was so sure, and Roselyn wasn't sure of anything, least of all of Madsen.

What if he took the diamonds and kept riding? Roselyn would have to face Pearson empty-handed and alone then, and that was a frightening and dangerous prospect.

She wanted to believe Madsen, but how could he deliver the diamonds to Pearson and still keep his word to his friend?

The answer was simple.

He couldn't.

On the one hand, Mama could be hurt. On the other, Madsen would be gone. An empty feeling settled in Roselyn's heart, for she knew, either way, she would lose.

She retreated from the kitchen and into the concealing shadows of the pantry to stack the clean dishes. As the tears fell, she cradled her bruised heart and slumped down against the shelves.

Not until the tears settled into hiccups did she notice she wasn't alone.

"There, there," whispered Fiona, crouching in front of her. She had dampened a hankie with a mixture of water and witch hazel and now dabbed the cloth to Roselyn's eyes and tear-streaked face. "This will take the puffiness away."

Then she lifted Roselyn's chin with a forefinger.

"Do you love Madsen?"

"So much I hurt," Roselyn said.

"I thought so."

Fiona hugged her to her heart and caged Roselyn within the protection of her arms.

"Happiness is never easy, sweetheart," she said, resting her chin against the crown of Roselyn's head. "But don't make my mistake. Don't throw happiness away."

She pulled back and cupped Roselyn's face between her palms.

"When you find someone you love deeply and truly," Fiona said, "grab onto him tight. Grab on and don't let go."

It was advice Fiona had acquired at a painful cost, and Roselyn nodded. The words were easy to understand but hard to do.

Scuffing the wetness away with the heels of her hands, she then told her mama of her worries about Madsen.

Fiona stood and pulled Roselyn up with her. While Roselyn sniffed and blew her nose in the hankie, Fiona shoved the jug of pulque and the bottle of laudanum back onto the shelf and hesitated, thinking for a moment.

"There's only one thing to do," she said, tapping the clay jug with a fingernail. "We'll steal the diamonds back."

Roselyn's eyes widened, and her mouth fell open.

"Steal from Pearson? Mama, don't joke. For a minute I thought you were serious."

"But I am serious. Madsen can't very well keep his word if he doesn't have the diamonds, now, can he?" Fiona arched her eyebrows. "So how else will he have them after they're delivered to Duke Pearson?"

The side door opened. Roselyn glanced over and saw Edgar come inside and cross in labored

steps to the coffeepot on the stove. Her mama had
a point and the only fix that might help.

"Think it will work?" Roselyn whispered.

Fiona's eyes gleamed, and she smoothed Roselyn's hair.

"Won't know, sweetheart, until we try."

"We?"

"Of course." Fiona chucked her under the chin
and started out of the pantry to join Edgar. "I'm
not about to sit here twiddling my thumbs and
worrying myself sick. We're in this together."

Roselyn grabbed Fiona's arm and halted her, a
new strength and resolve taking hold.

"No, Mama. Let me handle this."

"But Rose—"

"Think about it. If you go, Edgar will insist on
going." Roselyn shot a glance at the kitchen.
"He's not a young man, and his leg can't take
much more. If you don't want him to end up crip-
pled or worse, stay here. He needs you, Mama . . .
and you need him. It's time you two took care of
each other."

Fiona tightened her mouth, her eyes open wide
with anxiety and, finally, acceptance.

"Promise me you'll be careful?" she said.

Roselyn nodded, more frightened than she'd
ever been in her life. But she could do this. For
Madsen, she would do it.

Madsen spread his bedroll in an empty stall, set
his guns nearby, and stripped off his shirt. As tired

as he was, sleep eluded him. Instead, he lay with his hands folded behind his head and stared into the darkness at the rafters.

He felt the presence, and for a fleeting moment thought it was Bryce before he heard the soft swish of a cotton dress and the sound of easy steps padding through the barn. His body tightened in anticipation.

"Madsen?" Rose called.

"Over here, sugar," he said, standing.

When she rounded the corner, he pulled her into his arms, pressing her full length against him and kissing her with all the frustrated passion pent up within him. Rose melted into him and held him close, not a particle of air between them, her body as agitated as his.

"I was hoping you would come," he murmured, dragging his palms over her back and shoulders as if to reassure himself that she was real and not a dream.

"We need to talk," Rose said.

"Later." He nibbled the soft fragrant skin at the crook of her neck. "The sounds I want to hear right now from your sweet mouth don't need words."

Rose swallowed a lurid cry and pushed on his bare shoulders, sliding away to arm's length.

"Are you going to return the diamonds to your friend?"

Madsen closed his eyes in a tangle of scattered emotions. He had never felt so desperate to claim a woman and to be loved by her.

"Yes, Rose," he said, opening his eyes again. She was little more than a lighter shadow among the darkness. "I'm the same man you met in Colorado."

He heard her sigh his name as her mouth returned to his.

"Then we don't have anything to talk about," she said, clutching him with a desperation that matched his own.

Holding her flush to his body, he lifted her and moved to his bedroll, laying her down among the scent of hay and wild desires. Madsen tried to take it slow, to savor their stolen time together, but Rose was having none of it.

She wanted no tenderness, no gentle strokes. She wanted him the same way he wanted her—hard and fast.

Her fingers raked and kneaded his back, his chest, his shoulders, encouraging him. Her hot mouth skimmed his, pleading with him.

He slipped his fingers up her silky leg, peeling her dress away with him, and she opened for him in unbridled offering. He smiled when he discovered she wore nothing under her dress.

On a groan of impatience, he tore at the buttons on his pants, freed himself, and settled between her thighs. Her tight body rose to meet him and arched into his strength.

They rode the frenzied storm together, driving deeper and deeper, until they drove over the brink together and then collapsed with delirious sighs and sluggish thoughts. For long moments, he lay with his head pillowed on her chest, listening to her wild heartbeat while her arms cradled him in her softness.

"You better go back," he said, raising his head, "before Bryce comes out to bunk down."

Rose gasped and scrambled to her feet.

"I forgot about him," she said, smoothing her skirts.

The hunger Madsen felt for her was banked but not gone. Never gone.

He cupped her chin and kissed her, tasting her shiver, wanting her again.

"Dream of me," he said.

Madsen watched her cross the yard and meld as smoothly as candle wax from the dark into the light of the opened door. It dawned on him then that he had lied to her.

He wasn't the man Rose had first met in Colorado. Instead, because Rose loved him the way nobody else ever had, he would never be the same again.

Twenty-four

Madsen rode back into Uvalde inside a week, just as he'd promised Sully.

Rose had been unusually quiet during the trip. The impending meeting with Pearson weighed heavily on her mind, so Madsen didn't press her.

Midafternoon sunshine heated up Uvalde's dusty streets, and the town plazas were littered with sleepy old-timers whiling away the day in the shade.

As Madsen and Rose walked their horses around one plaza, they passed one old boy leaning his chair back on two legs. His head was propped against the adobe wall, and his hat was tilted down to block the glare of the sun.

He was a usual sight except that he thumbed up his hat and gave Madsen an imperceptible nod.

The alert eyes gazing out from under the hat belonged to Leander McNelly. That meant the Pinkerton agents were in town as well.

Without looking directly at Leander, Madsen nodded back on the way by. He wanted nothing more than to get this business done and get Rose back home safe.

They reined in at the doctor's office and discovered that Dill had taken Sully to a house on the outskirts of town. An elderly Mexican woman owned the house and occasionally rented out a room.

"By rights, he should be dead," the doctor said, shaking his head. "Reckon he'll make it, though. He's a good healer. I figure a couple of weeks of Miz Alphonso's cooking under his belt and he'll be back to raising Cain as usual."

Madsen and Rose got directions to the woman's house, thanked the doctor, and then took their leave.

"Want to go see Sully first?" Madsen said, stepping off the sidewalk.

"After we meet with Pearson," Rose said, gathering her reins. "Now that I know Sully's going to be all right, I want to get this over with."

She nudged her horse toward the saloon, where Pearson kept an office upstairs. They tied up at the hitch rail and dismounted, and Rose grabbed the jug of pulque she'd tied to her saddle horn.

"That's not for Dill and Sully?" Madsen said.

Rose shook her head and said, "A parting gift."

"What are you doing?"

"You'll see."

"That's what I'm afraid of," Madsen muttered, following her inside.

As they entered the saloon, a half-dozen cutthroats loitering at the bar angled their heads over their shoulders. Madsen took them and the spacious room in at a glance. It was early yet, so the saloon was nearly empty.

Six guns against two—not bad odds. Madsen figured he and Leander could dispatch this bunch while the Pinkerton agents nabbed Pearson red-handed with the stolen diamonds.

Rose sauntered to an empty table close to the bar, looking respectable and out of place in a brown skirt, a white blouse, and with her hair modestly pinned up at the back of her head. A hot glare from Madsen killed the leering smirks tossed her way.

"Afternoon, boys," she called, plunking the jug down on the tabletop and flashing an inviting smile in their direction. "Bring your glasses over. You won't be seeing me again, so the last round's on me and Mama."

When she got no argument from that rangy bunch, she turned to climb the stairs, leaving them to lap up their drinks. Madsen followed behind her, wondering what harebrained notion had wormed into Rose's head this time.

Another hardcase answered their knock and let them inside the office.

On seeing them, Pearson walked out from behind a walnut desk, one other hired gun hovering at his elbow. Madsen had expected to see more men here.

Apparently, Pearson felt confident in his position. Maybe too confident. Good, that would work to Madsen's advantage.

Duke Pearson was a brash, square-jawed Yankee

who dressed like a drummer in a flashy three-piece suit, with a gold watch chain and a diamond stickpin. He was as burly as a fighting bull, and his clothes seemed to strain to contain his belly.

He offered Rose a cursory greeting and sized Madsen up in a glance, taking in the Confederate-issue hat and the brace of pistols.

"Never heard of you," Pearson said.

"No reason you should."

"Are you any good with those?"

"When I need to be. Now if you're done being cordial, let's get down to business."

Pearson's eyes widened, then just as quickly narrowed in a withering glare. The two hired guns took a step forward.

An instant later, they were staring down the bore of Madsen's guns. Both men checked up, neither one having gotten close to slapping leather.

"We can keep it friendly, boys, or not," Madsen said, slowly thumbing back the hammers. "It's your choice."

"Maybe you don't understand," Pearson said. "It's not very healthy for a man to get on my bad side."

Madsen shrugged.

"I didn't suppose it was," he said, and suppressed a smile. "I'll take my chances."

Pearson studied him for a moment, judging him, and then barked an order for his men to back off.

"You're either a smart man or a fool," he said, grinning. "I can always use a man who knows his way around a gun, if you're interested."

"No, thanks."

Then Madsen thumbed down the hammers and holstered his guns. When he did, Pearson sobered and turned his attention to Rose.

"I'm calling in your mother's debt. You have something for me?"

"That's why I'm here," she said.

"What are you waiting for?" He put a meaty palm up and waggled his fingers. "Let's have it."

Without another word, Rose took the pouch from her reticule and dropped it into his outstretched hand. Madsen noted that Pearson's fingers closed around the pouch as greedily as if it were a woman's soft body.

Hefting the dark pouch once, twice, Pearson felt the weight and listened to the soft clatter inside. Then he smiled, turning his expression into an ugly smirk of satisfaction.

"Teddy Rawlings stepped in it up to his neck," Pearson said. "I knew he'd leave footprints. And I knew you'd find a way, Rosie, to follow them."

"We're quits, Duke," she said. "You wanted those. You've got them. Now I want Mama's marker."

Pearson opened his mouth to say something but changed his mind and snorted instead. Having the diamonds in his possession seemed to have restored his good humor, and Madsen figured his presence swayed Pearson into inventing a sense of Christian charity.

"Sure thing, Rosie," Pearson said, walking back

around the desk. "It's always my pleasure to do business with you."

He slipped a small key out of his watch pocket and opened a metal lockbox that sat on the edge of the desk. Once he'd retrieved Fiona's marker, he tossed the pouch inside the box, closed the lid, and pitched the paper across the desktop.

"Your mother knows where to find me when she needs money again." He sat and rested his elbows on the chair arms, steepling his fingers. "Now get out, both of you. I'm a busy man."

"There *won't* be a next time," Rose said, stuffing the paper into her reticule. "Count on it."

To make sure they left as Pearson had ordered, one of the hired guns hovered at the door like a buzzard on a fence post. The saloon below was quiet.

Too quiet to house drinking men.

Madsen gripped Rose's elbow and then angled back to Pearson.

"I'd be disappointed to hear that any of your boys were bothering her or her mother again," he said. "And I'm not a man to take kindly to being disappointed."

On a barked laugh, Pearson said, "You're nervy, mister. I like that. If you change your mind about a job . . ."

"I won't," Madsen said.

He cleared the doorway, only to step into a vicious swing of a gun that caught him from the side. Before he could react, the metal cylinder caved in his hat and crashed against his skull.

Madsen's fingers lost their grip on Rose.

He felt the floor rising to meet him and heard the deafening boom of a scattergun that was fired into the office. The acrid smell of gunpowder saturated his nostrils.

Then there was nothing at all.

Twenty-five

Jackie Trambull reeked of old beer, stale sweat, and cold-blooded opportunity. A menacing smile poked through his matted beard.

"Thought y'could pull one over on us, Rosie?" he said low and deadly, flattening her against the hallway wall.

Madsen lay opposite her, sprawled facedown on the floor. Dead or alive?

He was so still.

But Jackie gave her no time to mourn her loss. She stiffened her spine, refusing to cower. She wasn't beaten yet. Her gun was in the reticule that dangled from her wrist.

"I don't know what you're talking about," she said.

"Sure y'do. Our share of them diamonds."

"I don't have them. Talk to Duke Pearson."

"Now what good'll that do us, gal?" He chuckled. "That old lovebird ain't got 'em anymore."

About then, Preacher appeared out of the office carrying his sawed-off scattergun in one hand, Duke Pearson's metal box tucked under his arm.

He nodded to her, an easy gesture, one all the more threatening for its simplicity.

She never wondered if Pearson and his two men were still alive. The box told her they weren't.

"Looks like you got what you came for," she said. "Let me go."

"C'mon, now," Jackie said, fanning his rancid breath across her cheek. "We're all friends here, ain't we?"

"I don't need friends like you. Either of you."

Preacher's solemn expression never wavered, but Jackie dropped his pretense of a smile. Reaching a hand out, he brushed loose hair away from Roselyn's face. Her skin crawled.

"That's mighty uppity coming from a gal who's done been bested."

She slapped his hand away, hoping to gain the seconds needed to loosen the reticule's drawstring. It wasn't to be.

"Get your paws off me," she snapped.

"Watch it!" Jackie yelped. "That's my sore arm."

"We're wasting time," Preacher said quietly.

It was as much of a warning as he would offer. He shoved the metal box into Jackie's hand and then wrenched Roselyn's arm up behind her back and rammed her toward the stairs.

She stumbled but caught the wooden handrail for balance and felt the sting of a splinter gouging into her palm. Below, she saw that all six of the hardcases who worked for Pearson were either slumped in a chair or facedown on a table.

"You saved us some trouble," Preacher said in her ear.

She heard his smirk, and her heart sank. The laudanum Mama had mixed in the pulque had worked well.

Too well.

Judging by their slack jaws, none of them were stopping anyone anytime soon. Roselyn's gaze flew to the bar. Barkeeps usually kept the peace in their saloons, but this barkeep was nowhere to be seen.

She blinked and blinked again, her mind racing. Mama's plan to steal back the diamonds might have worked.

Then again, it might not have. It mattered little now, but Roselyn wished for one moment more with Madsen to let him know she had tried.

Just inside the saloon door, silhouetted against the bright sunlight, appeared a man in dusty denims, along with two men in frock coats. They stood sizing up the sorry bunch.

"You gents just back out the door there," Jackie called.

Instead of moving, they threw down on Jackie with six-guns, their shots chipping the wooden stairs and ricocheting off the banister.

On a yell, Jackie angled back to Roselyn and aimed his gun barrel at the side of her head.

"Out!" he shouted. "Nice and easy like and the lady won't get hurt."

They never moved.

Roselyn saw no reason for them to risk their lives.

"Please!" she said, inching down the steps. "Do as they say. There are four dead men upstairs already."

She harbored no illusions that Jackie wouldn't kill her. He would, without giving it a second thought. She was safe only as long as she served a purpose for him.

Lurching down each step, Roselyn stared at the trio with a full measure of appeal. They never took their eyes off her or holstered their guns as they backed into the street.

"Keep a'goin'," Jackie shouted at them. "Anybody comes near the door and she's dead."

Jackie cleared the stairs, with Roselyn and Preacher right on his heels. The pain radiated from her arm into her shoulder.

"Check the street," Preacher said.

Jackie ran over to the grimy window, looked out left and right, and then stamped his foot.

"Hellfire! Where's Willie w'them horses?"

"I'm not waitin'," Preacher said. "Give me the box."

Jackie whirled around, knocked a table out of his way, and spat out, "You long-haired, whiskey-drinking liar. You ain't runnin' out on me. I'm keepin' this box."

"Have it your way," Preacher said.

And then he fired both barrels at point-blank range. Jackie's soft gut exploded like an overripe watermelon. The box clanged to the plank floor when his body pitched backward, shattering the window and spraying the sidewalk and the street in a hail of glass shards.

Roselyn was too stunned to shake.

"Pick up the box," Preacher said in her ear, and shucked the spent shells.

She did as she was told.

Roselyn didn't know which hurt worse, Preacher yanking her arm up with a hard warning or the bright sun in her eyes when he drove her through the saloon door.

Even squinting, she saw no horses hitched out in front of the saloon. Two horses stood down the street to their right, beyond where Jackie's sightless body sprawled across the dirty sidewalk like a forgotten rag doll.

She spotted the men in frock coats crouched low across the street. One was behind a nearly full water trough, and the other one was at the rear corner of a buckboard.

Even from this distance, Roselyn could tell they weren't cowering. They were looking for a clear shot.

Otherwise, the street was empty. If the man in denims was there, she didn't see him.

"Let the woman go!" called a voice from the street.

Preacher saw the same sight she did and shoved her to the right, keeping his back to the wall, his gun barrels sticking out past her elbow and pointed toward the street.

"Stay where you are, boys," Preacher called back. "C'mon, Rosie. Move."

"I can't—" she began.

"Step over him," Preacher warned.

Bile rose in her throat from the stench. Every time she stumbled, the reticule clunked against her thigh.

If she could give the men a clear shot . . . and if she couldn't, she was dead, anyway.

She acted on instinct. Without looking at Jackie, Roselyn stepped over him, feigned a trip, and chucked the metal box into the dusty street.

A half-second later, she felt the grip on her arm release at the same time she saw the man in denims step out from around the corner of the saloon with his gun drawn.

From inside the saloon came Madsen's shout.

"Duck, Rose!"

Three shots blasted Preacher with murderous effect.

When the firing stopped, Roselyn was squatting on the sidewalk, hugging the wall below the broken window. Strong arms unceremoniously wrenched her up over the windowsill and pinned her against a solid chest.

"Are you all right, Rose? Talk to me, sweetheart."

Her eyelids flew open, and she stared into Madsen's blood-splattered and concerned face. Despite the quiver in his arms, he held her as if he'd never let her go.

"I'm fine," she said, and kissed him. "But you're a mess."

"Careful," he said, smiling. "My head hurts."

With her arms locked around his neck, he carried her into the saloon and away from the grisly scene outside. She caught sight of the man in denims handing the metal box to one of the men in frock coats.

"Madsen, the diamonds!" she said. "He's taking them."

"They're Pinkerton agents," Madsen said, lowering her until her feet touched the floor. "And the other fellow is my friend Leander."

Roselyn's world fell silent as the impact of his comment hit home.

"Then you kept your word, after all," she said, amazed. "To both of us."

Madsen nodded and kissed her again, his lips warm and gentle and persuasive.

"Why did you follow me to Texas?" Roselyn said.

"Because we make a good team."

His words were achingly tender to her ears. They caressed her battered senses with their sweet promise and entwined her heart.

"But why did you come?" she repeated.

His eyes probed hers with longing and caring and need. Her knees weakened. Tears welled in her eyes. The swarthy features of the man who owned her heart softened into a sensual dark blur.

"You're going to make me say it, aren't you?" he said.

"I'm afraid so."

Madsen cupped her cheeks in his palms and lifted his face to her in quiet appeal.

"I don't know why you love me, but I'm so damned glad you do. I want you to love me forever, because I've loved you, Rose, from the first moment I saw you. If you'll have me, I want to marry you and never be apart from you again."

"I thought you'd never ask," she said, breathless. "Oh, Madsen, you pick the most romantic settings."

"Is that a yes?"

Unaware of anyone or anything except him, and with her heart in her eyes, Roselyn answered his undeniable pull.

"Yes. Forever yes."

If you liked ONE WILD ROSE, turn the page for a taste of Veronica Sattler's breathtaking latest release, COME MIDNIGHT, also available this month from Zebra . . .

Who has time for love when the devil calls the tune? It's certainly the last thing on the mind of Adam Lightfoot, Marquis of Ravenskeep, when he—quite unwittingly, of course—summons forth the devil. To save his young son's life, Adam is willing to do most anything, and striking a reckless bargain with Lucifer—otherwise known as Lord Appleby—takes only a moment of consideration. What Adam *doesn't* bargain on is a young Irish healer named Caitlin O'Brien, her gift of sight—and her powerful determination to untangle the horrific mess he's landed in. And one dark midnight, they will discover that miracles are more commonplace than they imagine . . . as long as love is part of the bargain. . . .

One

"I shall never forgive you for this, m'lord— never!"

Lord Adam Lightfoot, fifth marquis of Ravenskeep, ran a bored gaze over his wife. Not for the first time in their seven-year marriage, he wondered what had possessed him to wed her. He supposed Lucinda had been pretty in a bland sort of way. Once. Now he couldn't get past the sour lines of dissatisfaction about her mouth, the irritating whine in her voice.

"Save your histrionics for the rustic set, m'dear," he drawled. "I fear I find them rather . . . tedious."

Lucinda shrieked, and lunged at him, her fingers curved like talons. Adam didn't doubt she'd have clawed his face if he let her. He caught her wrists an instant before her nails raked his skin.

"My souvenir from the French will suffice, Lucinda. I hardly require others to keep it company." Irritation mingled with disgust as he thrust her from him.

The marchioness eyed the line of newly healed flesh on his face; the work of a French saber, it ran from the top of his high, sculpted cheekbone to the edge of his perfectly chiseled lips. "What?" she sneered. "Afraid Vanessa Marley won't be able to abide you in her bed, m'lord?"

Adam wondered briefly where she'd learned about Vanessa; he'd hardly had time to break his latest mistress in. This only served to inform him Lucinda had already been in town too long to suit him. *Ton* gossip invariably found its way to willing ears. It was why he'd determined to keep his wife neatly tucked away on his country estate when he came up for the Season.

But Lucinda had tried to thwart those plains. She'd followed him up to London without his leave, which was bad enough; that she'd dragged their young son with her was reprehensible. He'd be damned if he'd let her use Andrew as a weapon to achieve her selfish ends!

"Well?" Lucinda carped bitterly. "It's true, isn't it? Vanessa Marley's the reason you're sending me back to Kent. You don't want the inconvenience of a wife complicating your disgusting—"

"Spare me your petty jealousies, Lucinda." Adam pinched the bridge of his nose with thumb and forefinger. Damnation, how he hated these scenes! "It isn't as if my lifestyle's a secret. I made it clear from the start, I'd no intention of giving it up. Or were you too busy congratulating yourself on snaring a rich title to pay attention?"

"You bastard! I did my duty. You had your precious heir—in less than a year's time! Why shouldn't I enjoy the Season in town? Other wives—"

"Your *duty*," he spat. "That's all it ever was to you, wasn't it, Lucinda? Bloody hell! It's a wonder Andrew exists at all, given the ice between your thighs!"

Ignoring her gasp, Adam closed the distance between them. He caught her arm when she raised it to strike him. A tight smile spread across his face, but it didn't reach his eyes. With his free hand, he cupped one of the breasts that filled the muslin bodice of her high-waisted gown. Lightly abrading its center with his thumb, he awaited the reaction he anticipated, and wasn't disappointed: Revulsion filled her face.

Adam made a sound of disgust and released her. The eyes that met hers were hard. Blue-white diamonds in a face that had been called indecently handsome despite the saber scar. "Did it never occur to you, Lucinda," he asked in a voice that held weary resignation, "there might be a reason I seek other beds? Fact is, my less-than-dear wife, a man courts *frostbite* in yours."

"Oh, very good, m'lord—place all the blame on me! Only, I know *better.*"

Lucinda stalked to the door connecting their chambers. Reaching it, she whirled to face him. "Everyone in England knows you for a rake, Adam Lightfoot. It's said you run through women as readily as Brummel changes his linens. Well, let me tell you something, M'lord Rut! You can bury me in the country, but you can't still my tongue. With every mile that takes me from London, I'll curse you with it, d'you hear? You'll rue the day you did this to me—I swear it!"

As she slammed the door behind her, Adam considered what she'd said. It was true, of course. He'd lost count of the mistresses he'd kept since he inherited, at seventeen. Yet he honestly hadn't expected those appetites to extend into his maturity. Tucked in the back of his mind was a hazy yearning he vaguely recalled from years ago . . . for a wife to love . . . adore, even . . . a brood of laughing children. . . .

Bloody hell, had he ever been that young? That naive? Had he actually expected to find a woman who'd be those things to him? Who'd make him want to retire contentedly to the country estate he now avoided like the plague?

He'd be thirty-four in July. When had it all gone sour? The war had done its part, of course. He'd seen enough carnage to harden a saint. Yet to be honest, he'd begun to grow world-weary well before he purchased his commission. He'd joined the regiment in '09. The year after he'd married. He'd already begun to grow tired of life. Pity he'd survived to . . .

His gaze fell upon a framed miniature on his bed stand, throttling the thought. A child's shyly smiling face looked back at him with eyes the exact color of his own. His son . . . the one thing in the world he gave a damn about. As long as he had Andrew, he'd something to live for.

He threw an irritated glance at the connecting door. Lucinda was well aware of his love for the boy. It was what had allowed her to think she could manipulate him with the child. The ploy had nearly worked. If he weren't convinced London was an unsavory place for the lad—

A self-deprecating snort truncated the thought. *At least be honest with yourself, old man! It's unsavory because of the life you lead here. Even now, you await not only your wife's departure but your son's. So that you'll be free for another night's debauchery!*

Another glance at the miniature had him swearing under his breath. Only this morning Andrew had begged to be allowed to stay. The pleading in the child's eyes said it wasn't merely because his mother had put him up to it. Yet Adam had steadfastly refused him, though he'd had longed to give in. The hardest part had been his inability to tell the child why. He could still feel the shame twisting his gut when Andrew had asked. He hadn't been able to meet his son's eyes.

How did a man explain to a six-year-old? That what had once been a careless option had become a necessity. That, since Salamanca and Vitoria, he needed the nights of dissipation to forget. To endure.

No, he could hardly tell a child about the bloodletting. The slaughter. The screams of dying men and horses . . . limbs and torsos torn apart by cannon, littering the ground.

Since returning from the Peninsula he'd found his mind haunted by agonized pleas from dying men. Young men, pouring out their lifeblood, asking for their mothers. Men hardly more than boys, whom he'd sent to their deaths in the name of duty. *Duty*. The word made him sick!

The memories gave him screaming nightmares.

So he kept the nightmares at bay . . . sometimes. If he was drunk enough . . . if the whore was clever enough . . . if . . .

With a disgusted snarl, Adam tore his gaze from the miniature, and rang for his valet. From outside on the drive, came the sound of carriage wheels turning on the cobbles. His own carriage, by the sound of it. *Finally departing, thank—*

Adam's bitter laughter obliterated the word he couldn't utter, even in his mind. The Deity had no place in his thoughts . . . or his life. Salamanca and Vitoria had left him believing in nothing and no one. Not even himself.

Better to think on the night ahead. Yet the forgetting had become harder. Even debauchery had begun to pall. He was all too aware he was fighting boredom along with the emptiness in his soul. If he had a soul. More likely, it had been devoured by the same beast that brought the nightmares.

Well, for now there was always Vanessa. An accommodating Cyprian with a voluptuous body and the practiced tricks of a whore.

And he mustn't forget m'lord Appleby. Though he'd met this latest among his reckless cohorts only a fortnight ago, Appleby showed promise. Of a certainty, he was one of the most intriguing and imaginative roués Adam had ever encountered.

Appleby had an inventiveness in the gaming hells that rivaled Vanessa's in the bedchamber. Surely, between the two, he'd be safe from the beast . . . at least for a time . . . wouldn't he?

A tapping at the door brought welcome relief from his thoughts. Calling permission to enter, Adam surrendered to the ministrations of his valet. Heretofore, he'd never bothered with a personal manservant, priding himself on a self-sufficiency at odds with the ways of the *ton*. But he'd won the highly touted Parks from Alvanley in a game of whist. Bored by the usual round of wagering one evening at Brook's, he'd wagered a prime piece of horseflesh, purchased at Tatt's only that morning. Wagered it against "the incomparable Parks," as Alvanley's envious cronies had called the servant. Poor Alvanley—the look on his jaded face when he lost! It had brought a measure of satisfaction, however fleeting; he might as well avail himself of the valet's expertise.

"I thought the striped might serve this evening, your lordship," Parks murmured a good two hours later. He held a waistcoat of subdued blue and gray stripes for the marquis's inspection.

"Yes, yes—whatever!" His irritation obvious, Adam allowed the manservant to settle the garment onto his shoulders. The tall-case clock on the landing had just struck nine. Not late by the *ton's* standards, but he'd had about all he could stomach of the valet's fussing. Blood and ashes, his cravat alone had taken six attempts before Parks was satisfied!

Unruffled by his employer's scowl, the valet helped him into a superbly tailored coat of deep blue superfine. Parks stepped back with a look of admiration. It had begun to rain earlier, and he raised his voice over a peal of distant thunder. "If I may say so, your lordship, we have achieved an image of the perfect Corinth—"

A frantic pounding resounded from the door. *Bloody hell—now what?* Adam wondered as he barked admittance. A glance at the mantel clock told him he was due to meet Appleby in less than—

A middle-aged woman rushed into the chamber: Mrs. Hodgkins, his housekeeper. "Begging your pardon, your lordship, but there's been— your lordship, forgive me, but I've terrible news!"

Adam eyed the normally unflappable servant sharply. The damned woman was *crying*. "Spit it out, Hodgkins." His tone was the same he'd used toward nervous junior offices. "What the devil's happened?"

The housekeeper made an attempt at speaking past the tears coursing down her homely face; her voice nonetheless cracked as she delivered her news. "There's been a-a carriage—oh, your lordship! Your carriage overturned, killing her ladyship and—"

"My son!" Adam's face was bloodless as he speared the woman with his eyes. "What of *my son*?"

"Alive, but badly injured, your lordship. He's—" She got no further. The marquis tore through the door, the sound of his rapid footsteps blending with urgent voices from the entry foyer below.

Adam flew down the stairs, trying desperately not to listen to the voice that jeered in his head. *You sent them away in that carriage!* You *did this to him! You!*

Jepson, his butler of many years, met him at the base of the stairs. The servant's lined face was tightly composed, if unusually pale. Then he saw the look on the marquis's face. The old retainer's eyes widened in alarm.

"Where is he, man?" No need for Adam to mention Andrew by name; they all knew how he felt about the child.

"Just arriving outside, your lordship. A passerby was kind enough to lend his carriage to—"

The front door banged open, snaring their attention. The blood drained from Adam's face as several liveried servants pushed through. Rain slanted through the open doorway, and their dripping attire puddled the floor. They bore a makeshift stretcher of some kind. A harsh cry died in Adam's throat as his gaze went to the small figure lying on it. Lying so horribly still.

It was nearly midnight when the marquis at last found himself alone with his son. The storm was reaching its peak. Thunder crashed overhead. Blue-white flashes of light flickered eerily at the windows. At Adam's feet, beside the bedside chair where he slouched, stood a half-consumed bottle of brandy; an empty snifter dangled from his hand. He eyed it absently for a moment, then shut his eyes in abject resignation. Half a bottle, and still no effect. But then, he doubted anything could provide the oblivion he sought.

His own chambers being closest, they'd brought the child here. Andrew lay in the middle of his father's huge tester bed. Adam's face twisted in anguish as he ran his eyes over the boy; he looked so awfully small and fragile against the great expanse of sheets.

A bandage covering a severe wound to the head obscured Andrew's curly dark locks. The bedclothes hid the splints and heavy gauze that bandaged a crushed leg; yet in his mind's eye, Adam could see them as clearly as the crimson-stained gauze wound about his son's head.

The physician, as well as a highly regarded surgeon they'd summoned, had left over an hour ago. Andrew still hadn't regained consciousness. Best to realize, they'd told the distraught father, he likely never would.

His son was dying.

Hissing an obscenity, Adam grabbed the bottle and poured himself a hefty measure. He raised the glass to his lips, tossed its contents down. The liquid burned a trail to his stomach. He wished to hell it could burn away his thoughts.

Guilt, terrible and unforgiving, ate into his mind. Like a cancer. A living thing that devoured from within. *You sent them away. The wife you took . . . used, but never loved. Dead, because of you.*

The son you've loved all too well . . . the son who, because of you, will soon—

"N-o-o-o!" The snifter splintered against the far wall as Adam's howl rose over the storm. Wrenching himself from the chair with a violence that knocked it over, he bent over the bed. Arms rigid, he drove his fists into the mattress and made himself look at the small, ashen face of his son. "You *can't* die. I won't let you! I—"

Adam dropped his chin and shut his eyes. The gesture, made by another, would have signaled prayer. But Adam Lightfoot didn't pray. Hadn't, for years. Couldn't. Not to a Deity who clearly condoned the things he'd seen. Who gazed impassively from a heaven that overlooked the filth that was war. A God who would allow this to happen to an innocent child, when it was the father who'd—

"I'm the one!" he raged. The clock on the landing had begun to chime the hour, but Adam's cry overrode the sound. "I'm the one to blame—not the child! Take me, and let the boy live—damn it! I'd barter my soul for it—I swear I would!"

At that exact moment, there came a sharp rapping at the door. Thunder rumbled overhead, but didn't obscure the sound. Nor the final strike of the clock on the landing, which had reached twelve.

Outraged that anyone would have the temerity to disturb him at such a time, Adam snarled an obscenity and stalked to the door. By Judas's balls, he'd have the bastard's head! Giving the doorknob a vicious twist, he thrust the door wide. "What the . . . ?"

He'd expected one of the staff, prepared to sack the feckless creature on the spot. But this was no servant. Before him was a man who wore the unmistakable hauteur of an aristocrat. Slender as a serpent, of average height, he wore the sartorially splendid garb of a dandy: a high, heavily starched cravat which had been tied just so. Tasseled Hessians, buffed and polished to a fare-the-well. Held at a fashionable angle was an ebony walking stick, its silver head carved in the likeness of some animal Adam couldn't make out.

The aging face bore unmistakable traces of dissipation; it was heavily maquillaged, the cheeks and lips rouged. A quizzing glass poised in one elegantly gloved hand completed the picture.

"Appleby. . . ." Adam scowled. "What the devil are *you* doing here?"

Discover the Magic of
Romance With

Kat Martin

__The Secret
0-8217-6798-4   **$6.99US/$8.99CAN**

Kat Rollins moved to Montana looking to change her life, not find another man like Chance McLain, with a sexy smile and empty heart. Chance can't ignore the desire he feels for her—or the suspicion that somebody wants her to leave Lost Peak . . .

__Dream
0-8217-6568-X   **$6.99US/$8.99CAN**

Genny Austin is convinced that her nightmares are visions of another life she lived long ago. Jack Brennan is having nightmares, too, but his are real. In the shadows of dreams lurks a terrible truth, and only by unlocking the past will Genny be free to love at last . . .

__Silent Rose
0-8217-6281-8   **$6.99US/$8.50CAN**

When best-selling author Devon James checks into a bed-and-breakfast in Connecticut, she only hopes to put the spark back into her relationship with her fiancé. But what she experiences at the Stafford Inn changes her life forever . . .

Call toll free **1-888-345-BOOK** to order by phone or use this coupon to order by mail.

Name_____

Address_____

City _____ State_____ Zip_____

Please send me the books I have checked above.

I am enclosing	$_____
Plus postage and handling*	$_____
Sales tax (in New York and Tennessee only)	$_____
Total amount enclosed	$_____

*Add $2.50 for the first book and $.50 for each additional book.

Send check or money order (no cash or CODs) to: **Kensington Publishing Corp., Dept. C.O., 850 Third Avenue, New York, NY 10022**

Prices and numbers subject to change without notice. All orders subject to availability. Visit our website at **www.kensingtonbooks.com.**